NOBODY SAVES YOU

NATALIE WEST

*For the only girl that could ever
truly change me for the better,
my awe-inspiring daughter.
You probably shouldn't be reading
this until you're older...*

CONTENTS

ONE
NOBODY CARES

Only one person was with her when she died. Well, technically three people, but they were melded into one. A true anomaly. Kind of disturbing, if I'm being honest. Their hand clutched a knife pressed flush against the girl's stomach, the blade just long enough to peek out her back. Excruciating pain radiated throughout her body until panic and nerves slowly drowned it out. Everything happened so fast. She was on the way to watch her favorite comfort movie when the dagger found its home in her flesh. Desperately, she tried to push back against the blade, but it stood firm. She knew this was the end, and she couldn't do anything about it.

The boy from high school, who would write love notes claiming to do anything for her, wasn't here to deliver. The coworker she wished would write her love notes barely spoke to her. Her brother, who promised to always protect her, was too far away. She was alone. Well, except for the presence of the three as one, of course. Nobody could save her.

As memories flashed across her dying brain, she didn't feel accomplished. She didn't feel regret. All she felt was an insurmountable rage before the lights went out. The trio, narcissistically named Dios, withdrew their blade. They tilted their head back and lifted the knife over their mouth so the blood could trickle onto their tongue. I believe I mentioned they were disturbing? In their mind, it was a way to absorb their victim's essence. From the outside looking in, however, it was not a good look. The girl toppled to the floor, her eyes dull and pathetic. Truly pitiable. Dios sheathed their knife and swiftly, silently, and creepily slithered out the window.

It's sad the girl couldn't put all that rage to good use. For revenge. And I don't even mean against Dios. See, for her, life itself is what deserved that vengeance. A life lived so mundanely and devoted to the service of others. Pieces of herself indiscriminately handed out, all at a cost. And what did she get in return? To be helpless in her final moment. To be abandoned by those who promised protection. To die alone in a room with a monster. So disgustingly pathetic that her name barely deserves a mention, but I guess I'll say it. Her name was Grace Abigail Ryder.

Or I should say *is* Grace Abigail Ryder. It's a funny thing, really. Our pitiful little bug doesn't seem to be rolling up. See, rage directed at life itself is powerful. It's the kind of fury that makes things interesting. So interesting, in fact, that poor Grace has risen from the dead. That's right. The light flickered across her eyes for one brief moment, followed by another and then another. Like an old projector spinning up while a sea of trumpets swelled, Grace was regaining power. Strange, forbidden power. Her deflated lungs filled once more, and her heart began to beat. Blurry vision focused on a red-stained floor.

Slowly, she sat up, clutched her head, and tried to come to terms with the preceding events. Who was that just now? There was a man in the room with her just moments ago. Well, she thought it was a man. Dios, as we've established, is a little more than that. That's when she remembered the stabbing. Frantically, she lifted her shirt in search of a wound. There was none. The only thing on her stomach was the ever so slight scar from her kidney transplant. She gave the organ, of course, didn't receive. I won't tell her, but she has a new one now. A better one, as a matter of fact.

The lack of a wound caused Grace to wonder if it had all simply been a dream. *No way*, she thought. A stranger had come into her apartment and stabbed her. She'd been holding a bowl of popcorn, heading to the living room when it happened. Sure enough, blood-soaked popcorn was scattered all over the floor, giving credence to her recollection. Honestly, I'm a little surprised the freak Dios didn't just eat one of those. Maybe it would've made the blood too salty? Or perhaps they were watching their cholesterol? Grace really liked the butter supreme overload popcorn. Regardless, it looks like Grace is starting to understand the truth. She just died. I know it seems like a weird thing to accept so quickly, but trust me, when you die, it'll be like nothing you've ever experienced. You'll remember it if you suddenly resurrect.

Grace tried to recall anything after the moment of her demise. Was she escorted across a river of the dead? Or perhaps she traveled through a ring of light? Did she meet god? She did, by the way, on that last one. Kind of, sort of. Semantics aren't really important right now. Unfortunately, those moments didn't come back with her from the beyond. She was just left with a pile of questions. How did she come back and was her murderer still here?

That last part appeared to be the most pressing. She sprang up and stumbled to the kitchen counter, desperately searching for a suitable weapon. Bread knife? No. Steak knife? Maybe. Butcher's knife? Why not? It seemed the biggest and most intimidating. Grace positioned the blade in front of her and slowly surveyed the area, plagued by doubts regarding its sharpness. After all, she frequently used it. She had chopped onions, apples, chicken, you name it, with that knife for years and never sharpened it once. Would it pierce flesh? As the thought crossed her mind, a vivid flash of phantom pain rushed to her stomach. She let out a scream.

"Come out, you little fucker!" A brazen explosion from the otherwise meek girl. There was that rage again. Love to see it. Her pace quickened around the apartment. She was no longer afraid of finding the culprit, but rather hoping to. "Come on. Come finish the job, you... you asshole!" I swear, she's usually quite tame. Not to mention, little Grace, they did, in fact, finish the job. You just didn't play by the rules.

"Come on!" A loud shriek rang from her lungs, the words dripping with disdain.

Just then, there came rapid poundings at the door. Grace snapped back to solid ground. Who could that be? She worried for a moment that it may be the perpetrator. What kind of killer knocks on the door of their victim, though? The knocking continued relentlessly until Grace finally made her way to check the peephole. It was her neighbor. She looked down to see half of her shirt drenched in blood. Which makes sense. She was just murdered moments ago, and resurrection unfortunately doesn't take care of dry cleaning. Grace began to panic. More poundings on the door. The noise needed to stop. She didn't want a big scene. A decision was made as she pulled open the door just enough to poke half of her body out. The half that wasn't stained red, of course.

"Hi, Trish!" A cheery greeting layered with slight panic. The knife was still in her left hand, just out of sight. Grace knew she had to answer the knock, but it would be in her best interest if nobody came in right now. What with the fresh murder scene and all.

"Are you okay?" the neighbor asked hastily. Trish was a kind, young, twenty-something who hosted a popular internet kids show creatively called "Miss Trish". Grace discovered it while babysitting her nephew one day. Ever since, she has always been flustered around the girl next door. It didn't help that the pseudo-celebrity was attractive, and Grace desperately desired to be cared for.

"Yeah. Fine. I'm totally fine!" Grace tried to regain composure.

"Are you sure? I swear I just heard you screaming. Are you safe?" Miss Trish's eyes got wide, and she leaned in and whispered, "Blink if you're not safe, but can't say it."

"I'm fine. Totally fine," Grace reiterated, trying really hard not to blink her now noticeably dry eyes. "It was a mouse." That was the excuse she landed on? A mouse? I get people being afraid of mice, but screaming bloody murder at them with a venomous rage seldom plays into the scenario. Let's see if Trish buys it.

"A mouse?" Incredulous. See? Miss Trish tried to peek around her neighbor. "Can I come in and help look?"

"Uh..." Grace entered panic mode again. "No, really, I'm okay. Plus, my apartment is a mess. Which is probably why I have mice." She died a little inside, knowing that Trish would now see her as a slob.

"I don't mind, really. I get it. You should see my place!" Trust me, Grace would love to.

"No really, it's not a good time."

"Are you sure?"

"Yeah, totally." Persistence may just win out. Grace hadn't forgotten that there could still be an intruder in her apartment. Which makes it a little confusing why she's not trying to involve the authorities right now. Perhaps panic over her rising from the dead? Is the worry of trying to explain that really worse than feeling safe? Or perhaps Grace doesn't feel unsafe at all and just wants to find her killer and enact that sweet revenge? Much more likely, however, is simply that Grace just doesn't want to be a burden.

"Is that what I think it is?" Miss Trish's tone starkly shifted. She stared intently at Grace's neck.

"What?" Frantically, Grace wiped her neck, thinking it was blood. When she checked her hand, however, it was dry. The color slowly flushed from Trish's face.

"You're not okay, are you?" She kept a kind tone, despite clearly being freaked out.

"Listen, I'm fine." Grace started to get impatient. "I just got startled by a mouse. It's not a big deal. I'm a little dramatic sometimes. That's all!"

"You have the mark of the dead." It was all Trish could get out as she pointed at Grace's neck. For there, just under her ear, lay a symbol. A twisted arrow going through a crescent moon. A symbol commonly known as the mark of the dead. Born only on those who have cheated death. It's a beautiful symbol, if I do say so myself. Fairly discrete location, but unmistakable. Several people have tried to imitate it with a tattoo, but the real thing emits a certain shine that cannot be replicated. You know it when you see the real deal.

A moment of silence passed between the two. Grace couldn't move her mouth. Her hand inched up her neck to cover the mark.

"I have to go now." Slowly, she backed away and shut the door on poor Miss Trish's worried face. "No, no, no!" Grace frantically whispered to herself. She died; of course she'd bear the mark. Quickly, she ran to the bathroom, dropping the knife in transit. The tip hit the floor, and it flopped to the ground without even making a dent. Not very sharp at all. It's a good thing Dios wasn't still there. Not that a knife could kill them anyway.

Grace scrubbed and scrubbed with soap, makeup remover, and—in a truly desperate moment—Clorox bleach wipes. It was all to no effect, aside from a slight burning sensation. The mark persisted. "Oh, god. Why me? Why'd this happen to me?" she called out. I'm sorry, but the alternative was dying a pathetic death. Was that really preferable? I think this is more than fair.

Hyperventilated breaths continued as she looked in the mirror, her eyes fixed on the cursed ink. She stared at its shape, its shine, its very meaning, and slowly her breaths spaced out. Slowly, she became calm. "Alright. You're a resurrected." Her hazel, undead eyes shifted to meet her mirrored gaze. "You. Are. A. Resurrected." One more time for the people in the back. "You are a *fucking resurrected*, and you *will* own this." She couldn't really understand why, but each time she spoke, the sting of her new reality faded away. It's easy to understand why, though, right? Remember when I said Grace harbored a vendetta in her last moment against her very life? Well, what better way to extend a middle finger to life itself than by refusing to die?

"You are a fucking beautiful resurrected, and you will own this!" Okay, that shout was way less subtle. Grace threw her fist out in front and gave her reflection knucks. A smile crept across her face.

* * *

Back on the streets, Dios was prancing along, avoiding street lamps and cracks on the sidewalk. They always felt great after a kill. While their primary goal was to convert the souls of humans, they honestly couldn't resist a good murder every now and then. Perhaps now is a good time to learn more about this yucky little trio?

Dios served the god Veritas publicly as a pastor, but in secret, they served a much more detestable being, the Silence. The Silence was a gelatinous orb of emptiness and despair. Like a black hole, it feasts upon the love, joy, and dreams of humans. Its followers are often tricked or forced into subservience, where they surrender those beautiful things to the being. What is left behind is a husk of a person whose only job is to act as a virus and infect all those they can. Now, as one may imagine, a being like that can't exactly roam the street easily. That's where Dios and a handful of others come in. They are known as disciples of the Silence.

Dom, Ira, and Orv were high-ranking servants of the blob with an insatiable craving for power. They each had something the others lacked. Ira had cunning as strong as her beauty. Dom was an amazing liar—or in his words, he was "influential"—and Orv was pure impulse, with an unnerving habit of getting what he wanted, no matter the cost. The Silence apparently thought the three of them would be unstoppable as one combined being. Personally, I also have to think it just thought it would be funny to take the three most independent and power-hungry people on the planet and force them to share. Which, admittedly, is actually hilarious.

The three can change their appearance to reflect any of them at will, but typically they move about the world looking like Dom. The fitted casual attire, perfectly combed hair, and white-skin maleness served them pretty well in the world. He's definitely the only one of them who could pass as a pastor for the nation's largest religion. Despite their appearance, each person could always speak freely.

"Let's have another! That bitch was a little sour," Orv shouted out.

"Orv, would you politely shut the fuck up? We are about to enter Main Street." Dom quickly quieted his cohabiter.

"Mmm, so much to eat downtown. Don't you agree?" Orv licked his lips.

"No more blood today, Orvy," Ira chimed in. "I'm thinking more like frozen yogurt?"

"Idiots, we are going home. We don't kill on our front doorstep," Dom said. "Plus, we had our fun already, and that girl's blood was definitely a little off-putting. As Orv said, she was sour."

"Nothing wrong with a little sour candy." Ira smirked.

"You're right! I want more! Let's go back and drain her!" Orv attempted to take control of the body, but was outvoted.

"How many times do I have to tell you? We don't return to the scene of the crime. If we want to keep up our hobbies, we have to be careful," Dom warned.

"Trust me, we know," Ira groaned. "Though I would love to go back and play in that beautiful red puddle she left behind."

"We could make blood angels!" Orv suggested, causing both Orv and Ira to laugh. Their voices rang out in unison in an unnatural frequency.

"And get blood all over this coat? Not a chance." Dom recoiled at the very idea. Since he put it out into the universe, he now needed to inspect the coat for blood.

"Don't worry, Dom, there's no stain. We weren't messy eaters," Ira reassured him. Dios turned the corner suddenly to find themselves amid a sea of street lights. They had made it to the downtown area. A few familiar faces passed them along the way, and they smiled and waved. The church Dios presided at was on this block. A massive building with gaudy stained glass windows on the corner right next to a burrito place. They entered the church, passed through rows of red velvet pews, and went into the directory.

"But I'm not ready for bed!" Orv protested as they entered a plain bedroom. All it held was a modest bed, a closet, and a floor-length mirror. Looking at this room alone, anyone could easily believe Dios to be a pious servant of Veritas who had taken a vow of poverty. Which was partially true. Dios wasn't much of a "nester". They spent little time at home, preferring to sow chaos out in the world.

"Don't be ridiculous. It's past midnight, and we have service tomorrow," Dom replied. "We have souls to save."

"Oh, good," Ira sighed. "That means I can sleep in while you do your boring little show."

"That little show," Dom started while hanging their coat gingerly on a hook, "is the only reason we can go on outings like tonight." Dios removed their shirt, folded it gently, and placed it in a hamper. A small, black spiral mark sat at the center of their chest. They approached a floor-length mirror and drew their knife. "Now, it's time to pray."

"Ooh, yes! I love prayer," Orv exclaimed. "My turn?"

"No," came Ira with an exasperated sigh. "Mine." The body morphed to reflect Ira's appearance. Long, wavy, red hair hung down over her bare chest. Piercing blue eyes stared into the mirror. "God, can't we just keep your body for this part, Dom?"

"Sorry, sweets. This is the way it works," Dom replied. "Besides, you look a lot better in that mirror, don't you think?" Dom forced a pervy smirk onto Ira's face.

"Ugh, yes, we get it. Because, tits." Ira rolled her eyes. "Every time." She lifted the blade to their collective neck and violently slashed across. Blood painted the mirror, and Dios' body fell to the ground, gasping for air. Despite this, they did not struggle. They did not reach their hand to their neck. They simply endured until, after a few minutes of gurgling their own blood, their neck healed and the bleeding stopped. Dios shot up and coughed, spitting the remnants in their throat onto the floor.

"The Silence has not forsaken us." Dom spoke the mantra through desperate gasps. "And our voice became one with the Silence."

"Amen," Ira said sarcastically. She raised her head and looked into the mirror. Blood soaked her body, and an unsightly wound lay across her neck, slowly healing. "Always such a shame to mar this beauty." Her hand lifted to meet the scar. "I despise it, even if it is just momentary."

"I think it's pretty! We should add more scars," Orv maniacally called out. "Next turn is mine!"

"Yes, Orv, you can perform the offering next time. Now, let's clean this up." Dios went to take care of the mess of their devotion. Quite a brutal sight, really. No matter how many times I see it. The Silence can be barbaric in its requests, but this is what it means to be a disciple. This ritual was crucial to determine if they were still in the grace of their lord. If they were, then the power of the Silence would remain with them, and the wound healed. If they were not, or if the Silence was in a particularly sour mood, they would bleed out and die. Dios has survived so many of these rituals, however, that it had just become more of a nuisance.

After cleaning the decoration provided by their offering, Dios lay in their bed, exhausted from a day of murder and suicide.

"Do you think they found her yet?" Orv postured. "Do you think she had loved ones? Do you think they're weeping over her corpse right now?" Dios let out a collective little chuckle.

Ira dismissed him. "Oh, please, Orvy. Did you see that place? Trust me, that girl was living all by herself. It reeked of loneliness."

"Absolutely," Dom agreed. "Definitely all alone. I don't think they'll find her until there's a foul odor."

"Oh, how I wish I could smell it." Orv cackled.

"Your imagination will just have to do, for now. Picture that bitch lying in her own blood, and let's go to sleep." Dom shut it down.

Only that "bitch" wasn't lying in her own blood. No, she was sitting on her couch, filled with confusion and unrest. Her kitchen floor was now spotless, with all evidence of her murder cleaned up. She thought briefly about leaving it. Sometimes, individuals who have been resurrected report their own murders. She could have left it for the police. However, police interactions with those with the mark of the dead vary. Sometimes it's a pleasant, concerned interaction that will trigger a full-blown investigation that, unfortunately, is often fruitless. Hung up by that old mantra—no body, no crime. Other times, however, authorities respond with complete apathy or even extreme hostility. I've seen a few resurrected end up in a prison cell after reporting their own murder. Crime cited as "pursuing the mark". Grace knew this. Best to deal with it on her own.

Someday she'd have the ability to track down her killer, but for now, all she could do was stare at her phone. The contact record for "Peter ICE" filled the screen, her thumb hovering over the phone icon. It's been hovering that way for almost fifteen minutes. Peter is Grace's brother. He and his family were all that she had left in this world after their parents passed. They died only two years ago, and since then Peter has always been adamant about being Grace's rock.

And a rock he was. Stable and unmoving. Grace did most of the legwork to maintain their relationship, and in exchange, Peter would come through during the hard times. So, why does this feel different? She wanted to call and tell him everything. She hoped he'd be okay with the mark. However, she knew there was no guarantee, and that rejection was possible.

It wasn't like they always got along. When they were kids, they fought almost constantly. A faint smile came over Grace's face as she remembered those arguments. No matter how bad they got, each one ended the same. Grace would say something dumb, like "get bent", and Peter would respond in kind with "can't bend steel!" Even though you can, in fact, bend steel. They weren't kids anymore. Could they survive a grown-up fight?

As she pondered, a wave of fatigue came over Grace. Coming back from the dead is exhausting, after all. I mean, sure, at first the adrenaline surge is incredible and will keep that heart pumping loudly for hours, but once that subsides, you'll feel so tired that you'll think you're dead again. Her eyes drooped. The phone slipped out of her limp hand and onto the floor as she collapsed. Fate made the decision as the phone landed just the right way to trigger a call to Peter. Fortunately, however, he slept with *do not disturb* mode on. Sleep tight, Grace. And maybe dream of something more pleasant.

* * *

The next morning, Grace woke to a sunray peering through her curtains. Groggily, she opened her eyes, only to cover them moments later with her hand. Her head was pounding, her throat dry, and every single muscle ached. I understand beating the reaper will leave you with a hangover worse than anything you've ever experienced. Grace groaned and rolled off the couch onto the shadier floor. No sun could reach her there—at least not for another thirty minutes or so.

When the brightness was gone, a new sensory intruder appeared. The buzz of her phone went off right by her head. Usually, it would have just been a slight annoyance, a Pavlovian response to check the notification, but to Grace, at this moment, the buzzing may as well have been a thousand bees in a tin can.

"Leave me alone," Grace grumbled, while still grabbing her phone. See? Humans are incapable of ignoring that intense itch to check a notification, no matter what state they're in. It was a text from Peter.

"2am phone call. Bad night or good night?"

Grace's first reaction was confusion. She remembered contemplating dialing her brother, but was almost entirely sure she hadn't. A quick check of the call log revealed she did. She sighed and begrudgingly put her thumbs to the phone.

"I'm fine!"

What a liar. Fine is not a word I would use to describe her present state. At that moment, she decided it wasn't worth telling the truth. Their next visit could be weeks away. She had time to figure out how to handle this news. Perhaps it was best to live her new reality for a bit before burdening anyone. Luckily, her brother never fully understood Grace's personal life. Anybody who made the effort to know how she spent her free time would know that a drunk dial at 2 a.m. was extremely outside the norm. It would be exciting, interesting, messy—which are all words I would not have used to describe Grace. Crowds were not so much her thing. Drinking alone? Even less her thing. Drinking with friends? Rarely an option.

Before throwing the phone back down, Grace glimpsed the time—1:30 p.m. This was enough to get her to shoot up. She hadn't slept this late since high school. What's worse was she was supposed to meet her only friend, Tommy, for brunch. Now she felt guilty. One of her five most used emotions.

"Aw, crap. I'm sorry, Tommy!" She scraped her phone back off the floor and checked her notifications, expecting a confused text or concerned phone call—nothing. How peculiar. She did, in fact, have plans with him. Maybe something weird happened with the phone? A couple taps and she was calling.

"Grace?" Tommy answered.

"Tommy! I'm so sorry! I'm running way behind and didn't realize what time it was," Grace frantically apologized. She didn't want to tell him why she was late, but also couldn't lie, so a half-truth it was.

"Huh? What are you..." Tommy paused. "Oh. Right. You wanted to get brunch this morning." It seemed like it just dawned on the man. "Yeah, I didn't see a text from you earlier, so I just assumed you weren't up for it." This was not a half-truth; this was a whole lie. Tommy forgot.

"Oh, yeah. No, I mean I definitely want to get together. Things just came up." Grace wasn't sure yet if she'd share with Tommy. I mean, eventually she'd have to. They've known each other for years, and she always shared with him, including that kidney I mentioned earlier.

"Yeah, yeah totally. It's just a bit late now." Tommy paused for a moment. "Actually, you know what? You cool coming here?"

"Right now?" Grace touched the mark. Did she want to go out and risk being seen? It was winter. Perhaps she could cover it with a scarf? "Yeah, I can do that." Reluctantly, she agreed as a desperate grab at normalcy. Perhaps this is the denial stage of grief? Though, I'm not sure if you still feel grief if the person who died was yourself. It's a complex emotion that I try not to familiarize myself with. Either way, it seems Grace has made plans and is going out into the world for the first time as a resurrected.

"Okay, awesome. Be here in like ten?"

"Ten minutes..." Grace looked at herself in the TV reflection. Although it was a warped image, she could tell her clothing was wrinkled and disheveled, and her hair was in knots instead of its usual wave. "Can we make it like forty-five?"

"Grace, come on. You're already late."

"Right, right. Thirty then?"

"Fine, thirty. I'll see you soon!"

Grace hung up the phone and got to work. Thankfully, she already took a full shower the night before to wash the dried blood off her body. All she needed was a spritz of hair detangler and some deodorant. After a whirlwind of twenty minutes, Grace paused to look at herself in the mirror. She gave a determined look as if to say "you got this", before throwing a scarf around her neck, hiding the beautiful mark. Then she hauled it over to Tommy's.

It was a short drive to her friend's apartment. Before she knew it, she was knocking at the door.

"Grace!" Tommy greeted her with overwhelming charisma.

"Hey, Tommy!" She extended her arms and gave him a big hug. "So sorry about this morning."

"Hey, don't worry about it. You know where to put your coat," Tommy said while getting a coat himself. Grace found that strange. Perhaps he planned for them to go out after all? "Okay, sis, so listen." Tommy paused and looked at Grace. "You know I hate to ask, but I have, like, a huge favor." He put his hands together and tried his best puppy dog face. Usually, this was quite effective. Tommy had a certain charm to him, but at this moment, Grace felt annoyed. A welcome change from her usual immediate accommodation.

"Um, okay. What's going on, Tom?"

"So, I'm watching my sister's dog, right?"

"Oh, li'l Chey Chey is here!" Grace's face lit up.

"Yes! Chey Chey is here. I'm watching her for the weekend." Tommy played into the excitement. "But, here's the thing. I forgot I told my mate I'd meet him to help with this project. He's making a couple of chairs, but he's having a mad hard time. Needs an extra hand to steady the wood and what not." Grace's face dropped. Why did she come here? She really didn't want to help build chairs. Who even does that?

"So, where do I come in here?"

"Well, I can't leave Chey Chey alone." Tommy looked around and then leaned in to whisper, "And my roommate has been acting supes strange. I can't trust her with him today. My sister would throttle me if anything happened."

"Alright, so you need me to watch Chey Chey. Got it." Grace was deflated, but also slightly okay with the role. Cheyenne, more commonly referred to as Chey Chey, was a fairly well behaved Jack Russell Terrier. Not as good as hanging out with her friend, but not as bad as making a chair.

"Yes, can you please, sis? I'll owe you. Next time we get brunch, I'll buy. On god." Tommy squeezed his hands tighter to grovel.

"Yeah, sure."

"Yes! Thank you, Grace. Seriously, you're the top. I am the bottom." Tommy bowed down humbly before putting on his coat. He was ready to go. Grace was a little surprised at just how quickly this was all happening. "And don't worry." Tommy stopped and pointed to his kidney, giving a shitty little smile. "I'll bring a piece of you with me." He let out a chortle.

"Always!" Grace laughed along, but she didn't really mean it. Tommy used that joke a lot.

"Alright, I'll be seeing you then." And with that, Tommy was gone. Grace now realized she didn't ask how long he'd be gone, or what exactly she was supposed to do. When does this dog even eat? It sounded like his roommate Chase was still around, but apparently acting weird. So, I guess he won't be much help. Sure enough, not long after that thought Chase appeared, peeking around the corner of his bedroom door. Grace nearly jumped when she saw him standing there. It was incredibly creepy.

"Holy hell, Chase. You scared me!" Grace shook it off. "Have you seen Chey Chey around? I'm supposed to be watching her, I guess." Grace started to search. Chase just stared. There was a twinge of malice in his eyes. "Nothing on you, I'm sure. Tommy is just really particular."

Grace thought the dead stare might be in response to being passed over for dogwatch duty. Perhaps the roommate was offended. Instinctively, she tried to soften the blow and avoid hurt feelings. When Chase continued his statue impression, however, she got weirded out. "Um, you know what? I think maybe she's in Tommy's room. I'll go check." She started to hurry past Chase, but stopped when she heard him whisper.

"Dead."

"What was that?" She ground to a halt. Grace was now face to face with Chase. That's a fun sentence, but it was not a fun encounter. Chase's eyes were dull and wide, looking straight into Grace's own. It was at this point that Grace thought the worst about Chey Chey's condition. "Chase. Where is Cheyenne? Is she... alive?" Chase pointed a bony finger at Grace.

"Dead," he repeated. In a panic, Grace raised her hand to meet her neck, checking to see if the mark was still covered.

There was no possible way he could know otherwise, right? The scarf was solidly in place, and all was concealed. Grace was briefly relieved, before returning to a solid state of disturbed.

"You know what? Maybe Tommy actually just took her with him." She started to plan an escape route. This was too strange. She'd connect with Tommy, and they'd come back to face this creep show together. "I'm just going to go find him and..." Grace paused. Something caught her attention behind Chase. A light flash of blue green. "I'm going to find him and..." The same flicker distracted her. There was something mesmerizing about it. She was drawn to it and sickened by it, all without fully comprehending what *it* even was. "Is someone in there with you?" Grace tried to peek around him.

"Dead bitch should stay dead." Chase leaned to cut off her gaze. That was the last straw. Grace was sick of this weird dude and his creepy flickering light. Something woke up in her.

"Okay, asshole. I don't know how you know about this." She lowered the scarf to reveal the branding. "But you seriously need to chill, or we're going to have a problem."

Chase's eyes were drawn to the mark, which started to glow a nice cool purple. I love that hue. A light hum filled the air around Grace, like a small orchestra warming up. This startled Grace and Chase alike. "What is that?" she asked mainly herself. Trying to communicate with the weirdo was proving to be pointless.

"Sonata Mor," Chase replied, a stunned and terrified look spread across his face. Huh, interesting. The first time she's not actually talking to him, and he has an answer to her question. And, what's more, he's actually right. Sonata Mor is exactly the right term for this noise and ability. I'll try not to spoil too much else. Things are about to get interesting.

"Huh? Sonata Mor?" As soon as Grace parroted the words, a small orchestra exploded into a cacophony of stringed instruments, swelling in anticipation. Her hair flowed in a wind circling around her. Frantically, she looked at her body, now covered in that same cool purple aura as the mark. She looked up at Chase. This time, she fully saw the flickering light for what it really was.

A creature stood a mere two feet behind the creeper. It looked like it was wearing a white hood stained in black blood that morphed into the creature's body. Its eyes were bottomless black holes, and its mouth sealed away with a dripping black ooze, making the shape of a large "X". The rest of the body resembled a human with stark white skin. Blotches of black patterned its chest, and a cloak connected off its back like webbing. This was a virus of Silence. Commonly referred to as silence themselves—lower case "s". They existed as an extension of the blob—grown within the void of a misguided human soul until they were big enough to take full control of their host, not unlike some parasites.

Glowing green strings extended from Chase's back to the silence's hand. Still immature. A fully grown silence would have no need for training wheels and could control their puppet from a long distance, no strings attached.

"What the...?" Grace had no idea what she was looking at. Unfortunately, she's not privy to the same information just explained to you. All she had was instinct, and that instinct told her that this thing was her enemy. The sounds of the strings hastened. "What the hell are you?" Grace asked, but before the silence would offer an answer, it twisted the strings and Chase instantly launched a punch. Grace's body swiftly moved to avoid it. "What the hell, dude?" Another twist leading to another swing. This one landed square on her jaw. She stumbled backward into the wall. Her hand quickly met the sore spot, lightly massaging the ache. The silence twittered their fingers around, and Chase bobbed and weaved in the doorway. A little showboaty for my taste.

"Whoa, okay. I think I get it." It clicked in Grace's head.

"Chase isn't the asshole here." The strings were pulled, and Chase dropped to sweep Grace's legs. Without thinking, she jumped over them like she was playing double Dutch. Grace nervously clenched her fists. She knew what she needed to do, but it definitely made her uncomfortable. Despite this, Grace went on the counterattack and threw a punch at the silence. As her fist soared through the air, a violin screeched out above the rest of the orchestra. It wasn't a pretty sound by any means. Her form was a little off. The silence pulled Chase up just in time to catch the punch.

"Ah! I'm so sorry!" Grace apologized as Chase was pulled in closer to the silence. "Not fair," she protested, before attempting another screeching punch. Once again, it failed to hit its mark. This time, it caught the poor boy in the side.

"Damnit. Chase, if you can hear me, I swear I'm not trying to hurt you! Also, could you, like, move, maybe?" The silence held its shield tight. Grace didn't know what to do, but it was obvious she needed to do something. This did not appear to be a symbiotic relationship. At that moment, Chey Chey came out of Tommy's room, barking profusely. I guess she didn't like the noise, either.

"Chey Chey? You're alive!" Grace let herself get distracted, allowing the silence to swing one of its meat puppet's fists right into the side of her head. A small burst of energy erupted from Chase's knuckles, causing her to fly through the wall into the next apartment. She crashed down onto a table, much to the surprise of a young couple sitting there.

"Whoa! What the hell is this?" the man cried out. The two jumped to either side of the dining room. "Do you know this girl?"

"Are you serious, Griffin? She literally just crashed through my fucking wall!" the woman exclaimed. Her name is probably Stacy.

"Does this happen a lot? Am I not safe? I thought you said you lived in a safe neighborhood?"

"Are you fucking kidding me right now?"

"Um," Grace stood up and cut off the budding couple's argument. "Sorry about that."

"You should be sorry, bursting in here like the fucking Kool-Aid man." Stacy was mad.

"Well, I didn't want to!" Grace retorted. Chase flew through the hole in the wall with a flying kick. Grace reactively put up her arms to cushion the blow. She stumbled back into a bookcase as Chase fell to the ground in the follow through. Grace briefly locked eyes with a pink stuffed octopus as she used the shelf to regain her balance. "Cute octopus," she complimented the renter in an attempt to mend her terrible first impression. The flattery bounced off Stacy. Chase quickly jumped up on his feet, and his weird little parasite emerged from the wall, strings tied tight.

"What the hell is that, Stacy?" Griffin freaked. See? I knew her name was Stacy. "Is this it? Is this how I die? Before we even have sex?"

"Griffin! Would you shut up, please?" Stacy turned her attention to the intruders. "And you three, I don't know what kind of weird shit you're into, but please get out of my apartment. And for the love of god, turn that music down. It sounds like a dying cat."

"Wait, you can see *both* of them?" Grace asked. "And you can hear that?"

"Duh. I think everybody in the building can hear that garbage."

"Wow, I have a lot to process," Grace said, but she did not have time to process. Chase, the real boy, launched an offensive strike.

"Cut the strings," a voice sang out in Grace's head. She

dodged the punch and caught a good glimpse of the glowing threads for the first time.

"How?" Grace asked out loud.

"With your sound," the voice replied in song. Another fist came flying toward Grace. She ducked just in time.

"What does that even mean?" Grace pressured the disembodied voice. She couldn't keep dodging forever.

"Gather it around your fist," the beautiful melody clarified. Our reluctant fighter looked down at her hand and imagined the noise flowing around it. To her surprise, sound waves collected around her open palm. The silence noticed this and panicked, launching a sloppy attack with its host. It was another right hook. Instinctively, Grace caught it with her hand and held it tight. "Here goes nothing." She adjusted her grip to grab Chase's wrist and swung him around. The sound waves in her palm propelled him across the room. This created some distance and exposed the strings.

A low orchestra bass began to swell—this time in tune. Thank god for that. She wound her arm around like a softball pitch and uppercut the glowing threads. A beautiful viola crescendoed as she sliced through them. There we go! Not exactly pro level, but a step in the right direction. I think she overestimated the amount of force needed to cut them. The windup was unnecessary. Chase collapsed, and the puppet master staggered backward.

"Hey, that was pretty good." Griffin applauded. "I think I get it now." He turned to Stacy, who was still not impressed. "This is your attempt to, like, wow me, right? A kind of dinner theater?" Stacy just stared back. Grace moved in on the defenseless silence, her orchestra playing a modest symphony in stride.

"I don't know what you are," Grace said, "but I've had a shitty day, and I really want to hit something bad." Energy formed around her hand again. "And you look pretty bad." She raised her arm, the aura swirling around it like a blade. Violins joined the mix, playing a heroic melody. The silence tried to run, but disconnected from its host, there was little it could do. Grace's hand slashed down across its body, slicing it in two. Black ooze spewed out as it rapidly disintegrated. Ooze that would be difficult to get out of that white linoleum. Hopefully Stacy didn't care about her security deposit. The aura around Grace died down, and her mark's glow faded along with the music.

"Hell yeah, dude! Hell yeah!" Griffin was pumped. "That was so sick! Alright, Stace. You did it. You wowed me. Now come take your prize." He opened his arms wide in anticipation of some form of physical affection. Stacy turned to Grace.

"Take your fucking boy toy over there and get the hell out of my apartment." She turned to Griffin. "You leave, too." She stormed off, mumbling about how she would never use the dating app Flitter ever again. Griffin stood there dumbfounded, unable to put his arms down. Perhaps he thought Stacy was joking. Sadly for him, she was not.

"Right, sorry!" Grace called out as she rushed to Chase. "And he's not my boy toy. I don't even..." She started to explain, but decided it wasn't worth it. She pulled Chase's arm over her shoulder and lifted him up. He let out a slight groan and opened his eyes.

"Grace? What are you doing in my apartment?" Grace was relieved to hear him speak.

"It's a long story. And this isn't your apartment." Grace helped Chase hobble to the door. It seemed a little easier than trying to lift him through the gaping hole in the kitchen. As she went to leave, she turned to Griffin. "Tell your girlfriend, or whatever, that we're really, really sorry." The rejected man just nodded and finally put his arms down in defeat.

When they got back to the apartment, Grace filled Chase in on what happened. Chase admitted the last few weeks were fuzzy, but he vaguely remembered being a weird jerk. The last thing he vividly recalled was going to the Veritas church with his family. I won't bore you too much with the specifics here, as I don't find Chase to be particularly interesting or important.

Grace had a lot to think over, however. To think the Sonata Mor would awaken in her. Not every resurrected has that. In fact, it's exceedingly rare, first appearing in ancient times. Only three others have had it since. Not a ton of rhyme or reason to why it shows up, but it's always a delightful surprise to see it. Things always get fun when it awakens. It's one of the few surefire ways to dispel the silence. Whether the host of this ability sees it as a gift or a burden can vary greatly depending on the person. I wonder how Grace will see it?

Despite the fact that Chase was now himself again and not a wandering puppet, Grace stuck around to watch Chey Chey. She had made a promise, and I guess she was seeing it through. They all sat down and watched some trash reality TV until Tommy finally came home around 9 p.m.

"Hey, Grace. How did it go?" Tommy came in, blissfully unable to read the room. Grace was less than thrilled that this hangout had turned into a fight with a monster and an eight-hour dog sitting venture. Chase was also annoyed because he felt obligated to stay around, despite wanting to see the girlfriend he'd been ignoring for weeks. As if he can save that relationship. Perhaps he felt he owed Grace, and guilt prevented him from leaving her alone? He obviously tried to get her to leave, but again, Grace stayed by her word. Chase even texted Tommy, trying to get him to tell her to go home. Tommy saw the message and meant to respond later, but completely forgot about it.

"Chase! You're up and about and looking normal. Good to see. Sorry, I just got your message now." Tommy laughed it off.

"That was some chair building sesh, huh?" Grace remarked. "Was it a good time?"

"Chair building?" Tommy said, confused. "Oh, yeah. Yeah, totally. Chair building was tight. Real clean time. Thanks a mil,

Grace!" It's hard to tell if he's ignorant or pretending he can't feel the annoyance radiating off Grace. It's also hard to tell which era of slang he uses.

"Sure thing, buddy. It was fine, friend. Anything to help, pal." Grace stood up, passive aggressiveness pouring out of her.

"Okay, okay, I get it." Tommy broke the act.

"Get what?" Grace didn't.

"You repeat things when you get mad, fam." He wasn't wrong.

"Well, I thought I was coming to hang out, not watch Chey Chey for eight hours with your roommate." Don't forget the fight with the ethereal being, Grace. You didn't expect that either.

"Yeah, well, to be fair, I didn't exactly expect Chase to be up and at'em, you know? And I really owed my bro a favor."

"Right, this bro who builds chairs that I don't know despite us being friends for a decade."

"I have a lot of other friends, Grace. You're not going to know all of them."

"Uh-huh." Grace grabbed her coat and scarf. It was at this moment that Tommy saw the mark.

"Whoa, Grace." She stopped and turned to him.

"What?"

"You died, bro?" He pointed at the mark. "Why didn't you tell me? I didn't know you just went through something like that. When'd you get that?" Grace was caught off guard. Tommy had a tendency to do this. Suddenly show a sweet side. Though Grace was seeing his entire persona as much more annoying than she used to.

"Last night," she answered meekly.

"Damn, fam. No cap?"

"Shut the hell up, Tom. You sound like an idiot." Grace smirked a little and continued to put her coat on. "I told Chase all about it. I don't really feel like talking anymore tonight."

"Oh, okay. Well, guess I'll just see ya around then?"

"Sure thing, Tom." Grace opened the door. "Oh," she paused. "And your kitchen has a hole in it." With that, she shut the door and was on her way.

"A hole?" Tommy repeated, befuddled. "Mate, what's she on about? You guys talk now or something?" He turned to Chase, who let out a heavy sigh.

"Yeah, it's been a day. Here, I'll show you," Chase said, getting up from the couch. "I already called the landlord."

TWO
NOBODY LISTENS

Grace fiddled nervously, buttoning a modest white blouse. She looked at herself in the bathroom mirror, zeroing in on the mark of the dead. Inhale. Exhale. Today was a big day. Grace was finally returning to work. It had been one week since she received the new branding, and she'd been holed up in her apartment the entire time. Multiple food deliveries and sick days later, here she is. Finally ready to head back out into the world.

As she eyed the mark, her mind went back, as it often did, to last week—to the fight with the creature. The entire encounter remained a mystery to her. What was that thing? What was that power? And what was that strange singing voice in her head? These same questions floated around over and over, but today she knew she had to start moving again. No answers were given to her. No strange voices sang what her next move should be. Life just continued.

She tried on a couple of cardigans, before deciding on a beige one with just enough lift around the neck. Between that and her collar-bone length hair, she felt confident she could obscure the mark. This day was bound to come sooner or later. She held no delusions that she could hide it forever, but didn't feel the need to advertise it either. Today, the snowball would start to roll down that hill, and she would just have to see where it ended up.

"First day back as the new me." She gave the mirror a pep talk. "Own it." A hardy nod and Grace was out the door. As fate would have it, she was leaving at the exact time Miss Trish was coming home. Grace gave an awkward smile and died a little inside. Of course, this would happen.

Miss Trish nodded and then looked back down at her keys, a gym bag in hand. She took a deep breath before facing Grace. "Hey, I'm so sorry for how I reacted the other night." Grace raised her eyes. "It's just. I've never met anyone who... you know..." She stumbled, trying to say the words.

"Yeah, me neither. It's no big deal," Grace reassured her.

"It is, though. After what you went through, to be greeted with that. I can only imagine how that made you feel."

"Well, it was all pretty new to me, too. I didn't even know it was there until you pointed it out."

"Oh my god. I broke the news... I am so sorry." Trish was taken aback.

"Oh! No! I didn't mean..." Grace stumbled, trying to ease any guilt. "Really, it's okay. For real." She was flustered. Save for the night she died, the two didn't really talk. It was honestly hard for Grace to look her in the eyes. To her, this woman was a pseudo-celebrity.

"Wait." Trish paused. "Does that mean *it* happened that night?" She put her hand up to her mouth and gasped. "Wait. The screaming. That's what it was about, right? Did someone..."

"No! No. Nobody did anything." Grace cut that line of thinking immediately. "It, um. It really was a mouse." Really, Grace? Back to the mouse? "I was cleaning on a chair, and it startled me. I fell backward, hit my neck on the island, and it was lights out." Okay, at least this is slightly more plausible. Falling into things and dying is a completely valid threat. That is, if this was a movie, and things like that actually happened.

"Oh my god, that's awful." Trish put a hand on her neighbor's shoulder in sympathy. Grace's stomach flipped. Human contact. What a rush. "Did you find that little asshole?" Grace couldn't help but crack a smile. She found Trish swearing a little endearing. Grace only really knew her from the Miss Trish show, so she enjoyed seeing the more adult side.

"Yeah, I got him." Grace continued the lie. "Real good."

"Good! He deserved it." Trish let go of Grace's arm. The two stood in awkward silence for a moment.

"Well, I should probably get to work," Grace finally said.

"Yeah, of course. Glad I checked in with you. If you need anything, just let me know. Okay?"

"Will do. Thanks, Miss Trish!" Grace let the name slip and immediately glowed red with embarrassment.

"Just Trish is fine." Trish chuckled. She gave a calming smile before heading inside. Grace managed to raise her arm ever so slightly to say bye. By definition, I guess that counts as a wave. Despite the awkward ending, Grace felt a little relieved. The first real interaction as her new self was out of the way. The fact that it wasn't a total garbage fire was a slight confidence booster. Probably just enough to ensure that she actually went to work.

Grace worked as a social media coordinator for a pet supply company called Pets YES. And yes, it is capitalized like that. Seriously. In every company memo, advertisement, and press release, it must be presented that way. A little over-enthusiastic, but humans often are when it comes to their pets. Grace enjoyed the job, but found the marketing mindset exhausting at times. The fact that she liked animals helped. Don't tell Grace, but everyone thinks it's a little weird she works there and doesn't have a pet herself. I believe there's a story there, but now doesn't seem like the time to dig.

As soon as Grace arrived at her desk, her boss, Tania, welcomed her. "Hey, there's our little guru. How we feeling?"

Grace put on her best smile. "Hey Tania! I'm doing a lot better now. Thanks for asking. Don't worry, I'm not contagious!" Grace floundered a bit. She always felt strange coming back from sick days, as rare as that was. In her head, she assumed everyone was worried about the germs she carried. This caused her to over-analyze every interaction.

"Glad to hear it. We lost a lot of time this last week." Tania wanted to ensure Grace was aware of the inconvenience. "Listen, after you get settled, let's meet and discuss how we can finally get some engagement around the new Waterfall Lake™ bowls." Grace nodded. Waterfall Lake™ bowls were a new line of water bowls that played calming waterfall noises when it detected an animal's tongue. It also had a bladeless fan that would bubble the water ever so slightly. It was overpriced and underwhelming. Pets YES was a company that excelled at innovation—just not particularly useful innovation. They prided themselves on their ability to push the envelope. This actually made Grace's job a lot easier. Easy to market the strange. Though sometimes she felt guilty about making these products appealing. The cat food bowl that would run around on spider legs came to mind. *Bring back the hunt* was the tagline for that one. Kind of clever. Entirely useless. Recalled after a week.

"You got it!" Grace nodded and then let out a tremendous sigh as soon as Tania turned the corner. So far, the mark has gone undetected. Or, at least, unmentioned. She sat and booted up her computer. Then she heard it. The voice of an angel.

"Welcome back, Grace. Glad you're feeling better." Grace looked up from her desk to see Cynthia Waters smiling politely. She had straight platinum blonde hair that tapered down into a rosy pink ombre, cutting off at the shoulder. It blended seamlessly with a cozy, yet fashionable sweater with long sleeves that covered part of her hands. High-waisted jeans completed the ensemble. No, that wasn't in the dress code, and no, it wasn't casual Friday. Neither of those facts seemed to bother Cynthia, or Grace, for that matter. Everything about her was perfect to Grace.

Cynthia was sitting at her desk, just a little distance away. The creative team all shared an open concept space, so there were no cubicle walls preventing interaction. Cynthia positioned herself about as far from Grace as possible, however. This was obvious, because her arms were extended in an uncomfortable manner, barely reaching the digital drawing pad. See, 99% of the office wouldn't care about Grace returning from a sick day—or in this case, week—despite Grace believing everyone would. However, Cynthia did not like to take chances in terms of illnesses. Grace knew this. Her earlier comment about not being contagious was likely for that particular co-worker's benefit.

"T-thanks, Cynthia." Grace pushed the words out. It killed her a bit, calling her "Cynthia." She knew all her friends called her "Cyn." She could never say it, though, always wondering if she'd earned the right. After everything she'd been through, you'd assume talking to a crush would be the least of her worries, but believe it or not, this was actually up there for the most difficult thing she'd done this week. And yes, that included literally dying. Cynthia nodded and then dialed back in on the rough sketch for Waterfall Lake™, arms still fully locked at the elbow. Not a great way to draw. She glanced up at Grace to ensure they were at least six feet apart. That's when she saw it.

"Whoa." Cynthia gasped. "Is that why you were out sick?" She gestured her stylus at Grace's neck. Grace quickly covered it with her hand.

"Um. Whatever do you mean?" Grace responded, overcorrecting her "stay cool" switch.

"No need to hide it. I saw it clear as day." Cynthia wanted to get up and continue this conversation a little closer, but she needed confirmation first. "So, is that why you were out?"

"Ugh. Yes." Defeated, Grace put her hand down. Why did it have to be Cynthia who noticed first? Now that she had received the all-clear, Cynthia walked over and leaned on the edge of Grace's desk. This was an effective way to activate Grace's panic button. Honestly, I'm getting a little annoyed by all these frantic emotions. Bring back the rage, Grace, please. That's the one I like.

"Damn. That's rough. I have a cousin who's a resurrected. You doing okay?" This was already encroaching on the longest non-work conversation Grace had ever had with Cynthia. The current record holder was about the office toaster not working. Short-circuited, not unlike our heroine here.

"Um. Yeah. Uh. It's something." Eloquently spoken.

"Oh, you probably don't want to talk about this right now." Cynthia stood up straight. "I'm so sorry. It's your first day back. In fact, you probably don't want to talk about it ever. That was rude."

"No, it's not that!" Grace finally got a sentence out. "I just. I'm just not sure how to talk about it yet. I've only really talked to Chase so far."

"Okay," Cynthia acknowledged, despite not having any idea who Chase was. "Well, I'm here to talk if you want. I know it's not the same as living with the mark, but, like I said, my cousin has it, and we're pretty close. He's actually told me a lot about it."

"Thanks, Cynthia." Grace smiled. "I really appreciate that." Now she's happy. This is more boring than panic.

"Absolutely." Cynthia went back to her desk feeling like she appropriately handled her previous bluntness. This time, she sat an appropriate distance away from her tablet. "Oh," she looked up at Grace. "And you can just call me Cyn, you know." There it is, the invitation Grace has dreamed about. I'm not kidding, either. She has actual dreams about Cyn giving her permission to use that nickname. She nodded enthusiastically. Toaster conversation be damned, there's a new champion for the longest interaction. Maybe the mark isn't so bad? Maybe she's finally seeing it for the gift it is? It got her this conversation, at least.

So far, all interactions have been great for our nervous girl. However, that could change quickly, because walking through the door now was assistant director Curtis Evans. Most of Grace's coworkers got along well, and a large part of that was because of hate-bonding over A.D. Evans. He was arrogant, belittling, and perhaps worst of all, a corporate yes-man. Tania filtered most of his bullshit, but whenever there were one-on-one interactions, they were seldom pleasant. At best, he infantilized you by assuming you didn't know how to do your job. At worst, he'd berate you for being an idiot. There are two Pets YES facilities in the area, and he split his time evenly between them. Unfortunately, it looks like the Seerstown location drew the short straw today.

Cyn gave Grace a look that screamed "ugh". Grace rolled her eyes. Evans didn't pay any mind as he walked past. He simply looked straight ahead. Everything about him annoyed Grace. His freshly pressed expensive suit, his slicked back, sleazy hair, the dead mouse under his nose, which he called a mustache, and his gross trailing green aura. Wait. Think through that again, Grace. Trailing green aura? Sure enough, following the semi-big boss was the same translucent green mist that appeared behind Chase just a week ago.

"No way!" Grace exclaimed a little too loudly, causing Cyn and A.D. Evans to glance toward her. It was at this point Evans noticed the mark, and gave a disgusted look. Grace shifted and readied her fist. This could get ugly fast. However, the boss just huffed and faced forward, never missing a stride. Frantically, Grace scanned the area, trying to find another one of those creatures. Surprisingly, none were found. She wondered if maybe the aura could be something else. When it came down to it, she had only just started seeing them, and they were still a mystery. It was not something else, however. As mentioned earlier, a strong enough silence can control their host from miles away and even act independently.

"Whoa, what was that?" Grace was so busy looking for a monster that she didn't notice her coworker, Sami Perez, had entered. Grace snapped her attention to him as he set up his workspace.

"Oh, hey Sami. Uh, what was what?"

"The massive mean mug boss man just gave you. I felt that ice from all the way over here." Sami pretended to shiver.

"It's because he's a dick," Cyn chimed in, shaking her head. "Assistant director Evans is a bigot. Why am I not surprised?" She must have noticed Evans eyeing up Grace's new ink and assumed that's what caused the icy glare. Pretty astute observation, actually.

"Well, yeah, he's a textbook misogynist, but I've never seen that look before," Sami said. At this point, Cyn realized she almost pointed out the mark to Sami and pulled back.

"Yeah, well, the great A.D. Evans doesn't need a reason to put a little flair in his stare, I guess." Cyn tried to redirect her comments.

"That was some extra flair, for sure. Hopefully, we don't lose you, Grace." Sami sat down and adjusted a pink stuffed octopus on his desk. "Oh, this is cute." Grace was honestly only half listening to this exchange. Enough to pick up that Cyn was sticking up for her, and maybe something about Sami's flair. It didn't matter. Her mind was on that green aura. What did it mean?

"It means he is diseased." That strange voice rang again in Grace's head. It wasn't singing this time. The occasion didn't call for song, after all. Grace slowly spun around in her chair, seeking the voice's source.

"Grace, you okay? I'm pretty sure he's gone now. Been in his office for a solid minute," Sami called out.

"Yeah. Of course. I just thought I heard something. Did you not hear that?"

"Uh oh. The intense flair stare is getting to her, Cyn," Sami teased.

"I didn't hear anything," Cyn replied, ignoring Sami's remark. "Maybe someone has their music on?"

"Yeah," said Grace, coping. "That's gotta be it."

"While I am always flattered to be referred to as music itself, I am most assuredly talking to you," the voice rang out again.

"Where, though?" Grace asked, knowing she wasn't imagining it.

"You are not ready to witness me."

"So you *are* somewhere around here."

"No. I am a figment in your head. It is not of import." Grace surveyed the area again. This time, she stood up and twisted in all directions.

"Okay, I was joking before, but now I'm actually worried. Is she good?" Sami asked Cyn. Cyn knew Grace was not good, but she also knew it wasn't up to her to say anything, so all she gave in response was a shrug.

"Halt your search," the ethereal voice demanded. "I am not present. I am within all living things."

"Which one is it? You're not here, or you're everywhere? Those don't make sense together."

"I assure you, they do." The voice was frazzled.

Grace noticed the pink stuffed octopus on Sami's desk. It looked familiar. Something about it. "Sami, where'd you get that?"

"This adorable little thing?" Sami picked it up and looked at it curiously. "No idea. Probably left by an admirer."

"One of your many?" Cyn chimed in. Sami flashed a devilish grin. Grace stepped closer to take a better look.

"What are you doing? Do not lay eyes upon the kraken." The voice lost its cool demeanor. "Spending time on the kraken is not worthwhile. The diseased one. That is who you need to worry about."

Now Grace definitely knew something was up. Who would refer to this rounded, cute octopus plush as a kraken? "Sami, can I see that for a second?"

Sami shrugged and handed it to her. That's when he spotted it. "Oh, Grace. I didn't know you were resurrected!" Finally, Sami noticed. "Good for you! Wear that proud, girl."

Grace didn't have time for this. "Yeah, it's rather recent." She grabbed the octopus from Sami's hand. Immediately, a jolt ran through her body, and a light hum vibrated off her skin. The frequency was still pretty low, so it was undetectable.

"You know, sometime you'll have to tell me what it's like to die. As a writer, I'd love to hear about that."

"Hey, idiot. Have some tact?" Cyn interrupted.

"What? I don't have a problem with it. I just want to know what it's like," he replied.

Grace was preoccupied with the sensation in her body and the obvious preamble of sound warming up. She recalled the deafening music from last time, and hoped to avoid that in front of Cyn. "I have to pee," was the best excuse she had. She bolted away to find a private location.

"Moron." Cyn hit Sami on the shoulder and went off after Grace.

Sami briefly recoiled. "Did she just take my octopus to the bathroom?" he pondered. "Yeah, I don't want that back."

Grace burst through a door into the stairway. This was the most secluded spot she could think of. A pretty good option, to be honest. Nobody used the stairs. She did a brief check for other bodies. The coast was clear. "Is this you?" Grace interrogated the octopus. "Are you the one in my head?"

"Of course not, child," the voice spoke and betrayed itself. Vibrations ran down Grace's arm, straight to her heart. There was no doubt that this little cutie was connected.

"Don't lie to me, it's so obvious!"

"How embarrassing. Yes. I am the one who has been speaking to you." With that admission, the low hum stopped. Poor plush couldn't hide from her duty any longer, it would seem. It was at this point something clicked.

"Wait. You were there when I fought Chase and that thing!" Grace remembered seeing the same octopus resting on the bookshelf.

"I have been here the whole time. I just do not always have things to comment on." The octopus gave up the act and started moving about with its small, adorable tentacles. Grace shrieked and dropped the plush. "Insolence!" the voice shouted. "You wanted me to admit the truth, and when I do, you toss me to the ground like common trash."

"Oh my god! I am so sorry! I just wasn't expecting you to move like that." Grace quickly picked the plush up.

"Calm yourself, it is fine. You are forgiven. I, also, have not fully gotten familiar with this body." The octopus nestled briefly in Grace's hand, before moving up on its tentacles in a triumphant pose. "Allow me to introduce myself, resurrected. I am Octavia. Ruler of sea and melody."

Ah, Octavia. I wondered when she'd show up. She was once a fearsome kraken who ruled over the dominion of the sea. A long time ago, she made a deal with a resurrected named Ragnar and was now bound to the Sonata Mor. Her current form is a little less fierce, and definitely not her first choice. I wouldn't bring it up.

"Octavia. Got it. I'm Grace." Grace was rolling with the punches.

"I know."

"Oh, of course you know." Grace bonked her forehead. "Because you're in my brain."

"No. Your companions have used your name several times."

"Right." Grace nodded. "You're a very observant plushy."

"I am *not* a 'plushy' as you say. I am the fierce kraken and protector of the Sonata composer."

"Oh no! I didn't mean to offend you. I just meant..." Grace went into her default mode.

"It's okay. Raise your head, child." It bears mentioning that Grace was not bowing her head. "I harbor no ill-will. I am here to guide you."

"Really? Thank you! I desperately need that." It was at this moment Cyn opened the stairwell door, just in time to see Grace excitedly hug the stuffed octopus, thanking it profusely. Grace's eyes shot to the newcomer, and she died a second time seeing who it was. Octavia returned to a still state.

"Hey," Cyn said, trying to ignore what she had just witnessed. "Wanted to check on you. Sami shouldn't have asked you that." Grace was a little confused. Once again, she had barely paid attention to him.

"Oh, yeah. Definitely. I know," she went along, cupping the octopus in front of her. "I'm fine, though. Really!"

"Sure," Cyn said skeptically. "Well, if you're ever not fine..."

"Cyn?" Grace cut in.

"Yeah, what's up?"

"Did your cousin... The one with the mark. Did he ever like... hear voices?" Grace couldn't believe she was asking, but she needed to know.

"No, I don't think he ever mentioned that," Cyn answered, perplexed. "Are you hearing...?" She gestured to the octopus.

"What? Oh, no," Grace lied. "Definitely not. It's just really cute. That's all!"

"Gotcha." Cyn looked sympathetic, pausing for a moment. "I'm sure what you're going through is overwhelming, and I can't say it would surprise me if resurrecting meant hearing things that other people can't. There's gotta be some kind of spiritual connection, right?"

She had a point. Coming back from the dead changes you.

Not usually in this way, however. Not every resurrected gets their own plush Octavia. "I'm just saying that if you are hearing things, I don't think that'd be weird." The remark landed.

"Yeah, I guess it wouldn't be." Grace let the words marinate as she finally started to calm down. Perhaps she was still hoping for things to be the way they had been. To be normal. That's just not her reality anymore. "Everything's definitely going to be different now, huh?"

"Doesn't have to be a bad thing," Cyn consoled her. Grace wasn't sure if it was her fatigue of hiding or just the words of the cute girl in front of her, but she found herself with a flash of confidence. She nodded assuredly and gently placed Octavia on the stair rail. In a majestic motion, she threw her hair up into a ponytail, fully exposing the mark. Cyn grinned.

"I had to do a lot for this thing, so I may as well show it off a bit, huh?" Grace laughed.

"Hell yeah! Looks pretty badass, too."

Grace's face flushed. "Oh, thank you, thank you." She did a slight curtsy. It was awkward, but luckily for her, Cyn found it endearing.

"Not to interrupt, but we do have a monstrosity in the building, remember?" Octavia re-inserted herself. Only Grace heard the intrusion.

"Right." Grace responded out loud. She wanted nothing more than to continue this exchange with Cyn, but Octavia had a point. "Hey, I do just need a quick moment." She forced the words out.

"Oh, yeah. Of course." Cyn was caught a little off guard. "I'll leave you two to it." She cheekily referenced the octopus.

"Ha, yeah." Grace couldn't think of anything witty to say as Cyn walked through the door, raising a hand briefly to say bye.

As soon as they were alone again, Octavia sprang back to life. "Phew, glad that is over."

"Yeah, totally." Grace agreed, but she didn't mean it.

"Now, about the abomination floating around this office. His silence is a strong one. We have to discover where it is controlling him from."

"Um, where *what* is controlling him from? And why does his silence matter, exactly?" Grace was trying to keep up. Ocatavia was never great at on-boarding.

"Right. Sorry, perhaps I am going too fast. It appears the Silence is not a widely discussed topic in modern day. Not as much as the last time I was in this realm."

"The last time? This realm?"

"Enough! History lessons come later. That thing noticed you earlier. We must make haste." Octavia wasn't being fully honest here. Sure, Curtis noticed the mark, but that alone wouldn't cause a silence to act out. It's true that the silence generally don't like the resurrected, mainly because they can't infect them. But rarely would any silence consider a resurrected a threat. What's happening here is that a cooped-up sea beast is looking for some action. "A silence is the name of the creature you fought last week. When you see that green aura around a person, it means they are infected and controlled by one."

"Okay. Got it." Grace gave a determined look, but her inquisitive side couldn't help itself. "And why are they called silence?"

Octavia groaned. She really wanted to kill something.

"Because they are an extension of a most unfortunate being called the Silence. A god aiming to rid the world of any pleasant emotion. Can we please continue?"

"Yeah, totally."

"Great. The silence—"

"It's just," Grace reeled the fish back in, "the creature is called a silence, but the god they are part of is also called the Silence?"

"Correct." Octavia sighed.

Grace stewed on that for a moment, much to Octavia's chagrin. "That's going to get confusing."

"They have been known as silence for as long as I have existed, child."

"Right, right. But it's still confusing. Like, what if you're talking about the god, and I'm talking about the not-god ones? And then in the heat of combat, or something, our miscommunication leads to our doom?"

Wow, she is really getting hung up on this. If Octavia was in her original body, she would have assuredly forced Grace to shut up by now.

"Ah, I see. We have dealt with this issue as written language has developed. The spelling of the god is with a capital S and the minions with a lowercase s. Problem solved."

"No. It isn't. Because we aren't going to be writing. What if..." Grace raised her finger triumphantly, signaling an idea. "What if we called the ones that infect people something else? Like... silent knights?"

Truly a cringe-worthy suggestion. One that can be blamed on her marketing experience. However, Octavia, unaware of any reference, seemed to like it, and her demeanor suddenly changed.

"Silent knight, you say?" She stroked her sewn on mouth with one of her chubby tentacles. "I like it. Henceforth they shall be known as silent knights."

Groan. Just like that, creatures who have existed for millennia have been rebranded.

"Yes!" Grace took the win. "So, A.D. Evans is being controlled by a silent knight?"

"Correct." Octavia was happy to be back on topic.

"Shouldn't it be close, then? The one with Chase was right behind him."

"Unfortunately, this one will not be as simple, resurrected. This one is not a mere babe. It is stronger and likely has been controlling its host for months, if not years."

"Wow, years?" Grace was stunned. "Huh, maybe that's why he's always been such an asshole?"

"Fret not, child." Side note, Grace was not fretting. "Every silent knight still leaves a trace that can be followed. There may not be strings like last time, but a true composer can always catch a trace."

"And that's me?" Grace pointed to herself. "You can also just call me Grace, by the way. Not that resurrected and child aren't endearing terms..."

"Yes, resurrected Grace. You are the bearer of the Sonata Mor. A gift with the power to purge a heart and rid it of the Silence." Octavia took her suggestion—kind of.

"So that's what it is. The Sonata—"

"Quiet." Octavia quickly stopped her. Grace instinctively took up a defensive position, searching for any potential threat. "If you speak the name, it will activate. Right now, the silent knight only knows you have the mark, not the Sonata. We should try to keep it that way."

Grace relaxed her stance. "Okay, power is voice activated. Good to know. Very anime." Grace logged the info away. "So, what do we do?"

"You will need to get close to the diseased one. That should allow you to pick up the trace from his aura, like how a shark picks up the scent of its prey by their blood."

"Alright, get close to A.D. Evans. Smell his aura blood. I think I can definitely..." Grace hesitated. "Try to do that."

"The moment is nigh, resurrected Grace," Octavia urged. "I will need more confidence than that."

"Alright, fine. I'll probably be able to do it." Grace attempted to bolster her gumption.

Octavia jumped onto her shoulders, aching for an adventure. You could almost see a gleam in those stitched eyes. "Fair enough. I will take it. Let us depart!" Octavia called out, and the two set out on their quest... right to Grace's computer. She sat and logged into her email. "What are you doing? I thought we were going to track down the silent knight?"

"I haven't logged in yet today. I need my work chat to show I'm active, or I could get in trouble." Grace verified her login through her phone. Octavia groaned. Cyn glanced up to check on Grace. The image of her frantically logging in while a stuffed octopus perched on her shoulder was quite the sight. Cyn darted a glare at Sami, before nodding toward Grace. Sami begrudgingly got up from his seat and walked over to the social media coordinator. "Plus, once I'm in, I can look at A.D. Evans's calendar," Grace continued, speaking out loud to Octavia.

Sami butted in, having heard what he assumed was Grace talking to herself. "Evans? He has that big board meeting today. I hear even the director's coming. He'll be tied up all day."

"Shit." Grace frowned. It took her a second to register that Sami was the one who answered. She shot her attention over to him, a little embarrassed that he heard her. "Oh, thanks, Sami. I completely forgot that was today."

"Yeah, yeah. It's going to be a big deal. I'd definitely stay away from him. He is a nasty, mustachioed snapping turtle before and after those meetings. Not that you should need any more reason to avoid him."

"Thanks for the heads up." Grace went back to pondering.

"Of course." Sami smiled and started to return to his desk, only to be met with Cyn's wide eyes, prompting him to turn around. "Oh, right. Grace, I also wanted to..." He glanced at Cyn. She was not blinking. It was terrifying. "Uh, I wanted to apologize about before. That was really messed up, I guess. I would obviously never pressure you to talk about—"

"It's okay, Sami." Grace stopped him. She needed to think, and honestly, she still didn't even remember what he said.

"So we're good?"

"Yeah, we're good."

"Great!" Sami gave two thumbs up and headed back to his

desk. He shot Cyn a smug look that screamed, "There, you happy?" Cyn was more confused than happy. Perhaps she was intervening too intensely. After all, it appeared to her like Grace couldn't care less. It's not totally unreasonable to assume Grace would care more. If this was even a few hours ago, those remarks would have sent her spiraling. At this moment, however, Grace was on a mission.

She verified the assistant director did, in fact, have the big meeting today. He had blocked off a chunk of time on his calendar beforehand, which she could only assume was for preparation.

"Damn, it's going to be hard to get near him today," Grace said, a little quieter now.

"I do not see the problem," Octavia scoffed.

"It's a private meeting with big wigs. I'm not exactly invited."

"Storm the meeting."

"I can't just storm the meeting."

"Why not? Ragnar used to storm a lot of things much more dangerous than a meeting. I have found it to be a very effective strategy."

"Well, I'm not Ragnar—whoever the hell that is—and this is the modern age. You can't just go storming into meetings and keep your job."

"You are no Ragnar, that is for sure." Octavia pouted. Grace leaned back in her chair, tilted her head parallel with the ceiling, and closed her eyes. This was a practice she did a lot while brainstorming. Whenever she needed an idea, she found this posture productive. Octavia toppled off her shoulder and quickly grabbed onto the chair to avoid a devastating fall to the ground. "You nearly dropped me to the floor again, you wretch!" Grace couldn't hear Octavia; she was too deep in thought.

"I only need to get near him, right? For how long?" Grace asked, still in generator mode. Please note that is what she calls it. Not my idea.

"Depends how intuitive you are," a disgruntled Octavia answered, climbing back atop Grace's shoulder.

"Can I have a ballpark here? Like what's the shortest and longest time it could take based on my intuition level?"

"For Ragnar, it would take three minutes, but he was more of a fighter than anything else. Matteo had better insight. He could pick up a trace in fifteen seconds." Octavia was talking about two of the previous Sonata composers. She failed to mention the most recent.

"Okay, I'm going to assume you're talking about other composers." Good job with the context clues, Grace. "So, then where do you think I fall between Matteo and Ragnar?" Octavia took a second to contemplate.

"I do not know you well. However, you do not appear nearly as skilled a fighter as Ragnar, nor do you seem particularly insightful, like Matteo."

"Thanks. This is great."

"For your first trace, we will want at least two minutes. That is a relatively low bar."

"Two minutes. Okay. So you think I can do it faster than Ragnar?"

"Resurrected Grace, I should hope so. Ragnar was an amazing warrior, but he had terrible insight. He made up for his lack of intuition by physically subduing his opponent until he caught the trace of the silent knight." Octavia glanced at Grace's modest arms. "I do not think that is an option for you."

"Hey! I'll have you know I was in gymnastics for like seven years."

"I do not know what that means."

"It means you're probably still right." Grace sighed, then sprang forward in her chair. Octavia held on this time. "So, I only need two minutes." She looked closely at the calendar. "If this is right, he'll probably leave his office for the meeting around 9:25. He strikes me as the kind of person who won't be the first to a meeting, but not the last either." Grace visualized the potential flow of events. "The walk from his office to the conference room may be close to two minutes. If I simply follow him during that walk, that should do it." Grace clenched her fist in victory.

"And if he notices you, we fight?"

"Whoa, whoa, whoa. We don't have to fight. It's a big office. There are lots of reasons I could be heading the same way. There's a bathroom near that conference room. I'll just pretend I'm going there." The plan was all coming together.

"I look forward to seeing your skills. Hopefully, the time you spent in the gymnastics will serve you well."

"You're not really using that word right," Grace observed. A quick look at the clock showed they had fifteen minutes before they needed to spring into action. This meant Grace felt there was time for an educational moment. "Here. Let me show you what gymnastics is." Grace pulled up a video on her phone. The screen instantly captured Octavia's attention.

"How nimble! Are these warriors training?"

"Well, they are training, but not to fight or anything."

"Then what could they possibly be training for?"

"For sport. Just to see what they can do, I guess? For fun, maybe?"

"For fun?" Octavia scoffed. "What a waste." She turned away from the screen in disappointment.

Grace nervously laughed. "Okay, not a sports fan. Noted." She began to put her phone away.

"Wait." Octavia stopped her. She pursed her lip and begrudgingly asked, "Perhaps we can watch just one more of these gymnastics on your magic rectangle."

"Of course." Grace smirked and resumed the video, keeping a close eye on the clock. This would prove to be an effective way to pass the time.

When it was 9:25, they took a screen break, and Grace got

into position. This apparently meant meandering near Curtis Evans's office. She was trying her best to play it cool, to not raise any alarms. This was accomplished by staring at an old black and white ad of a cat and dog cuddling, while a bag of the original PetYums™ treats sat beside them. Grace read the caption, "Good nutrition. Better Friends", multiple times. There was only so much she could study about this picture. Grace clutched her purse, which held an excited Octavia, thrilled to be back on the hunt. You could tell Grace felt uncomfortable wearing it, as it made it look like she was leaving. People thinking she was skipping work after a week off was the last thing she needed. Still, it was arguably less noticeable than wandering the halls with a stuffed animal in her hands.

Minutes were ticking away, and she could hear Evans still working in his office. Turns out, he was the type to be last to a meeting. This was due to a large hubris that enjoyed making people wait. Finally, at 9:29, A.D. Evans emerged from his office.

Grace tried not to look at him, zeroing in on the advertisement. As soon as she knew he wasn't paying attention, she began to tail. "So what exactly am I looking for here?" Grace whispered. "What does the trace look like?"

"You will know it when you see it." Octavia was thrilled to bits.

"Like porn. Great."

"Like what?"

"Why did I think you would get that reference?"

Evans stopped in his tracks. Quickly Grace tried to find something else to look at in the hall. This time, her averted gaze fell onto a motivational poster. A cat sat pleasantly atop a clothing line, winking at the camera. A speech bubble read, "I hung in there!" while the phrase "Celebrate Your Perseverance" filled the bottom in big, bold letters. Truly tactless corporate jargon. See, this is exactly the kind of environment that gives way to ideas like "silent knights".

"The board is real excited to hear about Waterfall Lake, Tania. I'll let you know how it goes," Evans said to Grace's supervisor, who was in the break room, grabbing her fifth cup of decaf coffee. She liked the taste. Grace exhaled a sigh of relief. He hadn't noticed them yet. Tania muttered something back to Evans, but who really cares? After a moment, he resumed his trek to the meeting, which he was now late to. A true power move. Grace followed. She squinted hard at him, trying to see anything unusual, but nothing was happening. The splitting off point was just up ahead. This was bad. Maybe she actually was more daft than Ragnar?

"Anything yet?" Octavia questioned.

"No," Grace grumbled. The moment of truth was here. In ten steps, Evans was going to enter the conference room, and Grace would have to veer off to the bathroom, a failure. However, Evans stopped again. Before Grace could pretend to look at something, the assistant director had turned around.

"Can I help you, miss?" he snarled. They've been made. Though it seems this guy doesn't even know Grace's name, so that works in their favor. Grace tried not to panic.

"I'm just going to the bathroom!" she practically shouted.

Evans sneered. "Is that so?" He looked at her mark again. The look of disgust screamed from every muscle on his face. Grace tried to scoot past him, but he sidestepped in her way. "You don't think I noticed you following me?"

"Um, following? What? Me? You? Like on social media?" Grace let out an anxious laugh. "For real, though, I just really need to pee. So..." Grace tried to move around him, and again he blocked her exit.

"Don't think I don't know what you are." He eyed her up and down as he leaned in closer, his mustache resting on a heavy frown. "Disgusting." He spat the word like venom.

"How dare you!" Octavia burst out of the purse. A.D. Evans stumbled backward and looked at the stuffed octopus in shock, and then back at Grace. It was at this moment Grace noticed a small green spark. It flitted in the sky just behind Evans, waving around like a leaf in the wind. "You are the disgusting one." Octavia continued her guard dog bark.

"It's... it's you!" Evans stuttered. Grace's eyes grew wide. They'd really been made now. Evans slowly backed away. Anger in his stare. "Mark my words... You both shall perish." As he reached the door, he took a second to collect himself, straighten his tie, and give one last leer before disappearing into the conference room. As he entered, you could hear him jovially say, "Greg! How were the links last week?"

Grace stood there, stunned. "What just happened?"

"He figured us out," Octavia responded. "He knows you are a composer now."

"Because of you?" Grace asked in a slightly accusatory way.

"Ah, yes, it would seem so." Octavia owned her mistake, but was not apologetic in the least. "I admit, I may have been a little overzealous."

"I actually get it. I've wanted to say that to him a lot in the past." Grace understood. "It was kind of cool to watch someone else finally do it."

"We are definitely on the clock now. So, please tell me you got the trace?" Octavia inquired. Grace looked ahead at the green spark still dancing in the air.

"Yeah." She smiled. "I got it."

THREE
NOBODY'S HOME

Grace felt like garbage. She had to ask Tania if she could go home early. The immense look of disappointment from her boss was almost too much to handle. All that hyping up she did this morning, only to return to the real world for roughly an hour and a half.

"I can't believe I had to leave after only two hours," Grace vented to Octavia, the trace still flittering in front of her. The two had taken to the streets. The composer was finding her first time following a trace to be quite straightforward. All she had to do was follow the green sparks. They'd flow and dance their way to another. The only downside was that she had to be pretty attentive to see where they led. Unfortunately, this meant driving was a no-go, and the duo had to go by foot. Well, Grace had to go by foot. Octavia caught a ride in Grace's generic, albeit fashionable, purse.

"I am afraid I do not really understand. There is a monster in the office. You would think it would be in everyone's best interest for you to take care of it," Octavia responded. Corporate life was, understandably, a mystery to the sea beast. While Tania didn't have a clue about the monster in the building, I happen to know that she would much rather have Grace working on the new social campaign than hunting it down. That monster made the company good money.

"I haven't taken a sick day since I got the job." Grace ignored Octavia and continued to replay her misery. "My record has been destroyed over this last week."

"Once again, composer, you have lost me." Grace fiddled nervously and checked her phone, half expecting a termination notice. Nothing. Octavia wished they would stop talking about the job. The whole walk had been like this. Which was strange. She found previous composers to be quite inquisitive when she showed up. Typically, they would ask lines and lines of questions. Perhaps it was the deadline they were put under? Needing to track down a silence so quickly really cut down the Q&A portion. The great kraken's embarrassment with her appearance didn't help either. After all, it took her almost a full week to make herself known. Not sure why she's so shy about being a plushy, however. The last time she returned was as a wooden puppet. Was that actually preferable?

"So, is there like a max radius a silent knight can be from its host?" Grace huffed, shifting gears.

Octavia's wish was granted—a legitimate question! She cleared her throat. "I would not say there is a max, per se. The furthest I personally have seen was about five miles from the host."

"Five miles?!" Grace groaned. "Any chance my power lets me fly or something?"

"Wings are wasted on those who never walked, dearest Grace." Octavia gave Grace a reassuring and squishy pat on the back. "But also no. The Sonata Mor has never provided the ability to fly." Grace sighed. In her mind, she believed they must have gone five miles already. It's actually been closer to two and a quarter, but she doesn't need to know that. She continued to follow the trace into a costly residential area. Big yards, multi-story houses, and sculpted evergreen bushes everywhere you looked. Not ritzy enough to include any fountains, but upper class for sure.

"The part of town I'll never be able to afford," Grace remarked with a heavy sigh. The spark continued into the yard of one particular house. A large Victorian style home with white siding and a red door. "Okay, it wants me to go toward this house." Grace stopped in the driveway.

"Fantastic! We are closing in. Onward!" Octavia swung her chubby tentacle out front.

Grace resisted. "I can't just trespass."

"I am not sure I follow."

"This is someone's house. I can't just go into someone's house."

"But our silent knight is most assuredly in there." It kills me every time they use that term—silent knight.

"Ugh, why couldn't it have been some place that's not private property? Like an empty parking lot or an abandoned mall?"

"Silent knights are drawn to areas with people. Most people live in these houses, do they not?"

"They do." Grace took a deep breath. Knocking on a door gave her immense anxiety. She'd have to harken back to her Girl Scout days for this one. "Okay, easy. I'll just go up to the door and ring the doorbell."

"Ring a bell? And alert the silent knight?"

"Well, I can't just barge in, Octavia! Besides, it's not like it can answer the door, right?" Octavia decided this was a fair point. Grace made her way up the walkway. "When someone answers, I'll be able to see if the trace goes inside or try to catch a glimpse of the silent knight. Who knows, maybe the trace will go cold once I get to the door." It did not. In fact, it only got stronger. The once tiny spark was now a bursting barrage of embers dancing in the air. No doubt about it, the silent knight was in there. Ugh, now even I'm saying it.

Grace put her game face on and rang the doorbell. Octavia squiggled with excitement. The two waited for a moment. Nothing.

"Once more," encouraged Octavia. "Summon the chime once more!" Grace took Octavia's suggestion and pressed the doorbell one more time. Again, nothing. Grace leaned over to peek through a window. All the lights were off.

"I don't know if anybody is home," Grace said with just a twinge of hope. Maybe she didn't have to talk to strangers or fight a monster at this moment after all. And no, she could not determine which one of those situations would be worse. Sadly for Grace, just moments later, the door cracked open a sliver.

"What do you want?" A young voice came from beyond the crack.

"Hi there!" Grace snapped back into place, trying to play it off like she wasn't just peeking in the window. It was showtime. "I'm with the Historic Homes Society, or HHS, for short. We were wondering if we could take a gander at this beautiful home and capture some of its historic architecture!" This was a surprise. I had no idea she was capable of lying like this. Was it convincing? Not particularly, but there was a level of commitment there. I suppose if you looked into her past, you would see a brief period where, to win a contest in her Girl Scout troop, she devised a series of clever rouses to sell cookies. Look a little further, though, and you'd see her return to each of those houses and apologize in tears the next day, offering a full refund. Grace's group did not win.

"Historic homes?" the voice beyond the door responded.

"Yes! And yours is a beauty. We've been wanting to check it out for ages." Grace continued to commit.

"This house was built in 2004." The voice disarmed Grace's lie. She couldn't believe it. Someone built a modern home to look like this? Who would have guessed?

"Um, yeah. Exactly. The early 2000s are historic now." Grace tried to save face. "Yup. That's it. After twenty years, a house officially becomes historic. Historic house right here. Absolutely historical. Brimming with history." Everything fell silent for a moment. Grace held a smile through the awkward quiet. That sure was something.

"Wait. You're that girl." Finally the voice spoke. Its tone changed.

"What girl?" Grace asked nervously. Suddenly, the door shut. "Shit!" Grace exclaimed, trying to figure out what had just happened. "That person seemed to know who I was. There's no way that was the silent knight, right?"

"Impossible. A silent knight does not speak on its own. It uses the one it possesses."

"Right, and we know that A.D. Evans is in that meeting for at least another hour. And that sure as hell didn't sound like him."

"We must get to the bottom of this," Octavia cried out. "Summon the chime once more!"

"Enough with the chime summoning! Is that really the best —" A booming air wave burst through the door, sending Grace and Octavia flying backwards. Splintered red wood rained down from the sky. The door was completely demolished. Grace got up on her elbows and looked toward the house. There stood a silent knight. Sparks of green flashed all around the creature as it looked forward with hollow eyes.

"What the hell?" Grace exclaimed. "I thought silent knights couldn't fight on their own?"

"Whatever gave you that idea?" Octavia bounced her way back to Grace.

"The last one used Chase to do all the fighting."

"You have much to learn about these monsters. A strong one is more than capable of battling on its own." The silent knight stepped into the yard. It moved apprehensively, analyzing Grace and Octavia, studying them.

"Well, why wouldn't you tell me that ahead of time?" Grace groaned.

"I find experience is the best teacher," Octavia lied. The kraken is usually quite chatty and loves to feel important. What she's ashamed to admit is that the thrill of the chase after a hundred years dormant really got the better of her. "It is swim time, composer."

"Don't you mean sink or swim time?"

"There will be no sinking," Octavia urged.

"Alright, let's do this." Grace stood back up and braced herself. "Sonata Mor!" The purple aura instantly swirled around Grace, and the stringed instruments erupted in quite the unharmonious tone. It sounded like a fifth-grade orchestra recital. Truly unpleasant. Even Grace had to cover her ears.

"There is discord within you, resurrected," Octavia observed.

"What?" Grace tried to shout over the screeching music. The silent knight bent forward and cranked its neck almost perpendicular with its body. A wave of energy formed by its would-be mouth, filling the air with a void before launching toward Grace. It crashed into her stomach and sent her and Octavia flying back in separate directions. The sound stopped abruptly. Honestly, kind of thankful for that last part. Grace moaned as she struggled to get back up. "It can fire energy balls?"

"It holds a power not entirely unlike your own." Octavia rolled back. "Some would call it the antithesis to yours. True silence. A void. Before we can fight it, we must do something about that sound of yours."

"Yeah, that was kind of not good, huh?" The silent knight advanced.

"One of the worst songs I have ever heard a Sonata composer produce."

"Gee thanks." Grace was back on her feet. Octavia pondered the problem. The silent knight bent down again and formed the void aura—that's what the ability is commonly called. Let's pray marketing doesn't get their hands on that one.

"Sonata Mor!" Grace tried again. Once more, a clashing song screamed out. The silent knight shot the void, and Grace did the only thing she could think of. She punched it. Hard. This had little-to-no effect and only pushed her backward. This time she stood her ground, at least.

"There truly is discord within your heart," Octavia reiterated as she hopped up on the composer.

"Oh, discord! That's what you said. I couldn't hear you before because—"

"Composer!" Octavia cut her off to draw attention to another flying aura. This time, Grace barely spun around to dodge it.

"So, it's going to keep doing that. Great."

"Focus, Grace. You are of a divided heart. One can hear it clashing."

"I don't know what that means!" Another void fired and dodged, all the while the silent knight kept closing the gap.

"In your previous fight, you found determination. You need to find that again."

"I am determined," Grace argued. The silent knight bent down to summon its only spammable move.

"Have you accepted your role? You must accept you are a resurrected now."

"I have! Since day one, pretty much. Remember when I was talking to Cyn? Totally talked about how cool I was with it." Grace firmed her stance. "I'm all in, baby." Grace braced herself for another attempt. She crossed her fingers. "Sonata Mor!" The instruments broke out into the same dissonance. Grace grimaced at the noise that was somehow worse than before. It distracted her just long enough that she could not dodge the void this time. It struck her in the chest, and she spiraled backward onto the ground, yet again. Will she get up this time? Cue that Chumbawamba song, and let's find out.

"Dammit!" Grace cried out. "I accepted it. I did. Why isn't it working?" Tears formed on her face.

"Are you sure about that?" Octavia rebutted. "Saying you are okay with something and being okay with something are not of equivalence."

"I... I did." Grace looked at the sky. "Right?"

"What was the first action you took when we started tracking the silent knight?"

"I came up with a plan to find the trace." Grace sat up and saw the knight marching toward her. It was coming to finish the job. She needed to get up, but her legs were weak.

"Incorrect. You checked your magic box for a thing called work chat," Octavia said with a slight tremble. She knew Grace couldn't take much more, and Octavia did not want to lose another composer so soon. Not after the last time.

"I... I didn't want to get in trouble," Grace realized.

"And the entire way here, what were you talking about?"

"I was upset about needing to leave early." It was sinking in now. "I was worried I was going to get in trouble..." Grace truly thought she had accepted that life would be different. She thought she could make a big declaration, and it would change everything. That's not how this works. Her heart knows that, and now, so does she. The silent knight got down and charged up the largest void aura yet. It knew Grace couldn't move fast enough at this moment. It was going in for the kill. "I was worried about leaving some shitty job with some shitty boss who doesn't even care." Grace let out a chuckle of disbelief. Octavia grinned. She could tell Grace was feeling it. "Why do I still even care?"

"Grab my tentacle," Octavia called out. It was time. Grace gripped onto the plushy, rounded appendage. "Listen carefully. You do not need pure resolve in this moment. You need only know that you must find it," Octavia assured her. "Now, call the music." The silent knight shot the void as the words escaped Grace's mouth.

"Sonata Mor!" The instruments awoke, this time in closer harmony. It was by no means a masterpiece, or even fully in tune, but the strings were at last working together. A purple sound wave zipped through Grace's body and onto Octavia, where it branched out into a massive tentacle. It was quite the sight—the kraken-sized limb sprouting from the tiny plush. It whipped around and bashed the void bomb away and out of the park. The silent knight took a step back. It finally had something to worry about.

"Whoa," Grace shouted. "That's so badass!"

"Heh." Octavia smirked. "This is not even my final form." The tentacle wound back again and slashed toward the silent knight. Its target was barely able to avoid the attack by falling to the ground. "Now we go on the offensive!" Grace looked at Octavia and nodded.

"Let's do this." With renewed energy, Grace got on her feet and raised the plush over her head, causing the appendage to rise high into the sky. The sun gleamed off the beautiful sound wave. "Sounds like payback." She swung down the plushy and massive sound tentacle directly unto the exposed silent knight. Violas and violins crescendoed, leading to a satisfying *bang*. Sparks went flying. Literally. The silence exploded into thousands of green sparks and black goo, before slowly dissipating into the air. The music came to a stop along with the aura, and Grace fell to her knees, exhausted.

"Victory!" Octavia screamed.

"Hey! Keep it down out there! Before I call the cops, asshole!" one neighbor shouted from the window. "What kind of person blasts classical music anyway? What a joke."

"Dad, chill," the voice of a girl responded from another room in the house.

"Sorry!" Grace exclaimed, before falling to her back and letting out a relieved laugh. Octavia rolled onto Grace's chest.

"I am proud of you, dear Grace. You may have only been able

to draw out one eighth of my power, but you defeated the knight, nonetheless."

Grace smiled. "Thanks, Tavi."

"Tavi?"

"Yeah, like a nickname. Octavia is a little long." The idea was intriguing to Octavia. She had never had a nickname before. She pondered whether it undercut her authority. "You don't like it?"

"No. It is acceptable," Octavia settled. "But only if spoken with the utmost respect."

"Of course, Tavi! Nothing but." Grace squeezed the plush and let out another laugh. Octavia didn't care for that as much. As Grace stared at the sky again, she truly felt lighter. She hadn't laughed like this in years, and yes, that includes the time before she was dead. "Wait, did I just have an anime power up moment?"

"You need to stop speaking nonsense." Octavia shook off the remark. Perhaps she was too flustered by the outburst of affection, but the guardian was being a little sloppy. For around the corner of the shattered doorway, a set of eyes peered out. They belonged to Jake Evans. A seemingly harmless nine-year-old boy. Trust me, though, Jake is far from harmless. Octavia really should have caught that. She said it herself. Silence don't talk on their own. Who did she think answered the door? Jake glared at the two before running out the back door. That's not such a good thing for our Grace.

It took the composer a while to get up, but eventually she regained her strength for the nearly three-mile walk back to her car. She wasn't happy about that and desperately tried to convince Octavia to "kraken up" to carry them back. Of course, that was impossible. The two of them could barely keep up that form for thirty seconds, and it was only one tentacle. No, the long walk would fall on Grace.

After a treacherous journey, she finally got back to her car, completely beat. As luck would have it, Cyn was leaving at that very moment.

"Hey Grace!" Cyn cheerily called.

"Hi!" Grace mustered up everything she could to pretend she wasn't dying of exhaustion.

"I thought you went home like a long time ago?"

"Yeah, I did. I just forgot my car here."

"Oh, I didn't realize you lived close enough to walk home." Cyn tried to understand. "And forget about your car."

"No, no. It's not like that." Grace waved her hand in the air, as if to brush the notion aside.

"Oh. Okay." Cyn was lost, but felt perhaps it was best to drop it. "Oh, you totally missed it!"

"Huh?" Grace really could collapse at any moment.

"Evans had this total meltdown while you were gone. Started bawling at the end of that meeting. Just began apologizing like crazy. Apparently, he's been fudging numbers to mislead investors and a whole bunch of other unsavory things. I couldn't believe it! I mean, I knew he was a jerk, but I didn't know he was corrupt. Security came, and they had to walk him out and everything."

"Whoa. For real?" Grace totally forgot about the puppet Curtis Evans. She realized it would make sense for him to have an awakening after the silence removed its hold on him. A similar thing happened to Chase, after all. "That's wild." She sounded somber. Chase was only infected for a couple of weeks, and it ruined his relationship. Grace wondered how long Curtis had been under control. Months? Years? How significantly did it ruin his life? Did he do those horrible things before he was infected? As much as she'd love to rejoice over her former asshole assistant director getting comeuppance, she had no way of knowing if he truly deserved it. What a boring attitude. Cyn picked up on Grace's vibe.

"Oh, I mean. Yeah, it was wild." She tried to adjust her tone to match the current mood, and away from the previous excited and gossipy one she started with. Though, after the interaction Grace and Evans had that morning, Cyn thought Grace would be more elated. Doesn't everyone want revenge, no matter how small? Personally, revenge would be more interesting. Cyn couldn't figure Grace out. She wondered if Grace was the type who loved her job and the company. "Sorry if I came in hot. Obviously, it sucks. I mean, he got away with that for so long. Pets YES will take a hit—"

"No, no! It's not that. It's just been a day," Grace interjected.

"Right, of course!" Cyn recalibrated. "You doing okay? Need anything?" Grace had to laugh inside. This is the girl of her dreams asking if she needed anything. From Cyn? Grace needed everything. But right now, she just needed to get home. The Sonata Mor can be incredibly draining. Especially when the sound is not perfectly in tune. Which it definitely was not.

"Thanks. I think I just need a bed." Grace attempted to finish the walk to her car, but her weak legs finally revolted, and she stumbled to the ground. Octavia went rolling out of her bag, trying to stay still. Cyn quickly ran to Grace's side.

"Whoa. You really aren't doing well." She helped Grace up and even scooped up the inanimate Octavia. I'm sure part of her has to think it's weird Grace carries a stuffy around, right? "You can't drive like this."

"Oh, sure I can! I'm just super tired. It's not like I'm drunk." Grace flashed a thumbs up as she quickly regained her balance, breaking free from Cyn's grip. The warmth of Cyn's arm still lingered along her back. She wondered if that counted as a hug.

"Tired driving can impair you just as much. Come on, I'll give you a ride today."

"No, for real."

"No, you for real, just let me help. Okay?" Cyn lost her patience. This was one battle she wasn't giving up on. Grace had to admit that a ride sounded pretty nice.

"Okay. As long as it's not any trouble?"

"None! I'm just right here." The two walked over to her car. Cyn hovered close by, just in case there was another fall. Surprisingly, Grace stayed on her feet. She remained awake long enough to tell her driver an address, before passing out for the duration of the twenty-minute drive. Even Octavia caught a little snooze. The pair have a lot of work ahead of them if one mediocre silence tuckered them out this much. Regardless, Grace is two wins up right now. Let's see if her streak continues.

The exhausted composer woke to a gentle nudge from Cyn. Groggily, she opened her eyes. It took her a few minutes to familiarize herself with her surroundings. All black interior, digital dash, and an EDM cover of a punk classic played lightly through the speakers. That's not usually the volume that type of music is played at, but Grace enjoyed hearing it nonetheless. Everything dialed in when she saw Cyn's welcoming face. Quickly, Grace adjusted her slouch and sneakily tried to dispatch the drool from her chin.

"I'm so sorry. I didn't mean to pass out on you like that." Grace still hasn't kicked that annoying apologizing habit.

"It's all good," Cyn reassured her. "Can you confirm this is, in fact, your place of residence, miss?" She did her best Ryde driver impression.

"Why yes it is, driver." Grace couldn't help but play into the bit. It was low-hanging fruit, even for an inexperienced flirter like Grace. Our composer was so tired that she didn't have the energy to second guess herself. "And don't worry, I'll be sure to give you four stars."

"Four? We use a five-star system."

"Well, you didn't offer me a complimentary water bottle, so I can't go five. I'm sure you understand."

"Water bottles are only for rides longer than thirty minutes. I'm trying to make money here. I'm sure you understand." The two let out a little laugh. "Here, I'll walk you up. Make sure you don't pass out in the elevator or anything."

"Probably not a bad idea." Grace got out of the car. Was she dreaming? "You really want that five stars, don't you?"

"Of course." Cyn went around to meet her. "I've got mouths to feed."

"Ah, gotta keep the family plate full."

"Yup. Especially when they only eat the fancy kibbles." Cyn smirked. The two continued with this kind of awkward banter the whole way. Trust me, it was tiring to listen to. Neither wanted to back down from the joke, and it wasn't even a good joke. It's done to death. Humans all think they're original. They're not.

When they got to Grace's apartment, they were met with a surprise. Chase was sitting against the door, waiting.

"Grace! You're back!" The uninvited visitor chaotically stood up.

"Um, hi, Chase." Grace didn't know what was going on. It was rare anybody came to her apartment in general, let alone unannounced. The timing was awful, however. Grace was considering asking Cyn to come in. Considering being the keyword. If she had gone through with it, I would've been shocked.

"Oh," Cyn froze. "I didn't realize you had," she looked Chase over, "company. I can just drop you here."

"No, it's not..." Grace tried to stop Cyn, but couldn't figure out a way to say "it's not what it looks like" without making it seem like she assumed that needed to be clarified. "I didn't know he was coming over," is what she landed on.

"No worries, I just wanted to make sure you got in safe." Cyn gestured to the door. "Mission accomplished. Have a good night, Grace."

"Thanks, Cyn. I'll see you later?"

Cyn responded with a thumbs up. "See you later." She made her way to the elevator, but stopped down the hall and turned around. "Don't forget to leave that five-star review, now." Cyn gave a little wink.

"Of course. Exceptional service." Grace smiled back. Once again, this was not clever banter.

"Your driver walked you up? Damn, that is next level service." Chase reminded Grace of his presence. Something that greatly annoyed her right now.

"What do you want, Chase?"

"Right." Chase snapped his fingers and hit his fists together. "Do you think we could talk inside?" he asked anxiously.

"Fine." Grace was not hiding her frustration well. Chase seemed too much in his own head to notice. As soon as they got in the apartment, Chase started pacing.

"Okay, what's going on?" Grace prodded.

Chase once again snapped his fingers and hit his fists together. "Alright, it's like this," he began. "So, you know how you kind of saved me from that thing?"

"Silent knight."

"What?"

"Silent knight. It has a name now." It had a better name.

"Okay. Silent knight." Chase let it sink in. "Wait, like the carol?" Finally, someone said it!

"Oh, shit." It dawned on Grace. "Yeah, I guess." She sounded disappointed.

"Alright. Well, you know how you saved me from the silent knight, then?"

"No, that won't do." Grace got withdrawn. She's doing that thing again.

"What?"

"Silent knight. It won't do. That's all I hear now." Grace waved her hand in the air and hummed the Christmas classic. "The song. That's all I think about now."

"Uh-huh." Chase was understandably confused. "So anyway. The thing. Are we back to just calling it a 'thing?'"

"For now," Grace agreed. Though make no mistake, her brain was storming.

"Okay, perfect. So, ever since you saved me from that thing, I've been seeing them in other places."

"Silent killer!" Grace popped back in. Come on now. She can do better.

"What? Like high blood pressure?" Chase was annoyed, but couldn't let that slide.

"Shit." Grace was back to the drawing board.

"Grace, can you just listen for a second?"

"Right, sorry. Once I get going, you know..." Grace gave a half-hearted giggle.

"I'm seeing the things other places. I've seen at least two now."

"Wait, you've been seeing them?" Finally, she's listening.

"Yes! They will just pop up randomly. And they always look at me with those creepy, empty eyes. But it doesn't seem like anybody else can see them. I'm freaking out, Grace. What are these things?"

"Well, the name is pending..."

"Grace!"

"Okay, okay. I'm currently learning about them myself. But, from what I understand, they are a creature or virus kind of thing. Not super sure. They serve an evil god and possess people. And I know I can see them because of the mark, but I don't know why you can."

"He has been touched by the Silence and your sound. He bears the weight of the truth." Octavia hopped out of Grace's purse, feeling well rested after the brief snooze. Chase yelped and stumbled backward against the kitchen counter.

"Did that just talk?" Chase sputtered.

"Did you just hear her talk?" Grace was shocked.

"Yes, he did. Once again, he has been inhabited by the ethereal. It means he can see them, and he can hear me."

Octavia bounced next to Chase on the counter. "Fear not, human, these things will probably not attack you."

Chase was reeling. "This is so not okay." He was already unhinged from everything happening. A talking plush octopus seemed to be the tipping point. "And wait. Did you say they *probably* won't attack me?"

"Nothing is guaranteed, but you are of little import to them as a severed. They cannot inhabit you again."

"What is it talking about?" Chase gestured to Octavia in panic.

"*She* seems to be saying since you were infected by one, you can no longer be controlled by another. You're immune, basically." Grace translated and looked to Octavia for confirmation. She nodded her bulbous head.

"Oh, well, that's nice." Chase was starting to come down. "But why do they have to look so creepy? I nearly have a heart attack every time I see one. I haven't been sleeping. I keep seeing them with their weird, messed up faces. And is that a cloak or their body? It's so gross!"

"It is both," Octavia chimed in.

"Both? Like their body is made of cloth?" Chase tried to comprehend.

"No," Octavia refuted, and Chase seemed slightly relieved. "It is more like they are shrouded in their own skin." His face returned to a horrified expression.

"That's it!" Grace exploded.

"What?" Chase and Octavia spoke in unison. Grace grinned before unveiling her thought.

"Silent shroud." She waited for it to land.

"What?" Chase repeated.

"The name! For the things formerly known as silent knights. They have cloak bodies. Silent shrouds. It's perfect!" Okay. I actually don't hate this one. Despite it sounding a bit like a comic book villain.

"Wonderful!" Octavia exclaimed. "Composer, I did not think it possible to surpass silent knight, but this captures a more sinister side." Chase looked at the two, dumbfounded.

"Thanks, Tavi. Now that we have that decided, we can finally get to the meat and potatoes—Chase's problem." Grace clapped her hands and pointed them toward Chase, whose mouth was hanging open.

"Uh. Yeah. Thanks. Glad we got that figured out," he mumbled while sliding down the counter into an upright fetal position. They had broken the poor boy.

Grace squatted down by him, and took a gentle tone. "Sorry, I'm sure this is a lot for you."

"You think?" Chase retorted, raising his head. "There's apparently an evil god, and something that disgusting was inside me."

"That's what she said," Grace cracked the joke. "Even the evil god part." Grace is probably trying to use the poor attempt at humor to overcome her discomfort with other people's pain, but I'd prefer to read it as indifference. That's a little more fun, don't you think?

Chase let out a chuckle and leaned his head back. "You really don't have an off button, do you?"

"Nope!" Grace put her hand on Chase's shoulder. "Listen, I'm getting pretty good at killing these things." Disclaimer: she's only killed two, and the last fight nearly ended her. "I promise to protect you." Then Grace gave a look I had never seen from her before. It was one of determination, but not the usual rage-filled one that I originally liked. No, this look was more heroic. Gross. Chase saw that same face and somehow found solace in it.

"Thanks, Grace. I just don't know what else to do."

"I got you, bro." She squeezed his shoulder.

Chase let out a relieved sigh and nodded. "Alright then. So, what do I do?"

"You can be our lookout." Octavia jumped down onto his

knee. "If you see one, send up a smoke signal, and we shall arrive to dispatch it."

"Just text me," Grace said, modernizing the approach.

Octavia frowned. "I do not know what that means."

"Yeah, totally. I think I can do that." Chase was getting energized. Coming to Grace was a gamble. Even though they spent that one day together, he knew very little about her. He really only knew what Tommy had said, and those things did not paint a confident picture. Seeing this side of her had him questioning if Tommy knew his friend very well at all. "There's one I have seen a few times now at the bar. Almost like a regular. It's been there just about every night."

"That's great! Did you happen to see who it was controlling?" Grace asked. "You may have seen puppet strings?" She pantomimed operating a marionette.

"I can't say I've seen anything like that..." Chase tried to remember.

"Only a composer can see the trace," Octavia clarified. "Chase may have been exposed to the truth, but unfortunately, he holds no power to actually do anything."

"That kind of hurts," Chase replied.

"Oh, I gotcha. So it could be controlling one of the regulars, but Chase wouldn't see it," Grace went on.

"Or it could be controlling someone from far away while looking for another fertile soul to reproduce within."

"Tavi."

"Yes, dear Grace?"

"Don't say that sentence ever again."

"Yeah, it kind of made me want to vomit," Chase agreed.

Octavia didn't understand the fuss and firmly planned to ignore the request. "It matters not either way. We must simply find it and swiftly destroy it!"

"Hell yeah!" Grace pumped her fist in the air. "Shroud number three, I'm coming for thee!"

"Ha, yeah!" Chase pumped his fist up, too. "And by three, you mean?"

"Third kill!" Octavia excitedly threw one of her round appendages up in union.

"You've only killed two, then?" Chase timidly asked.

"Mhm." Grace gave a hearty nod. Chase put his hand back to his head and returned to the fetal position. It appears he's once again feeling hopeless. Grace and Octavia exchanged a look, sighed, and attempted, again, to comfort the wreck.

FOUR
NOBODY KNOWS YOUR NAME

Brody Parch was devout. The kind of devotion that makes you sick to your stomach. It was Monday morning, and there he was, scrubbing the altar of the Veritas church. He wanted the marble to glisten and shine like the very grace of his god. Believe it or not, he actually did this twice a week. Which was ridiculous, considering service is only on the weekends.

Brody hated the idea of even a speck of dust collecting anywhere in the sacred space. Hymns played in the background while he cleaned and hummed along. Nervously, he checked his watch—10 a.m. It would be another half hour before the pastor woke. Brody had never seen a holy man sleep as late as this one. Sure, he showed up at game time when it mattered for Sunday morning service, but any other day of the week, he slept like the dead. Brody found it unbecoming. Slothful. A preacher should be available to tend to his flock at all times, or at least tend to the holy altar.

Brody stood up to admire his work. In his eyes, it was beautiful, but never beautiful enough. No chunk of rock, even marble, could ever be suitable to fully praise Veritas. One more check of his watch. He should have time for another wipe down.

Brody got back down to his knees, dipped his cloth in the cleaning solution, and wiped the base of the altar.

In the past, he would do this for the whole church. Ever since he was a teenager, he'd come to this building to maintain it. The current pastor, however, seemed to have issues with Brody venturing too far into the church on his own. While Brody hated that man, he also had to recognize him as an authority in the religion. This meant taking his orders, but resenting it.

Brody never pursued being a man of the cloth himself. Just like the stone he was polishing, he knew he could never be worthy enough. In his mind, he wasn't even something as presentable as marble. He was pea gravel meant to be trodden upon. Lowly in pain and pitiful at the foot of his lord. His fingers were cracked and bleeding from the constant exposure to the cleaning chemicals. Bandages wrapped around several sores to prevent any of that blood from getting on the holy ground. It truly was pathetic. Seeing such service, and to a god that probably never gave much thought to Brody. His unyielding loyalty makes me queasy. People like Brody are seldom interesting. However, boring Brody is about to get involved in something with a little more flair. For a boy stands at the church entrance.

"I need Father Dom!" the boy called out. It was Jake Evans. Brody looked up, horrified that someone would speak at such a volume in this venerable place and issue a demand at that. He pulled a cracked finger to his lips and let out a harsh *shush* before returning to his work. The boy began marching up the church pews. "Fine. I'll find him myself."

"I wouldn't." Brody perked up. The fact that Jake entered so boisterously, and without a proper bow, made the humble servant sick. What's more, Brody knew this child and the disgusting money he came from. Someone like that did not deserve an audience with even the most detestable of holy men.

Not to mention, Brody did not want the pastor to wake yet. Not when there was so much left to scrub.

"You don't tell me what to do, you shitty old man." The boy continued forward. Brody threw his cloth in the bucket and grabbed him by the wrist as he passed. Swearing in the church was too far, I guess.

"Listen here, Jake." Brody spat the name out as if he was uttering a curse himself. "You may be rich in this world, but that means nothing to God! If I were you, I'd start caring about your everlasting life. You can't lean on daddy forever. Learn some respect. For Veritas." Brody gestured to the giant mural on the back wall of the god. Glorious, vibrant colors radiated from the holy figure.

Jake glared at Brody, before ripping his hand away. He leaned in close with menacing eyes. "Your god can lick my balls." Jake gave a twisted smile, enjoying the look of shock on Brody's face. "Touch me again, and *my* god will watch as I rip your body apart." Brody fell backward, knocking over his bucket. The solution soaked into the luxurious red carpet surrounding the altar. Jake scoffed. "He's not going to like that, is he? Father Dom likes to keep up appearances."

"Enough, Jake." The hair on Brody's neck shot up. Perhaps he had lost track of time. Could the pastor really be awake already? Dios, taking on Dom's body, stepped from beyond the archway. "Can't you see Mr. Parch is just trying to do a kindness for the church?"

Brody stood up, distressed. "He's a demon, father." His loathing alternated between himself for soiling the carpet and the boy. "Send him away. He does not belong on this hallowed ground."

"Now, now, Mr. Parch." Dios walked down and put their hand on Brody. "Who would I be if I turned the youth away from our beautiful faith?" His attention shifted to Jake. "Young Evans. How are you doing? How's your mother?"

"A complete and utter whore," Jake shot back. Dios let out a sly smirk. They knew that would pinch the right nerve.

"See! Cast him away, father. Such vile things should not be said in the presence of Veritas," Brody pleaded.

"Mr. Parch." Dom's tone darkened. "I'm going to have to ask you to leave now." Jake stuck his tongue out.

Brody felt like he was going to burst. Kids can just be the worst, and Jake took that to a whole new level. Brody Parch would not stand for such insolence. "Your father really failed with you, boy." Brody got in Jake's face. Hoping to berate the boy into a pious life, perhaps. "You are an embarrassment. An unlovable little monster, and you do not deserve to step foot in this—"

Brody's last remarks were cut short as a knife found its way up his jaw. A small hand gripped the handle.

"Jake! In the church?" Dom scolded.

"I don't like this one." Jake spoke coldly as he twisted the knife, staring into Brody's horrified eyes. The pious man gagged and gasped while trying to wrestle the blade away from his throat. However, he could not out-muscle this nine-year-old. Jake wasn't ordinary, after all. I'll keep this brief, but he is what is called a spawn. Someone committed to the Silence from the moment of birth. In this case, it was because his mother was also one with the Silence. That same mother abandoned him almost immediately, and after a few failed foster homes, Jake finally learned he could make his own family by infecting someone with the Silence. Which is how he ended up with the affluent Curtis Evans.

With a swift movement, Jake pulled the knife from Brody's jaw and sliced his throat, finishing the job. Brody stumbled backward onto the altar. With his dying breath, he turned his head to the portrait of Veritas. As he looked upon his god, his blood poured out to wash that precious marble one last time. A final devotion.

"Jake! You just killed the person who would clean that up. Come on!" Dom scolded. Dios quickly went to the front of the church to lock the doors. "Honestly. You could have benefited from some parental guidance. I swear I've never seen a more annoying spawn."

"Parental guidance? From who? You? That's a great joke, Father," Jake said in a sarcastic tone.

"Of course not from me, you little shit. I'd never be able to stand you, just like all your other families."

"Oh, come on. That was beautiful!" Orv interrupted. "Murder on the altar of Veritas. The boy's an artist."

"He's a goddamn menace who better explain what he's doing here right now," Dom said as they grabbed Jake by the wrist and threw him into a pew. "Speak."

"Daddy is dead," Jake spat out. To be clear, Jake meant the silence inside of Curtis. Curtis is most likely not dead at this moment. I don't care to verify that, though.

"So?" Ira said. "Make a new dad. Maybe one that's not so disappointing. I mean honestly. Settling down in suburbia? How mundane."

Dom took back control. "Ira, please. A silence was killed. That doesn't happen very often."

"It was a composer," Jake revealed, and all three of Dios were at a loss for words. Jake delighted in their reaction.

"You're sure?" Dom finally asked.

"I saw her myself."

"A girl composer? Haven't had one of those in a long time," Ira acknowledged. "Girl power, am I right, boys?" She let out a little giggle.

"Take this seriously, Ira. The Silence hasn't dealt with a composer in a century, and that last one barely counted."

"Ah, yes, poor little Andrew. The one hit wonder." Ira smirked. "God, I wish I could've been there when he was killed. So young."

"Ooh, that means we can kill this one!" Orv cackled. "Killing a composer... I wonder what her insides look like?"

"Boy, what can you tell us about her?" Dom brought everyone back to task.

"She looked plain. If I had my powers already, I would've killed her myself." Jake clenched his fists.

"So you have nothing useful then. Great."

"I saw she had a stuffed octopus."

"Octavia?" Dom wondered.

"She's a plush?" Ira bursted. "Oh, that is too rich! I have to see it."

"And then rip her stuffing out!" Orv joined the chorus of laughter. If either was in control of the body, you'd expect them to be rolling on the floor right now. Dom wasn't enjoying this nearly as much as the others, however, so the body remained completely still. It's definitely unnerving to watch someone laugh that hard and not move in a way that matches. Another reason why Dios is just too much for me.

"If the composer has already met Octavia, that's a problem. We must fix this problem quickly," Dom said, and Dios turned to head to their quarters. They were immediately reminded of a more pertinent problem when they saw Brody's lifeless body. They groaned. "After we deal with Jake's mess."

"Jake the mistake!" Orv shouted out.

"Make yourself useful and go grab my saws," Dom ordered Jake, who simply flipped them off and sauntered out of the church.

"Jake, you little asshole, get back here and clean up your shit," Dom shouted.

"Better get moving, Father." Jake chuckled as he unlocked the church doors. "You never know when some wayward soul will come in looking for absolution." With that, he dramatically threw both doors wide open. "I'll be back later when you have a plan for this composer."

Dios let out a scream of frustration as the doors slowly closed behind Jake. "If that boy wasn't a legacy, I'd tear him to pieces!" Dom yelled.

"Yeah, yeah. Not great with kids. We get it." Ira was bored by this particular drama.

"Laugh it up, Ira. When he fully awakens, he's going to be a problem, and we'll have to keep cleaning up after him." Dios looked at the bloodied sacrifice upon the altar.

"At least this time he killed an inconsequential nobody." Ira shrugged. "Only bummer is we didn't get to kill this annoying fly ourselves." Dios dragged a finger through the blood, before inevitably going in for a taste. Their hand stopped right before it touched their lips. They shot a glance at the body and then at the Veritas mural.

"On second thought, better not," Dom decided before shaking the blood off.

"What a waste," Orv complained. Dios strode to the front to lock the church entrance again, before taking a seat in the nearest pew.

"So, after we discard old Brody over there, what are we going to do about this composer?" Ira questioned. Dios folded their hands to their head and closed their eyes in prayer. After a few moments, their eyes opened, as if a revelation had sparked from the great orb itself.

"We follow the sound," Dom answered.

* * *

Just a few miles away, Grace leaned back on her couch. A bowl of offensively sweet cereal rested on her lap, while an anime about an all-girl high school pop group played on the TV. Octavia sat on the arm of the couch and was way more invested in the show than I would have expected.

"So, this is modern music?" Octavia awed.

"Yeah! Well, part of it." Grace got semantic. "There's a lot of music in the world today. It doesn't all sound like this."

"I understand. Kind of like how there are orchestras and operas. Which would this be classified as, dear Grace?"

"Neither? Both? Things have diversified a lot." Grace took a break to crunch her sugar balls. Octavia nodded sincerely. "Speaking of. You said you've helped other composers in the past, right?"

"Correct."

"How far in the past are we talking? Like, are you immortal? Have you just been chilling all this time?"

"My aid has spanned centuries. And in some ways, I am immortal, but in many ways, I am not."

"Uh-huh." Grace didn't get it.

"I am summoned whenever a new composer awakens. When their song comes to repose, so does mine."

"Gotcha. That would explain some of the serious gaps in pop culture. So, when was the last time you were here, then?"

"Is now really the best time, dear Grace?" Octavia gestured to the screen, still playing *Pop Love: First Beat*. "They are about to perform the symphony that can get them into the regional contest. That is one step closer to their ultimate dream."

"Oh, totally. We can table that for now." Grace looked over at her new plushy friend. So much about this being was a mystery. Their intro was pretty rushed, and I guess now Grace wanted to scratch the info itch. It was just bad luck that she brought up the one topic Octavia was in no rush to talk about—her last time here. Or maybe it really is just that Octavia is addicted to this show. She always keeps me guessing that way.

Grace did her best to let the hyper-pop number play all the way through, before returning to her line of questioning. "So, have you always been a summonable guardian, then? Where do you go when you're not helping a composer?" Well, she tried, didn't she? Octavia simply shushed Grace and went back to cooing over the show. Grace took the hint and resigned to eating her breakfast. As soon as the song ended, Grace paused the show.

"What has happened? Is that the end?" Octavia looked to Grace. "Why have they all stopped moving?"

"It's okay. I just paused it for a second."

"You what? You can do that?"

"Yes! I figured while we talk, we can just leave it paused. It's clear you're not someone who likes to multitask during shows."

"But we were about to find out if they were successful in their endeavor."

"And we will find out... as soon as we talk a little bit." Grace pleaded with a big smile, "Please, Tavi?" Octavia sighed.

"Fine. I shall answer a few more questions. Then we will see if Glitter has conquered their opponent." Glitter was the name of the main girl group in the show. Spoiler alert, they don't win. Not this season, anyway. They won't go to the regional high school tournament until *Pop Love: Remix High.*

"You got it. Just like three questions."

"You may proceed."

"So, the one I asked before. Where do you go when you're not summoned?"

"That's a good question." Octavia put her tentacle to her chin. "I am not really sure."

"Really? So, do you not exist when there's not a composer?" Grace was trying to understand, but that concept wasn't correct at all. Octavia has another place she goes. She doesn't remember, because the two realms don't really mix. That's for the best. "Wow, that's trippy. So one day you were just summoned and joined the good fight?"

"No. I had a full life once. I told you I am the ruler of sea and melody. A terrifying kraken feared by all!" Octavia tried to look as fearsome as she could. This only made Grace want to squeeze the fluff out of her.

"Right. That was literal, then. You were actually a physical kraken?"

"The largest and most fearsome!" she proclaimed proudly. "I did not fuse with the Sonata Mor until I met Ragnar."

"Name doesn't ring a bell," Grace said facetiously.

"Ragnar was the strongest human I have ever met. The power he wielded with his sound was astounding. A perfect mix of power and beauty. Well," she backtracked, "perhaps a little more power than beauty. His song was loud and explosive."

"So every composer has their own sound?"

"Correct."

"Cool! What's my sound?"

"Screechy and unruly."

"Tavi!"

"You shall find your sound, dear Grace. It takes time."

"Yeah, yeah. Not for stupid awesome Ragnar, it seems." Grace was actually pouting over this.

"I understand it took Ragnar quite a while to find his sound, actually. Our paths did not cross until years after he came upon the power."

"Really?"

"Yes. He came to challenge me. A misunderstanding regarding a few missing ships from his rebel viking crew." Grace's eyes lit up. A duel? Missing ships? Rebel vikings? This had all the makings of an epic tale.

"You two actually fought? No way! Who won?"

"Exactly what I would like to know." Octavia referenced the TV.

"Yeah, yeah. After this story." Both parties would find themselves disappointed as a knock occurred at Grace's door. "Huh? Who is knocking at eight in the morning?" Tentatively, Grace got up and made her way to the peephole.

"Dear Grace, what about the show? What about *Glitter*?" Octavia frantically waved her tentacles around in the air, trying to reel Grace back in. That wasn't going to happen, for Cynthia was on the other side of the door. Grace's heart stopped. Here she was in her oversized shirt and baggy pajama bottoms. Not an ounce of makeup on, and hair resting in a nest above her head. It was obvious she was not expecting company. Let alone *that* company.

"Shit, it's Cyn," Grace whispered to Octavia.

"The maiden again? She seems drawn to you. Invite her in to finish the show. Or ignore her and return to finish the show." Octavia had one thing on her mind. Grace's heart nearly exploded when the knock came a second time. She couldn't figure out why Cyn would be here. Wait. Was this a profession of love? Grace started to daydream about her crush confessing her undying feelings until another rap-tap-tap took her out of it. It was do or die time. Grace inhaled and swung open the door.

"Hey, Cyn!" she blurted out immediately.

"Hey!" Cyn smiled, but then saw what Grace was wearing. "Oh, sorry to drop in like this. I realized last night that I kind of left you carless by taking you home," she explained. "I wanted to offer a ride, but I didn't have your number. Sami didn't have it either. In fact, nobody I talked to in the office seemed to have it. So, I sent you a message through the work chat, but there was no answer. I didn't want to leave you stranded, so I just kind of showed up." Take a breath after that one, Cyn. That was quite the rabbit hole. "But now I see that you're obviously still not feeling well, and this may be a massive intrusion." This was not a profession of love. Poor Grace. Her face dropped when she realized her appearance communicated "obviously still not feeling well".

"Oh, it's not a problem at all!" Grace rebounded. "Thanks for coming. Really. I didn't even think about the fact that my car was still at the office." She forced a laugh. "But yeah, I wasn't planning on coming in today." It wasn't because Grace was sick, obviously. After her realization yesterday, she found it hard to go to work. It seemed so pointless. Waterfall Lake™ drinking bowls could wait.

"Of course. Are you doing okay?"

"Yeah. It's more that I kind of don't care about work right now." Wow, Grace just went out and said it. Cyn was taken aback by the statement, but then resigned her shocked face to a pleasant grin.

"I totally get it," she laughed. "I knew you weren't a corporate yes girl." Cyn seemed relieved. She was still trying to figure out where Grace fell on that line, it seemed.

"Definitely not anymore," Grace confirmed. The two stood there awkwardly for a moment.

"Well, unfortunately, it would seem I'm a little more of a sellout than you." Cyn gestured to her work attire. Well, work attire for Cynthia. She really leaned into the casual part of business-casual. "So, I should probably head in. Next time you want to blow off work, though, feel free to let me know." She flashed a toothy smile that nearly knocked Grace over.

"Yeah!" was all Grace could get out while confronted with those pearly whites. Cyn stood there for a moment. I think she was maybe expecting an invitation to ditch right now. That was lost on Grace, who was too focused on surviving the unplanned interaction. "Well, I'll see you later, then," Cyn broke the silence. She waved and turned to leave.

"Cyn, wait." Grace's crush smoothly pivoted back around. "I can give you my number." Grace felt her face flushing red. "You know, so you have it for next time. I still don't have a car..."

"Yeah. That'd be great." Cyn lit up. The two exchanged numbers, said their goodbyes, and Grace returned to a very disgruntled octopus.

"What?" Grace asked, but she knew.

"You just expended all your inquiry time."

"What? No fair!" Grace tried to object, but Octavia simply gestured to the TV, immune to any pleading.

"But you were literally in the middle of answering a question. And that story sounded awesome." Octavia was unmoving. "Ugh, fine. Let's see if Glitter wins it all." Grace groaned. Once again, they don't. But the lessons they learn from coming together as a group is the real point of the *First Beat* season. Grace resumed play, and the rest of the day just sped by. The two binge watched TV, and Octavia put the shutdown on any further questions about her past—mostly as a punishment. I won't bore you with the details, but it went on like that until 7 p.m. when Grace finally decided to get ready.

Before Chase left the previous night, they all came up with a plan to catch the bar-hopping shroud. According to Chase, it had entered the campus bar every night so far. This meant Grace was going out on a Tuesday night for the first time ever. She and Octavia would scope out the situation and see if they could spot the shroud. Bonus points if they could find who it was attached to. Seeing as those severed from the silence still continue to see them, it was important that Grace figure out the host to issue a proper warning. This was less important to Octavia.

They'd be going to a very popular college bar where Chase worked. Don't underestimate how out of Grace's element this is. While she loved dance music, she never found herself in that scene, especially in college. Luckily, she was only two years removed from graduating, so she shouldn't look too out of place. At least that was the mantra she repeatedly told herself in the mirror.

Finding an outfit was the first obstacle. She had little in the way of "going out" clothes, let alone "going out on a Tuesday" clothes. Finally, she settled on a cropped sweater and her favorite pair of high-waisted jeans. Not exactly an inspired outfit, but perhaps slightly sensible. Last thing she wanted was to find herself in a fight while wearing a dress or skirt.

"You are quite the fair maiden," Octavia complimented.

Grace blushed, looking over herself in the mirror. "Why

thank you, Tavi. And you are cute as ever," Grace replied, trying to reciprocate.

"I do not desire to be cute." The exchange of compliments failed.

"Right, of course." Grace scooped up the kraken and checked her phone. "Nothing from Chase, yet. So, I guess we wait?" Grace tapped her fingers anxiously on the device.

"Why not go now? I understand we are heading somewhere that celebrates youth and vigor! Let us enjoy our time there before we end a shroud."

"Enjoy time at a bar?" Grace questioned herself. Was that even possible for her?

"Have you never done such a thing?" Octavia asked, and Grace withdrew. She thought about her college career. Replaying the many times she declined invites and opportunities. Did she miss out? Grace felt an ache she was becoming familiar with. Was it regret? Frustration? Anger? Perhaps it was all three, and all of it was aimed at the past. Grace clenched her fist and gave a hearty nod.

"I never have, but that changes tonight." Grace gave Octavia an intense smile and held up two fingers in a V for victory. The two have watched entirely too much *Pop Love* today.

"Huzzah! Then let us dance!" Octavia exclaimed. She wiggled happily, before striking a tentacle in the air for a stoic pose. "And then let us obliterate."

"Hell yeah!" Grace matched the energy, and with that, the two caught a Ryde to the bar known as Sparks. Grace liked to think they got a ride because she was planning to let loose tonight, and not because her car was still idling in the Pets YES parking lot. Whatever she needs to cope.

As soon as they arrived at the bar, Grace spotted Chase. He was pouring out a birthday shot for a fresh twenty-one-year-old. Grace pranced over to him.

"Hey bartender, pour me something good. On the rocks.

Shaken and stirred." Grace winked and pointed a finger gun. Chase politely pushed the drink to the patron he was serving, before turning his attention to the newcomer.

"That doesn't even make sense," Chase replied. Any greeting he had in him was immediately overwritten. "You want me to shake and stir your drink?"

Grace laughed. "I guess just a beer then, barkeep!" She just couldn't help herself.

"Do you really think that's a good idea?" Chase questioned.

"You heard her. Your finest mead." Octavia jumped out on the counter. Grace was admittedly a little embarrassed. Did she really need people thinking she brought a stuffed animal? She nervously created some distance between her and the octopus.

"Mead? That's not even the same... You both are killing me." Chase shook his head and leaned on the bar top. "But for real. What if..." Chase scoped out the area to ensure nobody was within earshot. "What if the shroud comes in?" he whispered.

"That's what we're banking on, right?" Grace spoke at a much higher volume.

"Then should you be drinking?"

"It's one drink, Chase. I'm not that much of a lightweight. I drink." Chase gave her a skeptical look. "At home sometimes," she clarified.

"That's just sad," he teased, before relenting and pulling an ice cold brew out of the fridge below. "Now I feel like I have to give you this. It's the lightest thing we have. On the house."

"I'll take it." Grace looked proud of herself as she accepted the drink. A couple of girls on the other end of the bar giggled and waved at Chase to come over. At the same time, a handsome young man gave him a glance and nodded his head. Both groups were vying to put their drinks order in.

"Now, if you'll excuse me, I've got to tend to other customers." Chase let loose his charming smile to all parties in waiting. "I will tell you if I see the thing." He tapped the bar before making his way over to flirt up a large tip.

"Alright. Us, too!" Grace called after him, but he was already working his magic with the gentleman now ordering. She turned around to face the massive dance floor. The place was packed. Way more people than she would have expected for a Tuesday, but that's what you get with a campus bar. DJ Feline Fine commanded the room, spinning all the right tracks to get the crowd going.

Standing there amidst all that energy, it dawned on Grace just how isolated she was. Most people probably don't go to these places alone. What's more, she was beginning to notice the occasional glance. The mark on her neck suddenly felt like it was two miles long. It may as well have been a spotlight. The sweater she wore did nothing to hide it, and her hair was half up. When she had made these aesthetic decisions, she was feeling much more confident. Now she was out and about, it was a different story.

"Shall we dance?" Octavia closed the gap Grace had been building, and the composer was reminded that she wasn't alone at all. However, tearing up the dance floor was anxiety inducing enough as it was, let alone with a plush octopus. The staring she experienced now would be nothing in comparison.

"Um, maybe in a moment?"

"Sure. We can just stand idly against this warped oak." Octavia patted the bar top. Grace felt Octavia's guilt trip, but not enough to cause any movement. "Did we not come to absorb the energy of the night?" Octavia wiggled her tentacles in a wavelike motion. "And culminate it all in the destruction of our enemies?"

"You have a very interesting balance right now, Tavi." Grace's eyes bounced around in a slightly paranoid fashion.

"You said you wanted to be more like Ragnar, right?"

"I don't think I *specifically* said that."

"Well, that is how Ragnar and I would spend the night. The celebration was just as important as the conquest." The Viking lifestyle was oozing out of Ragnar's backstory, but Grace knew she was no Viking. And that was an understatement.

"I get that. I do. But, I feel like I need something. I can't fully leap. You know what I mean?" Grace tried to explain.

"Not at all," Octavia bluntly responded.

"Right." The composer deflated. She surveyed the floor, searching for a spark—anything that would give her the push she needed to join in. It was then that she spotted Trish Miller. Yes, the star of the children's YouMovie channel. It was quite a sight. Her body moved to the music and lights in a beautiful and captivating way that could never be shown on her show. Make no mistake, other people were on the dance floor, but it belonged to her. Grace could tell Octavia was talking, but she was so zoned in that nothing registered. Her attention locked on the dancing girl. Trish was probably slightly younger than Grace, but she definitely wasn't in college. Right? People who lived in her apartment building don't go to the university. So, if she could own the floor in a place like this, why couldn't Grace?

"Alright, I'm doing it!" Grace finally found resolve.

"Drink from the skulls of those you have slain?" Octavia asked, delightfully surprised. Obviously, Grace missed something while she was captivated.

"What? No." Grace brushed it aside. "I'm ready to go dance."

"Ah, yes! Nearly the same thing. Let us dance!"

Grace cringed. Her new friend still had the unfortunate problem of being a plushy. However, Grace believed firmly in not leaving anyone out. On top of that, she was already getting a lot of looks anyway. People were going to judge her because of the mark, regardless. Could dancing with a stuffed animal really make it worse? Plus, who would she be if she abandoned Octavia because of something as silly as dancing? Especially after

Octavia had saved her skin the other day. "Alright," Grace decided. "Hop on."

She leaned her shoulder forward. Octavia squealed with excitement and boarded, ready to show just what those eight legs could do. Grace slowly danced her way onto the floor, wading into the crowd. The apprehension melted off the further she went. Chase watched with a smile as she disappeared into the horde of moving bodies. He grabbed what was left of her beer bottle from the counter—which was quite a lot. If liquid courage got her out there, it sure didn't take much.

Grace found a spot near the center of the dance floor, just far enough away from Trish. She had the courage to dance, not the courage to handle an impromptu run-in with an acquaintance. Grace wondered if that was the right word to use: acquaintance. Trish was there minutes after Grace resurrected. She knows almost the exact moment Grace died. Knowing that about a person has to make you more than acquaintances, right? Either way, whatever Trish was, Grace was not ready to go anywhere near that smoke show. It's not like she could get her attention even if she wanted to. Pretty much every guy in the bar kept vying for the part of Trish's dance partner. She would let them dance near her for a few seconds, before giving a subtle rejection by moving away.

Grace was done gawking now, though. It was time for her to add to the movement of the floor. The weight of eyes staring was a little less among the crowd. It was honestly difficult to discern most features on the dance floor, and that included the mark. She looked at Octavia, who gave a supportive pat on Grace's head. For a moment Grace stood there, listening to the music. Everything else slowly faded away. It was just her and the song. Then her body started to move.

There was a decent chance this was going to be a train wreck. Honestly, I was kind of expecting it. But, what can I say, the girl can actually dance! The music flowed through her almost effortlessly. Her hips swayed in time, and her arms and legs accented the hits of the beat. The rhythm and her heart were one. Octavia was delighted and joined in immediately, bringing her own charm to the dance. Free-spirited Grace isn't my favorite Grace, but it wasn't horrible seeing her like this. Song after song, the two of them tore it up. Of course, some people were staring. How could you not? However, they were not all bad stares. Looks like our composer is captivating a few potential dance partners herself. Sure, most of them found the plush strange, but also a little charming. Quirky is probably the right word for it.

Eventually, one of those stares came over to try his chances. He had shaggy brown hair, a deep blue bedazzled shirt, and was brimming with unearned confidence. I don't care what his name is. Shaggy hair made his presence known by pressing up against Grace from behind. Needless to say, this caused a slight startle. Octavia almost fell off Grace's shoulders. She was in the zone, and bodily contact was not something she was expecting. Well, at least not with another human.

Grace tried to sway away. Shaggy lacked anything appealing for her. However, this gesture seemed to be lost on the pursuer, who only followed crotch first. This was a first for Grace. Sure, it wasn't like she hadn't had suitors throw their hat in the ring before. In high school, she had a couple of guys make a move. I believe I mentioned one particular boy who wrote her a few love letters. Rejection in those cases usually included a long, drawn out conversation using any excuse available, excluding explicitly stating she was gay. Grace tried once again to move away from shaggy hair, and once again he refused to pick up on the signal. Does he think persistence is key here? Octavia noticed what was going on and whipped around to glare at the boy.

"Begone, imbecile," she shouted. However, while he could, in fact, see Octavia move, he could not hear her. This meant there was little impact outside of adding intrigue to the girl he now believed to be dancing with an animatronic octopus. Grace stepped away again. He followed. That was the tipping point. Grace flipped around to face him.

"Not really interested, thanks," Grace spelled it out. Shaggy hair just gave an annoying laugh.

"Come on, it's just dancing. Don't be so uptight." He shrugged it off.

"You're right. And you can dance over there, while I dance over here."

"Really? You think you can afford to send me away like that?" A smug look came over his face. "You're lucky I want to dance with you. With that on you and all."

"What a farce!" Octavia guffawed. Once again, shaggy did not hear this.

"Oh, please. I'm not looking to go home with anybody tonight. So, if dancing with Tavi is too weird for people, I don't care." Grace gestured to her plushy dance partner.

"Oh, nobody cares about that, sweetheart. It's the thing you have on the side of your neck." He pointed at the mark. Grace instinctively covered it. "A dead girl shouldn't be so choosy. So, come on. Let's have a little fun." He smarmily danced in closer. "After all, you've risen. I've risen." He gave a suggestive and crass wink while pointing downward. Truly charming. I'm surprised this guy doesn't have girls lining up.

Grace felt tears build up behind her eyes. She was embarrassed, offended, and mad. Her hand balled up into a fist. Just when something truly spectacular was about to happen, the moment was utterly ruined by a soft hand grabbing that fist and spinning Grace around.

"There you are! I've been looking for you." It was Trish. She had noticed Grace a while ago, but wanted to give her some space. When the pile of hair came into the picture, she decided to step in. She gave a savior's smile to Grace, which morphed into a frustrated scowl when she looked at the boy who was, unfortunately, going to live. "Did you need something? Besides a shower?" Trish said to him. The coward lost interest immediately when he saw Grace wasn't alone. He put his hands up and backed away.

"Freak's all yours, bitch," he shot before leaving. Grace started shaking, her fist aching to launch.

"He's not worth it." Trish tried to calm her down. "He's just a loser." What a letdown. I haven't seen Grace fight a human yet. Not one who wasn't controlled by a shroud, anyway. I wanted to see how she would fare.

"I knew I shouldn't have come here. Not for fun," Grace said through held back tears. Octavia lowered her head, feeling slightly responsible for this situation. While she didn't fully understand why, she could tell that the previous exchange really affected Grace.

"Why? Because of fuckboys like that?" Trish pointed in the general direction of shaggy. Hearing the peppy Miss Trish swear caught Grace off guard again. The juxtaposition made her crack a smile. "They make it their business to annoy people. Their opinions are worthless. Okay?"

"Okay," the composer acknowledged. Her heart rate lowered back into a normal range. Trish had a very comforting presence.

"Besides, you were amazing out there. I didn't know you could move like that!" Trish complimented as she released the grip on Grace's wrist and mimicked the dance moves. Grace shifted uncomfortably at the praise, but make no mistake, she was thrilled.

"Oh, stop. I'm just doing what I do." Awkwardly, she tried to navigate the compliment.

"For real, though! I couldn't keep my eyes off you." This just caused our girl to laugh nervously. "Anybody would be lucky to dance with you. No matter what that asshole said," Trish continued.

"Oh, you heard that, huh?" Grace's face returned to the previous sad look.

"Yeah, I did. He had no idea what he was talking about."

"Even with this?" Grace pointed to the mark.

"Yes. Even with that." Gently, Trish placed a hand on Grace's arm. "He was just talking out of his ass because he was a scared little boy. A boy may care about that, but it wouldn't matter at all to a real man." She gave a reassuring smile and squeezed. Grace felt her stomach turn in response. Maybe it was the dancing she saw earlier. Maybe it was the fact that Trish just played white knight. Maybe it was the way the dance floor light shined on her face. Whatever it was, something inspired Grace enough for her to say this.

"What about a woman?" She met Trish's brown eyes, which readily absorbed Grace's gaze. "What would a woman think about it?"

"Oh." Trish's mouth hung slightly open. Grace's eyes drifted to the plush red lips accenting. Her heart raced. Trish paused for a moment, before her touch slowly started to slide up Grace's neck. "A woman..." Her hand found a resting place right below the mark, outlining it. "A woman would think it's beautiful."

Electricity sparked across Grace's body as she heard the words. Almost unconsciously, she found her hand drawn to Trish's waist, lightly grazing the smooth bare skin exposed just below a purple crop top. The two pulled each other in as the bass pounded and flashing lights set the scene. Trish closed her eyes and waited in anticipation for contact, but Grace paused an inch away from her face. Thoughts of Cyn flashed in her mind. She questioned what she was doing. What was even happening here? Could she really be this smooth? Trish noticed the pause and opened her eyes to see Grace now looking away, lost in thought. She pulled back.

"Sorry. I thought..." Awkwardly, Trish placed her hand behind her head and averted her eyes. Octavia watched, confused. She wasn't sure exactly how to play this, but was prepared to roll discreetly off Grace's shoulder should the moment call for it.

"No," Grace called Trish's attention back. "It's not that. I just..." She began to explain herself to a now hopeful looking Trish when the ultimate moment killer drew her attention. A series of sparks passed behind the YouMovie star, giving way to a silent shroud. *Now when did that get in here?* I think Grace was both upset and thankful for the disruption. Her head was spinning, trying to make sense of what just happened.

"Composer," Octavia nudged.

"Yeah, I see it," Grace acknowledged.

"What do you see?" Trish brushed her tightly curled brown hair behind her ear, thinking Grace's remark was still part of their moment. *Sorry, Trish, it's time to get back to some regularly scheduled violence.*

"Trish, I am so sorry." Grace hated herself for ending it this way. "I kind of have something I need to do. Like really bad." Obviously, when Grace said it like that, Trish assumed a sudden call of the wild had occurred, and Grace needed to use the bathroom.

"Oh, yeah. Of course," Trish accommodated. "Please! I'll be out on the floor if you want to talk." Grace nodded frantically.

"You got it. Thank you. Sorry. The floor. Understood. I'll be back." Grace spouted the series of loosely connected words while making her way to the bar. She frantically tried to follow the trace of green sparks. It wove around the club like a tangled web, but where did it end?

"Chase!" She waved the bartender down aggressively. He placed a mojito in front of a young girl, before swapping his attention.

"What's going on, tiny dancer?" Chase smirked. "I saw you tearing it up out there!"

"Yeah, well, did you happen to catch the moment our party

crasher arrived?" Chase surveyed the dance floor nervously. However, he was unable to see anything of note.

"Um... Are you talking about that guy who came up to you?"

"Ugh, you saw that, too?" Grace turned bright red. "Wait. You didn't see what happened after that, did you?" Chase looked at her, confused. Seems he missed the almost-kiss. If only we all could be so lucky.

"No time for that, dear Grace. A silent shroud was sighted upon the dance floor!" Octavia jumped in. Chase's complexion drained pale as he desperately searched again.

"I don't see it?" Chase said anxiously. Grace turned around to point out the creature, but she, too, saw nothing. That is, nothing except the shower of sparks still circling the room.

"Did it leave?" Grace cautiously asked.

"Do not leave yourself unguarded, composer," Octavia warned. No sooner had the words been said before the shroud materialized from the sparks and lunged at Grace, tackling her against the bar. Its hands wrapped around her throat. Chase stumbled backward into the shelf, causing several low-end whiskey bottles to crash to the floor. He watched helplessly as Grace squirmed.

"Composer!" Octavia cried out. Grace tried to say the magic words, but the shroud's thumbs were pressing against her windpipe, preventing speech. "Let her go, deviant!" Octavia hurled herself against the creature, but unfortunately there's not a ton of weight behind her without the sound. She bounced off with minor inconvenience to the shroud. I'm not even sure it noticed. Octavia landed on the bar.

"Curse this soft body. You," she called down to a hyperventilating Chase, "help her!" Chase couldn't move at all, let alone speak. You'd think he was being choked, as well. "Weakling." Grace wildly tried to grab anything on the counter. Octavia noticed and rolled away on the bar. Her sights locked on an empty beer bottle. With steely resolve, she sped ahead with all eight tentacles, before hurling herself toward the bottle. She bonked it with just enough force to slide it a few inches closer. Grace's flailing hand found the impromptu weapon. She whipped it around onto the shroud's hooded head, shattering the glass. The creature stumbled and released its grip. Quickly, Grace pushed the shroud away and tried to catch her breath.

"Success!" Octavia threw a tentacle up in celebration. An exasperated Grace raised a thumbs up toward her partner.

"How's everyone feeling tonight?" DJ Feline Fine shouted out as he switched tracks to a high-powered EDM hit. The crowd screamed in unison. I guess that means they were doing well. Grace glared at the shroud, who blankly stared back.

"The time is upon us," Octavia urged. Grace acknowledged, nodding her head to the new track. Her heart tuned into the snare hits, until, in a moment of pure theatrical brilliance, Grace felt a brief pause in the song.

"Sonata Mor." Grace gasped the words out through her pressured vocal chords right before the music pushed into a heavy beat drop. Really, Grace? Did she wait for that? The purple aura surrounded her, and the strings began to move harmoniously. This was new. The violas and violins found their place within the timbre of the dance hit playing in the club. The shroud tilted its head, analyzing the composer before vanishing.

"Oh, hell yeah!" DJ Feline Fine screamed into the mic. "Mew crew, we got something special tonight." He turned the faders up and quickly got to work finding the most complementary mix. Apparently, he felt this was a duet now. His bedazzled, gold cat ears perked in excitement. Everyone's eyes landed on an incredibly confused Grace. There were some cheers, some gasps, but overall the energy was palpable.

"What the hell just happened?" Grace looked to her plushy sherpa.

"It appears you are now part of the grand show," Octavia responded.

"Not what I meant, Tavi."

"I know. The shroud has vanished. That appears to be its gift."

"Its what?"

"Just like composers can harness a special ability with sound, so can shrouds with the void. What I am unsure of, however, is if this one's gift is invisibility or teleportation."

"Those sound equally bad." The shroud reappeared behind Grace.

"Behind you!" A lost voice finds its way. Chase finally got to his feet, just in time to issue the warning. Grace spun around and created a sound wave around her arm, blocking another attempt to tackle her. The shroud bounced off the makeshift shield and fell backward. Cheers came from the crowd, who could now see the horrifying creature along with the gang.

"Ooh, alright. Another contender finds their way in the club. Some kind of burnt marshmallow man," DJ Feline inaccurately described the shroud. To be fair, the spotlights up there really make it hard to make out details. The shroud performed its vanishing act while still lying on the ground.

"Thanks, Chase!" Grace called out while rapidly searching. It seems this foe could appear from anywhere.

"Glad you finally found your voice," Octavia added. Chase nodded, trying so hard to control his shaking. He wasn't succeeding.

"You're both my eyes right now, okay?" Grace continued to spin around. The violins faded away, replaced by a timid and anxious cello. Feeling the change up, the DJ quickly transitioned to a breakdown. The entire club felt the apprehension. Waiting in uncertainty. A collective gasp filled the room as the shroud appeared from above, looking to give Grace the ol' silence's elbow. Grace whipped around, but saw nothing. She didn't think to look up, I guess. The attack came colliding with Grace's unsuspecting head, shooting her to the ground. The composer bounced off the floor and into the crowd.

"Cheap trick." Octavia quickly rolled to her protégé.

"Oof! That one had to hurt!" Feline Fine with the commentary. Grace looked over with blurry eyes, just in time to see the shroud disappear.

"Grace!" A voice cut through the muffled crowd and music. A caring hand was placed on her dizzy head. Grace turned to see a worried Trish hovering over her. "Are you okay?" The voice came in sharper.

"Oh, hi, Trish," Grace groggily spoke, her string instruments in disarray. "What are you doing in my kitchen?" That's not a great sign.

"She hit her head rather hard." Octavia squiggled to Grace's side.

"Holy shit! It can talk." Trish was taken aback by the revelation of the talking stuffy. To her credit, her concern for the dazed girl on the floor overruled her knee-jerk reaction to move away. Grace was finally losing the double vision.

"She can do a lot more than that." Grace slowly sat back up.

"Good, you are back to your senses. Have you found the trace?" Octavia got down to business. The interaction between the two enthralled Trish.

"I'm trying, Tavi. It's all over this freaking bar." All around, green sparks flitted in varying levels of intensity. Attempting to make sense of them truly would be a struggle all on its own, let alone while you're fighting for your life. A ramp up began on the track, the countdown to the drop. Feline Fine was calling his, or rather Grace's, shot.

"Hm..." Octavia pondered to herself. "Usually, the trace would be a good way to keep track of such a foe. If it truly is everywhere, then it must be teleportation. Looping in and out of the void." The shroud appeared again from the sky, hoping to reprise its sweet chin silence. This time, the sonata guardian saw it coming. Octavia rolled into Grace's hand and launched a massive sound tentacle toward the airborne silence. It collided with the shroud's side and sent it flying into the wall. Cracks spread from the point of impact. The loud thud happened seconds before the beat drop. Feline Fine was close on that one. They can't all be perfect transitions. Grace's violins came in sharply, with a staccato melody. She regained balance on her feet.

"See? She does a lot more than talk." Grace chuckled toward Trish. "Thanks for coming to my aid... Again." Trish looked up in awe at this entirely new side of Grace. Bouncing purple sound waves flowed around her, complementing this unrelenting confidence. Trish wondered if this was really the same girl who had been living next door all year.

"What a purrfect counter!" Our self-appointed commenter rolled his tongue into the microphone. The people on the floor formed a circle around Grace and the shroud. It resembled a middle school formal, except everyone here was having fun. Well, mostly everyone.

"Are you stable, dear Grace?" Tavi called up.

"In the ways that matter."

"Grand." Octavia and Grace watched as the shroud teleported again. "I appreciate this new sound." Octavia shivered, absorbing the classical and dance music mashup. The beat pounded, and the waves around the pair pulsed in sync. Grace stood in the middle of the floor, gripping Octavia, and thus the protruding sound tentacle, like a sword.

"Yeah, it feels good."

"Keep alert." The two turned slowly in a circle, trying to predict their opponent's next move. Grace noticed Trish still kneeling in the center of the battlefield.

"Trish, you gotta clear the floor. I don't want you to get hurt," Grace called out.

Trish nodded and took off for the edge of the crowd. "Beat

the shit out of that thing!" she shouted as soon as she found her spot. Grace gave a bemused nod. Trish swearing is always cute, apparently. The shroud tried to take advantage of the brief distraction by appearing in Grace's blind spot. Luckily, Octavia was playing lookout. She quickly whipped her tentacle toward the encroaching enemy. The shroud, however, was able to grab the incoming sound wave with both hands. It clapped its hands violently against it, dispersing the sound tentacle into a shower of particles.

"What the hell was that?" Grace was stunned.

Octavia grunted in frustration. "I am sorry, dear Grace. I was not strong enough. I need a moment to recharge."

"So it, what, just destroyed your tentacle?"

"In a manner of speaking. But fret not, composer. Tentacles grow back." The shroud disappeared and reappeared right beside Grace. It grabbed her by the back of her neck and threw her forward. Grace tapped into her gymnastics days and sprung off her hands, flipping back onto her feet. Seven out of ten. Octavia bounced off the floor and sprang back up to Grace's shoulder. Eight out of ten.

"Whoa! Is she a cat, mew crew? Always landing on her feet," Feline Fine commented. Grace had fallen on her back nearly a minute ago, however. So no, she doesn't always land on her feet. In fact, it seems like she falls over quite frequently.

The silent shroud decided to take advantage of Octavia's forced respite. Quickly, it launched a barrage of stealth attacks all around Grace. Our composer put her hands together in an X and focused the sound in front of her like a shield. This worked for the first three assaults. Left, right, behind—Grace called it all correctly. The streak ended as the shroud came up from the floor and upper cut poor Grace. She flew up in the air as it vanished again. Thankfully, Octavia regained just enough charge to create a small tentacle that extended to the ground, allowing her to slow the descent. Lightly, Grace touched the floor. She immediately took a knee. Little octopuses swirled around her head.

"Okay, I think I chipped a tooth on that one," Grace said, checking her teeth with her hand.

"I must say, dear Grace, you take hits to the head almost as well as Ragnar!" Octavia praised.

"Not something I ever wanted to compete in."

"Come on, Grace!" Chase's voice cut through the crowd. His hands were still shaking. It seemed he was actually getting nervous. Trish happened to be standing next to him and noticed.

"She's got this," she reassured Chase. Surely the woman who displayed that intense confidence moments ago wouldn't lose, right? Grace shook the fog out of her head and tried to follow the trace one more time.

"I can't figure out where it's coming from, Tavi. This trace makes no sense."

"Then do not use your eyes, composer. Use your ears. Feel the music," Octavia advised.

"What do you mean? Aren't I feeling the music already?" Grace referenced the shaky strings playing around her.

"Shut it all out. Everything. Only the music," Octavia clarified. Grace trusted her mentor. Her eyes closed as she sealed away the distractions. It felt like before, when she went out to the dance floor. Once again, she was allowing herself to really take in the music around her. This was risky, sure, but it's not like her sight was doing her much good anyway.

"Alright, I think it's time we pumped this into overdrive," the DJ purred into the mic. "Let's end it with a banger." Feline Fine pulled the fader and spun a hot new track. Triumphant. Grace joined in with a sweet melody of violas. Every hit of the kick drum drew her in deeper. Everything melted away until it was just Grace and the music. Only this time, she could feel it filling up the entire room. Sound waves waded and crashed against her skin. Each individual frequency danced along her body. And in that sea of sound, she noticed it. A black hole of silence zipping around the room.

"There you are." Grace smirked. At this point, a new instrument emerged into the mix. Loud, glorious trumpets emanated from Grace and played in tandem with the synthesizer blaring over the speakers. It was a nice changeup. As the brass swelled, so did the sound waves around Grace and Octavia. A second tentacle sprouted from the kraken, who promptly used both appendages to hold herself up on her own.

Octavia continued to survey the room. Grace noticed something else forming in the song. She could feel it right in front of her. Decisively, she reached out and grabbed it. Noise concentrated in her closed palm, and when she opened her eyes, she held a sharp, little sound wave. Almost like a tiny dagger or spearhead. She gripped it tightly and steadied her arm. The silent shroud was teleporting rapidly around her. She could still feel it. All she needed to do was wait for the right moment.

"Are you feeling what I'm feeling, Tavi?" Grace asked.

"I am, composer," Octavia acknowledged. "On your signal." The music began to build again. Rapid snare hits, leading to the biggest drop of the night. It cut off in a second of pure anticipation. Grace's trumpets blew a sustained note that carried past the last snare hit. DJ Feline Fine tapped the pause button and waited with bated breath for the queue. This time, he was determined to hit his mark.

"Now!" Grace called out. The music resumed with a blitzing synthesizer drop. Grace's horns and strings came together in an amped melody. Octavia lifted herself on one tentacle and shot the other just behind Grace, where it plucked the shroud out of the air and gripped it tight.

"Gotcha," Grace said as she pivoted and launched the sound dagger toward the unveiled enemy. The sharp waves made a clean slice all the way through the monster's neck, and the shroud lost both the match and its head simultaneously.

The crowd erupted in cheers and cries of disgust as it exploded, and a black goo rained down on the poor souls in the immediate area. Trish and Chase were so relieved that they hugged, only to remember they didn't actually know each other. Quickly, they returned to an awkward, albeit happy, stance with plenty of space between them.

"Mew crew! Mew crew! What did she just do?! Looks like we have a winner! Let's get that meow mix dinner!" DJ Feline Fine mashed a celebratory air horn and let out a horrendously long meow into the microphone. Slowly Grace's sound faded out alongside the music. "Now, who's still here to party?" Our DJ friend quickly segued into the rest of the evening. If the crowd cleared out, it'd be bad for his rep, so keeping the people engaged was his top priority.

"Composer! That was inspired." Octavia wrapped her small plush tentacles as far around Grace's neck as she could. I guess that counts as a hug? Is Octavia a hugger now? Trish and Chase came running up as the crowd quickly filled in around them. A line formed in front of the bathroom for those waiting to wash the goo off.

"Now that was awesome." Chase was pumped. Quite a 180 from the shriveled mess he was before.

"Grace, are you okay?" Trish asked for what seemed like the millionth time.

"Yeah! I think." Grace sheepishly grinned.

"You hit your head so many times, are you sure? How many fingers am I holding up?" Trish held up three.

"Seventeen?" Grace joked.

"Stop! I'm being serious!"

"Three, Trish. I promise I'm okay." Grace proudly put her hands on her hips. Suddenly, the room began to swirl. Perhaps she spoke too soon. "I probably should sit down, though." The group escorted her to a bar stool.

"Chill here for a sec. I'm going to grab some water," Chase

said as he hopped over the bar to resume his regularly scheduled duties. He laid a fresh glass of ice water in front of the main attraction, who greedily consumed it.

"So, I know you've been through a lot, but any chance someone would like to let me in on what just happened?" Trish rested against the bar top. She monitored Grace with concern.

"Besides a badass show?" a passerby hollered. Grace felt a combo of embarrassment and empowerment. She wasn't expecting to make such a spectacle.

"They're called a silent shroud," Grace responded.

"A what?" Trish leaned in. DJ Feline Fine was cranking the volume up as far as it would go on an industrial electronic tune. To say it sounded like a factory jam would be putting it politely.

"A silent shroud!" Grace shouted, but she was so tired. If she kept screaming over the music, she might pass out.

"Perhaps let us take this outside," Octavia bellowed. Her voice can really carry.

"Oh, good idea." Trish agreed with the toy. "Can you stand?" She leaned in close to speak directly in Grace's ear. Grace tensed as Trish's breath brushed along her neck. She nodded speedily. I'm not sure the girl can handle much more excitement today. Chase gave her a thumbs up as the three left the bar. Dancers cheered as Grace made her grand exit. She shyly waved at her adoring fans.

The cool air felt amazing on Grace's warm skin as they exited. No coat required. Trish led them just down the brick wall of the establishment.

"Alright. So, I live next to a superhero?" she teased. "That was amazing, Grace! How long have you been able to do that?"

"About two weeks?" Grace put her hand behind her head.

"She is learning rapidly," Octavia proudly stated. Grace lit up. "Not as fast as Matteo, but fast." The light went out.

"Right. And I don't think we've met yet?" Trish politely turned her attention to the plush.

"I am Octavia. Ruler of sea and melody!" Octavia struck a valiant pose.

"Of course." Trish rolled with it. To her credit, she was very used to talking to puppets and stuffed animals on her show. "I'm Trish. Producer of children's entertainment." Octavia bowed her head, and Trish responded in kind. "So two weeks." Trish turned her attention back to Grace. "Does that mean...?"

"Yeah, it happened after I died," Grace said matter-of-factly.

"Whoa. Is that something all resurrected can do, then?"

"Not remotely," Octavia chimed in. "Dear Grace is the latest in a line of composers wielding an ancient power against the devilish Silence."

"Well, when you put it that way, it doesn't sound like a big deal," Trish joked, incredibly impressed by the credential, if not a little overwhelmed.

"Civilian, I assure you, it is a big deal." Octavia missed it. She hopped back into Grace's purse to settle in for a rest. Trish giggled. Grace couldn't help but smile. The evening was by all counts a success. Even I have to admit, the fight was entertaining. Grace may not know what to think of these butterflies in her stomach, but right now she was trying to just enjoy the moment. Trish felt the same.

"Energy is pretty intense in there, huh?" a voice spoke, approaching on the sidewalk. Grace turned to see a woman with curled red hair, a gorgeous turquoise bodycon dress, and six-inch heels. It was Dios. They were using Ira's body right now, so unsuspecting Grace did not recognize the bombshell in front of her. In fact, she focused more on regaining her composure. Too many pretty girls talking to her today.

"Yeah, the DJ is really lighting it up," Grace responded. Dios looked at Grace. They could tell she looked familiar, but fortunately for Grace, Dios didn't make a habit of remembering the faces of those they've killed. In their opinion, why would they? They probably didn't think they'd ever see their victims again. Dios decided perhaps she was just a steward of the church.

"Is that right?" Ira posited. "There definitely were some special sounds coming from this club, that's for sure." It appears Dios did exactly what they were told. They followed the sound. Grace's fight must've alerted them like a beacon. Luckily, no trace of that sound lingered.

"Definitely go check it out." Grace smiled. Dios was already done with her, however, and moving to the door. "I guess she's going to." Grace felt another dizzy-spell and leaned against the wall.

"Whoa!" Trish laid her hand on Grace's arm. "Maybe we should catch a ride home, yeah?" Trish offered. Grace simply nodded in agreement. "Okay, perfect. I'll order a Ryde."

"You really should get your steed back, dear Grace," Octavia suggested, half asleep. Grace groaned.

Inside the club, Dios made their way to the bar. They sat down next to our favorite mass of shaggy, dumb hair. He nearly fell out of his seat when he saw the gorgeous figure standing beside him.

"You going to buy me a drink, or what?" Ira seduced. Shaggy moved his head up and down like a dog begging for a treat.

"Anything and everything you want," he said eagerly. Ira smirked. College boys were too easy.

"Anything?" she said suggestively.

"Oh, yeah." Poor kid's heart was about to beat out of his chest. I worry about the durability of his pants, as well.

"Tell me, stud. Anything interesting happen in here tonight?" She leaned in close. Shaggy scoffed.

"Just some dumb undead bitch making a big scene. I wouldn't call it interesting." Dios perked.

"Resurrected?"

"Let's not talk about her, baby." Shaggy flashed a smile. "Tell me about you? What's your drink? Favorite position? If we have time, you can tell me your name."

"No, no, no, not so fast, big boy." Ira put a finger to his mouth. "What did this resurrected look like? Is she still here?" This caused shaggy to groan a little. He really does not like obstacles.

"I don't know. Not worth my time, you know?" He nibbled Dios's finger. "Now, maybe let's be done with the talking, yeah?" He raised his eyebrows.

"Couldn't agree more." Ira knew he was no longer useful. She placed a hand on his chest and leaned in. Shaggy opened his mouth for what would most assuredly be an awfully wet kiss. However, his expected ecstasy turned into sharp pain as something shot into his heart, radiating from Dios's hand. He stumbled backward and rapidly tapped his chest.

"What the hell?" he spouted. It felt like he was stabbed, but there was no wound. "Did you just tase me, bro?" Shaggy asked in disgust. I'm afraid that was no taser. We just witnessed an infection. A seed had been planted in his heart, ready to feed on his every flaw. Judging from what we saw tonight, I'm assuming that seed will grow very fast.

"Have fun nurturing that, puppet." Dios patted the boy on the head and moved along.

"Hey, don't you..." He started to protest, but slowly forgot what he was upset about. "Don't you... Um... I need a drink." His attention shifted back toward the bar, and his brief encounter was but a foggy memory.

"You're looking for the dead girl with the sick sound and the stuffed octopus?" Another guy came up to Dios, eager to succeed where the last victim failed.

"That's the one," Ira confirmed.

"She just left with her friend a minute ago." He gestured to the door. Dios remembered the two girls they talked to on the way in.

"Ah, perhaps we've already met, composer," Ira said as they turned away and headed for the exit.

"My name's Shawn, by the way," the desperate would-be suitor called out. I think he expected a prize for his intel, but Dios paid no mind. Shawn should just be happy he survived the encounter. Chase overheard the exchange and found it strange. That woman had just gotten to the bar, yet she was leaving already. Why would she be interested in Grace, purely based on the description provided? His eyes tracked Dios out the door. Quickly he shot a text to Grace:

"Someone spicy looking for you at the bar. Be careful." He tapped his phone nervously before returning to his duties.

The frosty night air greeted Dios again. They looked around the corner where Grace and Trish had been standing. Thanks to a very fast Ryde, however, they were already gone.

"Shit. I knew there was something about that girl," Dom said.

"Calm down. We don't even know for sure they were talking about her," Ira snapped back.

"Come on, Ira. You know it just as well as I do. I know you sensed it."

"I'll give you that. She did look familiar."

"At least we know what she looks like now."

"If that was the composer."

"We saw her face. Now we can take her face!" Orv cackled.

"If that was the composer," Ira reiterated. Dios looked at the cars driving past on the busy street, scheming their next step. It probably won't be the best thing for Grace if they cross paths again too soon. If you think about it, Grace is just starting to learn what she can really do. It would be very anticlimactic if this ended right as it was getting good.

FIVE

NOBODY REMEMBERS

Dirty slush lined the building, and piles of neglected snow melted down into black ice in the alley behind Sparks. Muffled music pulsed off the stained brick as the midnight crowd went wild inside. Amid this lovely scenery lay a solitary soul. They were flat on their back, staring up at the single star peaking through the haze of city lights. Green and white pixie cut hair with fair skin. A baggy hoodie and straight leg jeans were their only defense against the cold.

They watched the star intently, as if expecting it to move. Slowly, they reached a hand to the back of their head, where their fingers were greeted with something wet. Bringing the hand back into view revealed a web of blood between their digits. I guess their hair was green, white, and red now. The blood got boring quickly. They dropped their hand to their side and continued staring at the lone star.

"Oh my god!" a girl shouted down the alley. "Are they okay?!"

"Stay right here, babe. I'll check." Her boyfriend played hero and ran up to the poor individual in the alleyway. "You okay, man?" he asked. The person turned their head and tried to focus on the features of their would-be savior. Trimmed beard, gold chain, tight black shirt. Each feature came into focus one at a time.

"I'm..." The person started to talk, but didn't know how to answer. Were they fine? Bleeding from the head was seldom a good thing.

"Shit, here." Beard chain threw an arm under alley person and lifted them to an upright position. "I'm going to call an ambulance, okay?"

"No." A gut instinct kicked in.

"What? You've got a lot of blood on you, man."

"Not a man." The person hopped off beard chain's shoulder, revealing a black bandana wrapped around their previously hidden arm.

"Whoa, whoa. I'm sorry. I didn't know." The bearded fellow shot up and backed away after seeing the accessory. "I don't want any trouble, okay?"

"Thanks," is all the person said before exiting the alley. Gold chain gave them plenty of space to move past. As soon as they were out of sight, the would-be good Samaritan quickly ushered his girlfriend into the club.

The crisp night air blew against black bandana's face as they left the bustling nightlife and headed toward the quieter part of downtown. It seems they didn't know exactly where they were going. Our new point of interest seems to be suffering from a fair bit of confusion. One road led to another alley, which led to another road that led to main street.

An eerie feeling hung in the air as the dense quiet contrasted the typical bustling energy of the area. Shops that welcomed multitudes of visitors during the day were now all darkened and adorned with closed signs. Black bandana stopped briefly in front of one such dress shop, where their reflection lined up with a gaudy display gown. It felt strange. They just stood there for a moment at odds with the mirrored image. A faint tickle of a former life flashed in their mind, before they eventually shuddered. Whether that was due to the dress or the weather was unclear.

At that moment, something skittered behind them and pulled their attention away. They looked over just in time to see a pair of cat tails disappear into the alley beside the shop. With nowhere else to be, they followed. They peered down the dark alleyway and saw a lone black cat jump up onto a dumpster. It turned to face its follower. A half skull mask rested upon its face, purely white, save for two lines of black ooze dripping down from the eyeholes. Two fangs protruded from the mask, giving it the appearance of a baby saber-tooth tiger. A skeletal, white line ran down the cat's back, leading to two fluffy tails.

Actually, cat isn't the right word for this thing at all. This is what is called a "hush". They are interesting and mischievous little creatures. While they share quite a few similarities with the visual aspect of silent shrouds, I assure you, they are born from a different path. They are drawn to the void, however, which means they often serve the needs of the Silence, most of the time coincidentally. One of these in a town can really bring out the negative energy. Oddly, our stranger doesn't seem afraid of it. Even more peculiar, hushes feed on sound, and Main Street is as quiet as it gets. So, what is it doing here?

"Hi." The person greeted the hush as they inched closer. "My name's... Nova." They pulled the name from a faint itch within their brain. Hearing it aloud, it felt correct. Nova paused a few feet in front of the creature. The two inspected each other for a moment, before the hush jumped down and slowly approached.

"You're unique," Nova said as they squatted down. They reached their hand out, stopping just short of actually touching the hush. The beast looked at the hand and sniffed it out. A moment of perceived consideration passed before it pressed its bony head firmly into Nova's palm.

"Good kitty." Nova smiled. Once again, not a kitty. "Are you lost, too?" The hush rubbed against Nova's arm in response, before swiftly climbing up onto their shoulder. Nova giggled as the hush paced between their shoulder blades. After a couple of laps, it stopped right beside Nova's head wound and began to lick the blood.

"Hey now. Easy, buddy." Nova winced. The hush disregarded as it took one more lick and then nuzzled its head roughly against the wound. "Hey, hey, hey!" Nova instinctively reached back to put a hand between their head and the little creature. When they touched their hair, however, they could no longer feel any wound. A couple of quick taps, and they realized there was no pain, either. In one swift motion, they scooped the hush and held it out in front of them.

"Did you just... heal me?" they asked. The hush tilted its head. Kind of cute for an agent of chaos. Nova pulled it in tight for a big hug. "Thank you!" The hush nuzzled in Nova's armpit. If they could make any sound, it would surely be purring right now. "Do you need a name?" The hush nodded. Now that's a novel idea. A hush with a name. Nova squinted their eyes and analyzed the cat intently. Their eyes moved from the skull mask to the spine, and eventually to the twin tales.

"I've got it. Mata! Like Nekomata." They seem to have drawn inspiration from the folklore about the two tailed cat. The hush wiggled in approval. Nova smiled and perched the little monster back on their shoulders. Mata quickly got cozy and curled up in the sweatshirt's hood. Luckily, it was mostly a spiritual being and weighed next to nothing, so it didn't pull down the collar. Nova gave Mata a little pet before making their way back to Main Street, no clue where they came from or where they were going. Truly an intriguing pairing, though. This was a worthwhile detour.

"Now that's an interesting pairing." See? Someone agrees. A woman stepped forward into the streetlight. She wore a long, plain black dress that went past her ankles, and a headdress resembling a habit, with a black lace veil coming down over her eyes. Even standing in the light, it was hard to see her against the night sky and darkened buildings. "A severed and a hush," she said with curiosity. Nova turned to place themselves between Mata and the stranger. They took a defensive stance. "Do not worry, sweet girl. I wouldn't dare harm something so..." She searched for the word. "Rare."

"Not a girl," Nova said.

"Of course you aren't, sweetie." The woman moved in closer. She was out of the light now and nearly disappeared altogether. She reappeared right in front of Nova. They tensed up as she brushed her hand under their chin. "You know hush's don't usually do that." She gestured to the creature nestled comfortably in Nova's hood.

"Hush?" Nova asked.

"Hush," the woman whispered playfully, placing a finger to her lips. "It's the name given to this charming little creature." Nova watched intently as she circled around and placed a hand on Mata. "Poor thing. You seem lost." She shifted her eyes to Nova. "You, too."

"Just leave us alone."

"Oh, sweet baby." She wrapped her arms around them from behind. "It's okay." Nova froze. Mata tilted their head at the newcomer. The woman glided Nova back within her eye line. "I'm on my way to see someone. A pastor. Won't you accompany me?"

"Why?" Nova kept their guard up.

"I'd like to get to know you better. Perhaps find you a warm bed to sleep in."

Nova relaxed their stance. They couldn't remember much, let alone where home was, and the possibility of a warm bed sounded nice amid the February cold.

"Okay," they hesitantly agreed. "But if you harm Mata..."

"Mata? Is that the hush's name?" She looked at the comfy creature. "I wouldn't dream of it." The woman turned the pair around, looping her arm in with Nova's. "Now, shall we?" Nova didn't object, and they were off to the church.

* * *

"Do you think they're okay?" Grace asked Octavia. She poured thirty ounces of the finest medium roast coffee into a giant cat mug, complimentary from Pets YES. It was the morning after the big fight, and both were feeling much more refreshed. Trish had gone home late the night before, after getting the full rundown of the situation. Glad we missed that. I can only handle exposition so many times.

"Does that still cause you concern?" Octavia questioned as she pulled herself onto the rim of Grace's mug and inhaled the scented steam. She let out a sigh of approval.

"I just wish I could've followed the trace, you know?"

"Dear Grace, you could barely follow the trace to the shroud. You had little chance of following it to the host." Octavia plopped back down on the counter and looked up at the composer.

"I'm sure the world is a scary place for them now, is all. Wish I could help."

"You spared many others by taking down such a formidable shroud. You have done plenty." Octavia took a hearty stance. "It was quite a treat to witness you finding your sound last night. I was beginning to worry you may not have it within you."

"Thanks, Tavi!" Grace ignored that last part. "Couldn't have done it without you. Though I do have to ask why so many of your lessons happen when I'm about to die?" She brought up a good point. That has been the guardian's go-to move lately.

"It is hard to explain the power you possess," Octavia justified. "You must be in a scenario where you can feel it. Frequently, that requires the pressure of danger." She put a discerning tentacle up to her mouth and nodded assuredly.

"Uh-huh. Is that how Matteo learned? What was his power like?" Very sly, Grace. She was itching to learn a bit more about previous composers. Ragnar had been talked about to death, but Matteo had only come up a few fleeting times. Naturally, Grace was unaware of any others.

"Matteo was a true savant," Octavia said, taking the invitation to go down memory lane. "The music flowed through him effortlessly. His instrument was a sound rapier. Ragnar, of course, wielded an ax. If Ragnar was power, Matteo was finesse." Grace bemoaned that Ragnar still managed to enter the conversation, but she decided to hone in on something else.

"Instruments?" Grace inquired.

"Yes. That is the name given to the weapon a composer forms with the sound. Every composer develops their own sound, as you know. They also develop their own unique way of handling it," Octavia explained. She could already see the follow up forming in Grace's eyes. "Your instrument appears to be throwing knives."

"Throwing knives?"

"From what we saw last night, that is my best approximation."

"That's kind of badass!" Grace was feeling pretty cool at that moment and proceeded to take a cocky big gulp of her coffee. It was still entirely too hot. She quickly realized her mistake and slammed the cup down, exchanging it for a bottle of half-drunk water nearby. Grace had a tendency to have multiple beverages in play. She chugged the bottle dry. Octavia just looked on, confused.

"Dear Grace, perhaps you should let it cool first," she cautioned.

"Yup," Grace coughed out. "I'll keep that in mind." She gave a wink in an attempt to regain some style points, then immediately grabbed her cup again. Thankfully, before she could take another ill-conceived sip, a knock came at the door.

"Another visitor! It sure has been a lively week," Octavia observed. It seemed like Grace had a lot of people dropping in lately. Definitely her most social week of all time. Yes, of all time. I'm not exaggerating.

Grace set her mug down to check the door. Would it be Cyn again? Or perhaps even Trish? A lump formed in her throat. She never did settle things with Trish over their almost kiss. The night before turned into more of an info dump than anything else. Either face behind that door would get her heart going to the point where the remaining thirty-one ounces of coffee would be unnecessary. Brazenly, she opened it without checking the peephole.

"Chase?" Grace said with just the right amount of relief and disappointment.

"You really need to answer your phone," Chase scolded as he quickly entered the apartment.

"By all means. Come in."

Chase began pacing. "I was worried about you."

"Why? We killed the shroud. You were there."

"There was this super hot but sketchy woman looking for you last night."

"A hot woman was looking for me?" Grace spoke with just a tinge of pride. She did not seem to be putting the appropriate weight on the word "sketchy".

"Yeah, she came in shortly after you left. As soon as she learned a resurrected girl was there, she hightailed it back out of the bar. I texted you right away. When you didn't answer, I thought she caught up to you and did something. I half expected to find a corpse in your apartment!"

"A couple of weeks too late for that," Grace quipped. "But yeah... totally didn't get that message." She laughed apologetically. "So, what did this mystery hottie look like?"

"She had red hair. Was wearing this tight greenish dress."

"I saw her!" Grace came alive. "She was looking for me?" Down, Grace.

"You saw her? When?" Octavia asked incredulously.

"It was right after the fight. When we went outside. Maybe you were in my bag already? She said something about the bar being electric or something."

"I vaguely remember hearing the voice of another as I nodded off."

"Do you think she wanted an autograph?"

"Grace, you should approach this seriously. The Silence has many warriors. They are not all shrouds," Octavia warned.

"Really?" This was the first time Grace had heard about another enemy type. "But, I mean, this woman didn't look like anything even close to a shroud. She looked completely normal. Well, except for being super hot." Octavia shook her head. "Chase's words!" Grace added, defending herself.

In this instance, Grace seemed to believe anything related to the Silence would have a similar aesthetic. This was obviously not the case. The mention of this person's exceeding normalness did not ease Octavia's worries. In fact, it had the opposite effect.

"There are some we call disciples of the Silence, who are of humanity. They are fierce, and they are not to be trifled with."

The words had an effect on Grace. She tightened her stance. "Okay, okay. So, they could look completely normal and still be evil. Would they have an aura?"

"Anything entwined with the Silence will have an aura." Grace relaxed slightly after hearing this. "Of course, if they are a disciple, they could easily mask it beyond your current level of intuition." And Grace was tense again.

"Cool. Cool. So, if you had to compare them to the shroud I killed last night, they would be..." Grace gestured, looking for some measure of comparison.

"The shroud from last night would be but a mouse in a den of lions," Octavia said gravely, and maybe just a touch hyperbolic. Sure, disciples of the Silence are stronger than shrouds by a good margin, but a mouse in a den of lions isn't exactly the metaphor I'd go with. Maybe more like a mongoose? Either way, the comment landed. Grace now understood what they could be dealing with.

"Alright. That's..." Grace trailed off. Panic was growing in her chest. "But, I mean, we don't know for sure she was one of those, right?"

"Right! Maybe she was a reporter, and she just wanted to interview you. She didn't look super evil." Chase jumped on the coping train.

"We need to accelerate your training." Octavia ignored them.

Grace sighed. "I thought that required the 'pressure of danger'." Grace did her best Octavia impression.

"Correct. Do you not feel pressure?"

"Because some hottie who may or may not be a disciple of an evil god was looking for me?" Grace scoffed. "Yeah. Yeah, I am feeling the pressure." Her facade melted immediately.

"Then we must train. You have only just begun to find your sound."

"Alright, well, I'll leave you two to that, then." Chase initiated an exit strategy. "Glad you're alive, Grace." He did his signature snap and fist-hit combo as he made his way out.

"Wait, Chase," Grace called him back. He closed his eyes. So close.

"Yes?" he begrudgingly replied.

"I need your help with something first."

"Chase is not required for the training, dear Grace." Octavia spoke the words that made Chase relieved, if not a smidge insulted.

"Not that. There's something else I need to do." Grace tied her hair up and put her coat on. "I have to warn someone about the horrors that they may begin to see."

"Not that again," Octavia groaned. "I thought we had already concluded that there is no reliable way to find whomever was severed last night."

"Not them." Grace picked up an unhappy, little octopus in her hands. "There's someone else who needs to know." She turned to Chase. "And I need a ride."

"Where?" Chase asked apprehensively.

"To where the one percent live."

* * *

It was quite the mood in the car. We have a sourpuss, a reluctant cab driver, and a girl who hasn't managed to shed her dogooderness. The three of them were cruising down the most affluent neighborhood in all of Seerstown. That's right, we're on a journey to visit Grace's former scumbag boss, Curtis Evans. Former applies to both of those words now, as he's no longer her boss or presumably a scumbag. I guess Grace is worried that the supernatural he is now privy to may scare the mustache off his face.

"Holy shit. What happened to this place?" Chase commented on the utterly destroyed front yard as they pulled up to the Evans' household.

"Yeah... I guess they haven't had a chance to clean up." Grace gave a guilty ha-ha.

"Wait, was this you?" Chase suddenly felt like he was escorting a felon back to the scene of the crime.

"Well, just some of it! A shroud did most of it."

"Do not be modest, dear Grace. We were responsible for the devil's share of the destruction!" Octavia bragged. Chase shrunk down.

"In self-defense!" Grace said, trying to maintain her image.

"And vengeance!" Octavia was not helping the cause.

"Is this guy going to call the cops when he sees you?" Chase asked as he shifted the car into park. He stared intently at Grace.

"I don't know if he'll even know I fought the shroud controlling him."

"I remembered."

"You remember our fight?" Grace was surprised and also starting to feel a little guilty. She remembered a couple of punches that landed on Chase's person during that scramble.

"Well, bits and pieces. But I know you killed the shroud controlling me."

"That's because I literally carried you back home and told you."

"Right," Chase resigned. She had a point. He also thought about how utterly confused he'd have been if left to his own devices. "Fine. Let's talk to moneybags and get out of here quickly, just in case he starts to remember what you did to his house." Grace nodded in agreement. The three made their way to a screen door shoddily attached to a splintered frame. A sad holdover. Chase gave Grace a disapproving look.

"That was all the shroud! Scout's honor." Grace threw her hand up as if taking an oath.

"Summon the chime!" Octavia popped out of the purse to shout the order.

"Not that again, Tavi. Please." Despite her dispute, Grace did, in fact, ring the doorbell. No answer. Grace looked around. Curtis's car was in the driveway. Sure, based on Cyn's story, it sounded like he may have been arrested, but someone like Curtis surely would've made bail, right? Grace didn't care to go prison touring today. Plus, if he wasn't here, why even have the temporary door?

"A.D. Evans?" Grace called inside. "Are you in there? It's Grace Ryder. We... um, used to work together."

"Perhaps we should summon the chime once more," Octavia suggested.

"Do you just really like doorbells?"

"What do you want?" A gruff voice broke up the interaction.

Grace turned her attention back to the door and jumped when she saw Curtis suddenly standing on the other side. Stained white t-shirt, old gym shorts that didn't fit right, and a nasty stubble crowding his mustache.

"Oh, hi! Um, like I said, we used to work together." Grace tried to recover from the startle.

"Oh..." Curtis said, defeated. "What did I do?"

"Excuse me?" Grace asked.

"I did a lot of bad things to a lot of people. I assume that's what this is about, right?" His head hung low. This was a man terrorized by guilt. Guilt for something he didn't really do. Or perhaps there's something else weighing on him.

"No. It's not that," Grace assured. "I mean, yeah, we weren't exactly friendly, but I don't think that was all your fault." Curtis looked up with puppy dog eyes. "I know you weren't really you."

Those eyes got wide. "You know?" His voice trembled.

"Yes. I do. We all do." She gestured to the group. Chase gave a little wave, and Octavia hopped up on Grace's shoulders.

"We are here to illuminate your mind." Octavia disregarded any possible effect she could have on him. As expected, Curtis was stunned by the talking plush. They always are. However, his reaction went well beyond. He took three steps backward and tripped onto a staircase. Shakily, he held a hand out, as if trying to push them away.

"You're... you're her."

"Are you okay, Mr. Evans?" Grace reached for the door handle.

"No!" Curtis shouted. "You need to leave."

"Excuse me?"

"Now. Leave now. Before... Before he sees you." His voice turned to a whisper. Chase started to sweat, feeling like eyes were watching them.

"Uh, Grace. Maybe we should listen," Chase warned.

"Before who sees me, Mr. Evans?" Both Grace and Octavia

were invested. "Are you okay? I should've killed the one controlling you."

"Not the Silence." Curtis spoke and shocked everyone.

"You know of the Silence?" Octavia inquired. Curtis couldn't stop trembling.

"Please, just go," he pleaded.

"But, they've only just gotten here, daddy." A cold voice slithered out from around the corner. Curtis closed his eyes, and tears started to roll down his cheeks.

"No, no, no," is all he could say, shaking his head as he withdrew into the fetal position.

"Hello, composer." Jake Evans came into the light, one hand resting behind his back. "Care to come in for a chat?" Chase started to back away from the door. Grace peered intently at this newcomer. Was this little boy the reason Curtis was so shaken up? How did he know that Grace was a composer? Hair stood on the back of her neck as the thought crossed her mind. She wondered if this could be one of the disciples Octavia mentioned.

"Composer. Be on guard," Octavia advised.

"What did you do to him?" Grace shot the question.

"Daddy?" Jake looked at the puddle of a man beside him. "Daddy did something bad. He's learning from his mistakes right now."

"Are you a disciple?" Grace came right out and asked it! You have to admire the forwardness. When Grace starts to get mad, she is much more direct. And she was getting mad. Her fists started to clench. However, something stopped her from going full blown rage. It's not because he's a child, is it? Jake had a way of making just about every adult he's interacted with hate him, regardless of his age. Grace is the type with a code, though, so perhaps she's conflicted. Jake simply guffawed at her question.

"Please. If I was something that pathetic, I'd do the world a favor and slice my own throat."

"Then what are you, child? How do you know of composers?" Octavia asked. She wasn't fully ready to believe this boy had nothing to do with the Silence.

"Why don't you come on in and we'll talk about it?" Jake smiled and opened the door with his free hand. His other hand was still resting behind his back. It's pretty obvious he's hiding a knife back there, right? Jake may be a psychopathic spawn, but he's still just a kid. Stealth techniques aren't in his repertoire.

"Why don't you show me both hands there, big guy, and then maybe we can talk?" Grace picked up on it. As I mentioned, it was incredibly obvious. Jake cackled.

"Are you worried about what I might be holding in my hand, composer?" he asked. Chase continued to back away. He was a good two feet behind Grace at this point. "Are you worried it's something I could kill you with?" His head tilted as he looked into her eyes.

"I don't know. Is it?" Grace was apprehensive, ready to say the magic words if she needed. Jake flashed an evil grin.

"Okay, okay, fine. I'll put it away." In a swift motion, Jake exposed a long, sharp knife and rammed it into the neck of his would-be father. Blood splattered against the patio door and Jake's face, contouring his twisted smile. Grace was stunned. It all happened so fast. Curtis's mouth twitched, trying to speak, until finally Jake let go of the knife and Curtis collapsed. "There." Jake held up both of his now empty hands. "Now will you come in?"

"Did that toddler just kill his fucking dad?!" Chase shouted as he nearly slipped off the back step.

"Sonata Mor," Grace summoned with anger. This time, as the sound crescendoed, it didn't start with strings, but a low bass synthesizer hum. I see. So, Grace really is finding her own unique sound. It was coarse and choppy, but not unpleasant. Jake's eyes dilated, admiring the power.

"Now that's different from last time."

"What are you?" Grace was staring daggers at the boy, but that was all she launched at him. Right now, she used the Sonata Mor as more of an intimidation technique. Jake's boyish appearance really was messing with her. Chase's attention went between Grace and the car. Everything in his body told him to run, except for one stupid emotion.

"Me? I'm just a little boy." Jake babied his voice and puckered his lips. Then he burst out laughing. "I'm not interested in fighting."

"Nonsense!" Octavia called out. A sound tentacle shot out and met the ground with a crash. Surprisingly, she followed Grace's lead of intimidating over action. Octavia was more tactical, however. For her, it was more about ensuring she could get information out of Jake before slamming him into the ground. "You are a swift and merciless killer. Fighting is probably all you know."

"Fighting is long and drawn out. A waste of time," Jake countered. "Killing should be quick and fun."

"You are one messed up kid." Grace quickly tried to determine if there was any humanity in this boy worth saving.

"Enough." Octavia ended the standoff. Her tentacle swiped forward, slashing through the door and speeding toward Jake. A beautiful, wordless aria accompanied Grace's heavy synth bass as it soared toward the target. Jake's stupid smirk wasn't going away, however. He stood completely still, unflinching, as the tentacle came crashing into a green force field that surrounded the boy. The sound wave pushed against the shield, trying to break through. The scene caught Grace by surprise, but not Octavia. She was determined.

"Composer, I require more sound," Octavia requested. Her tentacle still provided pressure, all with the hope of wiping that smile off the little shit's face.

"Right." Grace tried to focus just like she did at the club, but this was different. There wasn't an external song to prime her heartbeat. Nothing to latch onto except her own sound, which was still just a bare-bones saw bass.

"Grace," Octavia pleaded, but to no avail. A pulse shot out from the shield and evaporated the sound tentacle. "Dammit!" Octavia cursed.

Jake cackled. "It won't allow me to go down in such a pathetic way," he said, showboating. "Please, don't underestimate a child of the Silence."

Octavia tensed her fluff. She finally realized what he was. "So you are a spawn."

"A what?" Grace needed clarification.

"One who was born within the yolk of Silence."

"It means I come from a long line of people who fuck up composers like you," Jake bragged. A sly look painted across his face. "In fact, I wouldn't be the first in my family to spill blood like yours." He peered right at Octavia. She trembled with rage.

"Who is your mother?" Octavia asked, waiting to pounce on the wrong response. Her tone shifted. It became dark and pointed. Grace picked up on the change. She had questions, but now may not be the time. Jake, on the other hand, seemed immensely pleased.

"Just some whore," he responded callously. "But I understand my great grandmother was quite accomplished." If Octavia had blood, it would be boiling. "Killed some shit composer back in the day." The chains broke.

"You shall pay recompense!" Octavia screamed. In an instant, the guardian absorbed all of Grace's sound. The aura surrounded the kraken and her alone. Grace's synthesizer cut off, replaced by a violent opera. "I am sorry, dear Grace, but I am taking it all." The sound focused into a drill-like twister in front of Octavia as she levitated off Grace's shoulder. High a capella tones bellowed out in a minor key. Grace couldn't comprehend what was happening. She could still feel the sound, but it felt removed. Like someone was playing a song in the next room, and she could only feel the bass through the floor.

"Trying again?" Jake heckled. "Be my guest." A sharp tentacle shot out from the vortex toward him. As expected, it collided with the green shield. The sound wind drilled down into a fine point, focusing all the pressure in one spot. Jake watched with all the superiority he could muster until a crack started to spread in front of him. The shield was weakening.

Finally, the edges of his lips fell. I don't think he believed that could happen. He felt an unfamiliar emotion start to creep in—fear. However, Octavia's tentacle was also weakening. She focused everything she had into the attack, and it still might not be enough. Shrill sopranos sang in a staccato pattern. Each beat pushed the tentacle drill further. The cracks almost enveloped the entire shield now. Just a little more.

"Impossible." Jake watched helplessly as his defenses crumbled. Grace glanced over at her companion. She saw Octavia was putting everything into this. While she didn't fully understand, Grace could feel it radiating off the sea beast—unquenchable vengeance.

"Come on, Tavi!" Grace cheered. Octavia felt the support, despite the composer having every right to be upset. When it came down to it, Octavia did just kind of hijack her sound. A low synthesizer came up from the ground floor, and wisps of an aura began to spiral off Grace and onto Octavia. The weakening sound wave regained its balance, and the staccato pulse of the singing blended in unison with a relentless bass line. The cracks diversified and spread all across the shield until it finally shattered. A pulse released from the shield as it imploded, silencing Grace and Octavia's sound completely. Tie ball game! Grace and company no longer had a weapon, and Jake Evans no longer had his precious shield. The look of shock on his face was something to savor, however.

"That... That shouldn't happen." His cool was all gone. Jake was now just a scared boy, facing the potential consequences of his actions. Luckily for him, his opponents were both running on empty.

"Sonata Mor!" Grace called out, but nothing happened. "Sonata Mor!" She tried again. Same result.

"Dear Grace," Octavia stopped her. "That was all we had. We failed."

"We can't let him get away," Grace responded. She started to advance, but fell to her knees. Jake nervously laughed at his fortune.

"I guess we'll have to reschedule our chat." He backed up slowly. Chase inched forward. I think he was debating whether he could really tackle this child psychopath. On the one hand, yes, he was currently a defenseless nine-year-old. On the other, Chase had just witnessed him commit patricide in cold blood. Jake picked up on Chase's advances, pulled the knife out of his surrogate father's neck, and wielded it in front of him.

"Don't think about it," Jake warned. That was more than enough to encourage Chase to stop in his tracks. Jake backed away slowly, before running out the back door. Déjà vu, anyone?

"Chase! Get him!" Grace ordered.

"No way, Grace. I'm not chasing a knife-wielding child of the corn." Chase had a point. I have no doubt Jake would come out on top in an altercation. He's kind of a wildcard. Grace pounded the floor in frustration, before falling over. She rolled onto her back and took in that same view of the sky she experienced just days earlier. I think she was getting sick of feeling spent on this particular piece of land.

"I'm sorry, Tavi."

"Do not apologize, dear Grace." Octavia sounded defeated.

"I know it was important to you. I could feel it. It wasn't enough."

"I will have my day." Octavia moved over to Grace. "It is I

who should apologize to you. I am ashamed of how my behavior affected you."

Grace turned to meet the look of one sad octopus. "What do you mean?"

"I selfishly took everything. All your power. We are linked, bonded by the Sonata Mor, with the ability to give and take the sound. I took advantage of that. I took advantage of you, dear Grace. For that, I am ashamed." She hung her head low.

Grace was seeing a new side to her sherpa. With the last of her strength, she booped Octavia on her plushy little head. "I mean, I would have preferred you asked first, but we're cool. I get it." She tried to comfort Octavia, but to little success. "So, our sound is linked? That's pretty cool." The sad plush continued to look down, lost in her guilt. Grace let loose a big smile as a new thought crossed her mind. "That kind of makes us a girl group, huh?" That did the trick.

Octavia looked up with a renewed sparkle in her eye. "Like Glitter in *Pop Love*?" she asked in awe.

"Exactly like Glitter in *Pop Love*." Octavia couldn't help but squeal with excitement before returning to a more dignified look.

"And just like Glitter, we have our own ultimate goal."

"Make it to nationals?" Grace joked.

"To eradicate the Silence and all who follow it," Octavia pronounced. Our lovely kraken has bounced back. When she starts riding the line between adorable and ultra-violent, that's when you know Octavia is herself.

"That was my second guess." Grace let out a laugh.

"Should I pull the car up, or...?" Chase butted in. Grace and Octavia suddenly remembered he was there.

"Chase, you're kind of part of our girl group, too!" Grace teased.

"Yeah, yeah. So, the car?" Chase tried to stay on topic.

"It is true that you stood by our side on two occasions now.

That is commendable," Octavia acknowledged. "Perhaps an invitation to the group is in order."

"I don't want to be in your girl group," Chase protested. "I just help out sometimes, preferably with much less dangerous things."

"Aw, come on, Chase." Grace regained enough strength to sit up now. "You could be the pretty one." Grace smirked. Chase blushed.

"I'm getting the car," he said as he removed himself from the situation. Octavia climbed aboard Grace's shoulder. The composer looked over at her friend.

"I sincerely promise that next time, we will work in tandem," Octavia said with sincerity.

"I know we will," Grace agreed. "And, whenever you're ready, you can tell me why you hate that elementary schooler so much." Octavia nodded. She wasn't fully ready yet. "Besides the obvious reasons," Grace added.

Chase pulled the car onto the yard and over the walkway, stopping right beside Grace. I guess he figured a few tire tracks in the grass couldn't make it any worse.

"Need help getting in?" Chase asked from the car.

"No!" Grace responded, slowly getting to her feet. "I think I'm getting my legs back." She slapped her thighs like one slaps the hood of a car. "Alright, Tavi. I sense a *Pop Love* marathon when we get back."

"What an extravagant idea!" Octavia agreed. "And then, we train." Grace groaned a little. She was less excited about that idea. After getting in the car, Grace pulled her phone out and held it up to show Chase.

"Apparently, I need to check this more. Now let's see how many missed calls and messages I've got." Grace said it facetiously. Apparently, she's trying to make a point to excuse her previous unresponsiveness. This attempt, however, falls flat, as there are three missed calls and a text. Two calls from Pets YES and one from her brother, Peter.

"Oh, shit." She was surprised. "I guess I do need to check my phone more."

Chase checked the screen. "Three missed calls? Just while we were dealing with the creepy kid?" He was surprised. For Chase, that volume of messages wasn't abnormal, but for Grace, he didn't expect it.

"Well," Grace spoke coyly, "technically the calls from work came in before we left, I guess?" Chase just shook his head. Grace didn't dwell on his judgment, however. She was too busy opening the text from Peter:

"Call me back ASAP" was all it said. It was rare for him to reach out first, and the tone of the message gave Grace an uneasy feeling.

"I should probably make a call," Grace explained to the crew. Chase turned down the music and gestured as if to say "go for it". Grace exhaled. A lot had changed since she last talked with her brother. What could he want? Her thumb tapped the phone icon to start the call. Peter picked up almost instantly.

"Grace, thank god!" He sounded relieved. "Where are you?"

"Uh, hiya, Peter. I'm just driving with some friends. What's up?" she said awkwardly. Her brother's jumpiness definitely had her confused.

"Driving with friends?" Now he sounded disappointed. He gave a heavy sigh. "Grace, why am I getting calls from your work doing a wellness check?"

"They what?!"

"Yes. They called me as your emergency contact. Apparently, your car has been parked there for days now, and you haven't been coming into work? Nobody has heard from you."

"That's not true. I saw Cyn yesterday!"

"Who? Nevermind. It doesn't matter. What is going on with

you? Why are you skipping work and without a car, for god's sake?" Peter probed.

"I don't know, I just had a hard time..." Grace paused, trying to search for the right way to explain.

"A hard time? That's why you call in, Grace. You don't just skip out on work. How inconsiderate can you be?" Grace fell silent. To be clear, Grace earnestly forgot to call in. The last couple of days haven't exactly been normal. Regardless, it had been a while since she got a good scolding from her brother, and it didn't feel too great. Adding insult, Grace tried incredibly hard her entire life to be "considerate". So, that being called into question for this one incident stung. None of her previous efforts seemed to matter right now. After a few seconds of quiet, he came back softer. "What's going on, Gracey?"

"It's hard to explain." Grace felt a lump in her throat. Falling back into this role—that of the bumbling younger sibling—filled her with all the familiar emotions of a former life. Her brother sighed.

"Okay. How about dinner, then? Tonight. The kids would love to see you, too." Grace banged her head back against the car seat. Was she ready for that? Peter sensed the hesitation. "I promise not to drill you with questions the whole time. Just let me see my sister, and maybe you can relax a bit. Share only what you want." Relaxing was probably not on the menu. Regardless, Grace accepted.

"Sure. That sounds nice."

"Perfect. Five o'clock?"

"I'll be there."

"See you then, Grace." Peter hung up. Grace held her phone by her ear for a moment to process. She decided it would ultimately be good to see her brother. It was time. And seeing the kids may be just the escape she needed. For one night, maybe she could forget she died, resurrected, and found herself at odds with an evil blob god.

"You good?" Chase tested the waters. He could tell the convo was charged. To his credit, he tried very hard not to listen, but a sedan hardly allows space for privacy.

"Yeah, it's all good," she lied. "I should probably go get my car today, though. Mind if we take a quick detour?"

"Oh, I wasn't letting you go back home without your car." Grace looked out the window to see they were already entering the Pets YES parking lot. "I'm not risking being brought along on another death journey." Chase playfully smirked.

"Oh, please. You love coming on adventures."

"Not even a little bit." Chase held firm. He really didn't care for it.

Grace tapped him on the shoulder as the car came to a stop. "Keep telling yourself that." Grace got out, with Octavia still perched on her shoulder. The octopus seems to be dozing. "Thanks for having our back today. I'm glad you're no longer being controlled by a parasitic monster."

"That makes two of us." Chase gave a casual salute. "Any time I can help. But in the future, maybe let's keep my help away from the action?" Grace laughed at the suggestion.

"I'll see what I can do," she said, as she shut the door and waved goodbye. After Chase drove off, she turned to face the corporate building. She had no desire to go in, but decided it was probably best to at least show them proof of life.

"You okay if we make a brief pit stop before our anime binge?" Grace asked Octavia, who was now completely fast asleep. The image of Octavia sleeping always came dangerously close to inciting cute rage in Grace. She held back the urge and gently scooped the plush and placed her in the purse. "I'll take that as a yes."

* * *

A few miles away at the local church of Veritas, Nova was waking up. They were given a modest room in the directory. As their eyes cracked, they began to survey their surroundings. The space was small. Stained wooden floors gave way to a hideous floral wallpaper. A single oak cabinet in the corner carried the room's entire decor. Sunlight peeked through the window onto Mata, who was curled up by Nova's feet. They realized the human was awake and got up into a big stretch, before nuzzling their new friend's face.

"Good morning, Mata." Nova smiled. The hush paced in a circle until Nova sat up and threw their feet over the edge of the bed. The night before was a blur. They briefly became acquainted with Pastor Dom, before being ushered away into a bed. It's funny. Nova had learned the name of the pastor, but never bothered asking the name of the woman who brought them here. The call of sleep was too powerful, and to be perfectly honest, they didn't care. In fact, the only reason they knew the name of the preacher man was because of Dom's sense of self importance.

Nova could hear muffled talking coming from the next room, and I suppose they felt they needed to at least thank their host. They got up and made their way over, still in their clothes from the previous night. Except for the hoodie, of course. That was removed, revealing a graphic t-shirt of a moth perched atop planet Earth. I don't know what that's supposed to mean. Mata strutted right behind.

"Ah, there are our sleepy little ones." The woman warmly greeted the pair as they emerged. She pulled out a chair for Nova. "Please, do join us. I've prepared something to eat."

"Breakfast?" Nova asked groggily as they took the seat. Dios sat across the way, studying their new tenant.

"Oh, honey, it's already lunchtime." The woman giggled as she grabbed a plate of pan-seared chicken with rice and asparagus. "Passed actually. I was getting worried I'd have to put this in the fridge." She placed the plate in front of Nova. Mata jumped up on their lap.

"Thanks." Nova was gracious, but still confused. Just who were these people? Did they know each other before? Our amnesiac is still struggling with their memory, it seems. The woman looked like she was also in her apparel from the night prior. In fact, she did change her clothes, but the variances were incredibly slight. It was no wonder Nova didn't notice.

Dios was in full pastor garb and presenting as Dom. "Mira tells me you're experiencing some trouble remembering things. Is that true?" The pastor jumped right in. Nova deduced Mira to be the name of the woman in black.

"Just bits and pieces," Nova spoke carefully. They petted Mata with one hand and dug into the chicken with the other.

"Very interesting. And the..." Dom gestured to the hush, not wanting to reveal too much by saying the creature's name himself. Dios was unsure how much the newcomer was aware of.

"Mata," Nova filled in the blank.

"Ah, yes. Mata. Quite the creature, don't you think?"

"Never seen anything like them." Nova lowered their head so Mata could greet it with a bony nose boop.

"They are remarkable." Mira sat back at the table. "And this one seems to fancy Nova quite a bit." She shot a veiled glance at Dios, who returned one in kind. They weren't fools. Dios knew that a hush seldom cared for anything besides destruction. In fact, they would not admit it out loud, but its presence had them slightly on edge.

"And you don't know why that is?" Dom tried to get Nova to crack a facade. He wasn't convinced their guest was fully being honest. Of course, Dios could sense that Nova had been severed. However, memory loss is not a common, long-lasting symptom of being severed. Most people remember what they did as puppets to the Silence. That was Dios's silver lining lately. Sure, silent shrouds were dropping, but they knew that meant insufferable guilt for all those who were freed.

"We just met last night," Nova sharply responded. They could sense hostility. Nova wasn't a fan of the preacher. They seldom cared for holy men, but this one especially rubbed them the wrong way. Very keen intuition.

"Uh-huh." Dom still didn't believe it. "Well, please, enjoy your meal, and then let's see where we can get you set up on your feet, yeah?"

"Dom." Mira cut in like a knife. "You're not casting away those in need, are you?"

"Of course not!" Dom boisterously replied. On the inside, Dios was fuming. Of course, they wanted Nova and Mata gone. They saw the pair as nothing more than a liability. Mira, on the other hand, saw so much more.

"Good." Mira turned to Nova. "You're welcome to stay here as long as I am."

"Which will be how long, again?" Dom impatiently tapped their fingers on the table.

"Until our problem is taken care of." She took a sip of her tea, not even looking at the frustrated disciple.

"Naturally." Dios was barely holding it together.

"It's bullshit! Let's just skin the little shit." Orv finally broke through. Dios quickly turned away to hide their face. Nova tensed up. A sudden threat unbecoming of a pastor, and in a different voice. What was this, Dom and Mr. Hyde? Kind of, actually. Except in this version, everybody is terrible. Mata was bothered very little by the abrupt change, but did look up when the pets stopped. Mira leaned in toward the preacher.

"Manners," she sternly reminded Dios. Nova looked over at her, their guard on high alert.

"What's going on?" They grabbed their kitchen knife. Mira let out a heavy sigh.

"You see, Dom isn't just one person," she explained. Dios spun around.

"And we're sick of this boring little show!" Orv shouted.

"Idiot!" Dom pushed the rabid dog back down. "Could you not have shut up for ten more minutes?" Nova watched as the preacher argued with himself.

"You can put the knife down, sweetie. It's all bark. They won't hurt you." She could see Nova's grip tightening on the sharp kitchen utensil, their eyes locked on Dios. "Or Mata," she added. Nova briefly shifted their eyes to Mira, before returning to the threat. They weren't taking any chances right now.

"Oh, please, kid. Dom and Orv may be idiots, but Mira and I know you're special." Ira joined the conversation. "So, put the silly little knife down. We don't want to have to kill you." The woman's voice coming out of Dom's body solidified Mira's remarks. Nova realized that this truly was more than one person or a very talented actor. They kept the knife at the ready, but they engaged with their words first.

"What is this? D-I-D?" Nova asked.

"This isn't some geeky game, loser," Dom sneered.

"D-I-D, not DND, you imbecile. Honestly. Dissociative Identity Disorder. They're asking if our psyche was split into three personalities," Ira explained, before turning her attention back to Nova. "No. It's not that at all." Dios decided to display their full talents. No reason to hide. At this point, they either had to kill Nova or fully bring them in. Before everyone's eyes, they changed their body into Ira. Nova was startled, but impressed.

"Amazing," they admired.

"I know," Ira said and looked down at her body. "I love how my bust looks in this pastor shirt. It's giving sacrilege."

"You can shape-shift?" Nova asked. "Into anything?"

"No." Ira sighed. "Just into one beauty or two different flavors of douchebag."

"Oh, shut up, Ira. We all know my face is the winning

number." Dom took offense. Nova couldn't take their eyes off the show. It was like they were in the front row at the circus. Slowly, they put their knife down.

"There we go. See, harmless?" Mira assured them.

"I should slit your throat and dance in your blood for calling us that!" Orv snapped.

"Don't mind that one. He doesn't get to drive much."

"You prissy, little bitch!"

"Orv, please. You make the worst first impression." Ira calmed the animal. Nova petted Mata and thought for a moment. This was a rollercoaster, but they found themselves drawn to the ride. Did they trust any of these people? Not a chance, but they knew Mata wasn't your usual cat. These new acquaintances didn't seem usual either. Both were anomalies. Perhaps it was fate that Nova stumbled into this world. After all, not just any group could shed light on their new friend.

"I'll accept your invitation." Nova brought them all back to task.

"To stay by my side?" Mira beamed.

"For now."

"Oh, joy!" Mira clapped her hands. "This is wonderful news."

"In exchange for something," Nova cut back in.

"How about your life?" Dom sneered. "You aren't doing *us* the favor, kid."

Mira raised a hand to silence Dom, and then gestured with that same hand for Nova to continue.

"I want to learn about Mata. How to take care of them. Where they came from. Any threats."

This request was a little surprising. There must be something significant between the two. Not many people would put themselves under the care of a strange woman and a tricycle of psychopaths, just to find out how to protect a pet they had literally just met.

"I think we can do that." Mira looked at Dios, who

begrudgingly agreed. "Wonderful. It's a deal then." Mira held out her petite hand. Nova looked at it for a moment, fully contemplating the potential consequences, before finally reaching over and shaking it. Mira grinned. Dios grimaced.

"Now, how about you four get more acquainted? I'll grab a towel for our guest." Mira rose from her seat. "I'm sure you'll want to wash up?" Nova nodded. They didn't love the idea of being alone with Dios, however.

"I think I'll just finish this in my room," Nova referenced the remainder of their lunch.

"Fair enough. I'll be there in just a moment with your toiletries." Mira understood. Dios tapped the table aggressively, still not thrilled about the deal. "That means you can come help." Mira squeezed Dios's shoulder.

"Naturally." Dom groaned. Nova grabbed their plate and returned to their room along with Mata, while Mira and Dios went in the opposite direction. The supply closet was located squarely on the other end of the church. When they got into the worship space and were out of earshot, Dios gripped Mira's arm and swung her around to face them.

"Just what is your game here?" Dom interrogated.

"Hands," Mira warned. Dios released their grip to appease her. "You really don't see the value of taming a hush?" she continued.

"They are chaos incarnate. No loyalty to the Silence."

"No, but for some reason it has loyalty to Nova."

"Do we really have to spell it out for you boys?" Ira asked. "I, for one, love the idea, Mira. Let's shake things up around here."

"Yes, that's all great in theory, but do any of you know how to actually train a hush?" Dom questioned. No response. "Yeah, that's what I thought."

"Ideally, we won't have to rely on them. But we know very little about this new composer, except for the fact that she's a woman. You know what that means."

"A win for feminism?" Ira joked.

"It means she has the potential to be a true successor," Mira stated, which caused Dios to burst out laughing.

"Oh, come on, Mira. You think she's the Maestro?" Dom scoffed. "Why? Because the first one had tits, too?"

"Such a vile little mouth," Mira snapped. "It's unprecedented, and it means we have to be on guard. I hope our new composer goes just as easily as the last, but until that happens, we need all the weapons at our disposal. The Silence would not have summoned me here if this was not important."

Dom grunted.

"We'll play ball, Mira," Ira assured her. "But, as soon as the composer is dead, so is that amnesiac and their little hellcat." Mira ignored the statement. Neither approving nor denouncing the plan.

"What is that whore doing here?" a voice yelled out from the front of the church, pulling everyone's attention. Jake Evans stood amidst the pews with clenched fists. He glared at Mira with eyes that could kill.

The corners of Mira's mouth weighed down as she looked upon him. "Hello," she said, disgust dripping from her words, "my son."

SIX

NOBODY'S FAMILY

Jake was shaking with rage. Every ounce of his devil-may-care attitude had vanished. Big day for him, actually. He's showing a wide range of emotions outside his usual arrogance. It's easy to understand why, though, right? Mira is the mother who abandoned him, after all. Dios watched with unbridled joy as the two reunited.

"Jakey! Just in time," Ira's voice came through. "You remember mommy dearest, don't you?" She stoked the fire. Jake marched down the aisle. Mira scowled at the advancing boy until he was a foot in front of her. No words, just action. Jake wound up and swung a violent punch at Mira. His fist went all the way through her with no resistance, causing him to lose balance and fall onto all fours. Mira's body dissipated. He put everything into that assault. Punching through air was immensely unsatisfying.

"Crude. Inelegant. Embarrassing." Mira re-appeared, sitting in the foremost pew. "I knew you'd be just like your father. Disgusting." Jake whipped his head toward his mother.

"Shut up. Like I'd care what some whore thinks," Jake spat. If I didn't know better, I'd think he was on the verge of crying.

"And an astounding lack of vocabulary on top of it all. Please," Mira got up and glided over to the boy, "at least try to diversify your insults." She towered over him. He looked up with those angry eyes right before she slapped him down to the ground. "Now," Mira turned her attention back to Dios, "where were we?" Dios clapped enthusiastically.

"I cannot tell you how long we've all been waiting to see that!" Dom exclaimed.

"Again, again!" Orv pleaded. Mira ignored the encore. Dios savored one last look at the aftermath before continuing their walk with Mira.

"Failures!" Jake hollered, getting back up to his feet.

"Jake, if I were you, I'd really just call this one," Ira advised. "Or don't. Whether you leave or get beat up doesn't matter. It's a win-win."

"The composer just confronted me." Jake brought up Dios's unfinished business. "In my house." Dios gave full attention now. Mira also perked up. Talk of the composer was on topic.

"Go on," Dom prodded.

"She broke my shield," Jake revealed.

"She broke the Silence's guard?" Mira was intrigued. Jake looked away from her, refusing to acknowledge anything she was saying. "Oh, please. Don't be such a child."

"Why are you even here?" Jake asked, continuing to avert his gaze.

"Back to being useful." Dom snapped his fingers. Mira ignored the question. Jake exhaled aggressively. He wanted nothing more in that moment than to fully awaken and bring everyone to their knees. The troubles of being a pre-teen, am I right?

"Her and her little plush. They were able to break it. However, they could barely move after. I think that's their limit," Jake reluctantly answered.

"That's good. It means she can't sustain that kind of power,"

Mira noted. "Still, to destroy the Silence's guard is no meager feat. For a new composer, it's almost unheard of." Mira shot a look at Dios as if to say, "I told you so." They are correct. Grace may be hard on herself for not being on the same level as previous composers, but that last attack was impressive. I think it had a little more to do with Octavia, however. Grace isn't able to structure her sound efficiently, yet. She's not polished. It was Octavia who organized Grace's sound.

"I don't suppose you got anything useful. Like a name? Address? Detailed bio tracker?" Ira asked. Jake smirked. He did have something.

"I know her car."

"We can work with that," Dom acknowledged. "Did you get the license plate?"

"As a matter of fact, I did." Jake dangled the info. Dios just glared. "Fine." Jake sighed. "You're no fun at all. It's FCK-BOI." Dios clapped their hands.

"Alright. Perhaps it's time we paid a visit to our puppet friend at the police station," Dom suggested. Mira nodded in agreement.

"I'll tend to the newcomers, while you check in on our lead," Mira gave the directive. Dios grumbled, annoyed that Mira felt she could bark orders. Regardless, the trio dispersed in pursuit of their given task.

"Wait!" Jake called out. "That's it? Are you kidding me?" Mira ignored him, disappearing into the storeroom.

"You want more, boy?" Ira responded, eyes still locked ahead. Dios shifted to Dom's body. "Then maybe work on becoming useful. Awaken already." Dom said the last words as the entrance swung open. "And then die in battle," he whispered under his breath.

The massive doors slowly came to latch, and Jake was alone at the altar. He looked down at his quivering hand. Jake wasn't used to feeling this way. Vulnerable. Looks like more than one shield was broken today. He violently shook his body in frustration, before snapping back into a rigid stance.

"I'll awaken. And after I prove myself to the Silence by killing that composer, I'm going to enjoy ripping all of you apart." Jake allowed the imagery to flood his brain. The thought of Dios and Mira bloodied at his feet brought that smug smile back. He glanced over at the supply closet, his long-lost mother still behind the door. Boy-scorned pointed his finger like a gun and mimicked a bang. With a new motivation ahead of him, Jake left the cathedral.

* * *

Grace shut the door to Tania's office. I hope you don't mind; I spared us the boring meeting with the boss. Basically, Grace still has a job and is using up her dwindling vacation. Tania was ready to toss Grace out until she saw the mark of the dead. After everything that happened with the assistant director, the last thing Pets YES needed was more bad publicity for firing a resurrected shortly after they had died. Some people would be all for that kind of story, but another group would most assuredly boycott. Regardless, Grace was indifferent about how things played out. She was prepared to be fired, but wasn't mad that she was still employed for the time being. Fighting the Silence doesn't exactly keep the lights on.

As she was on her way out, she made a detour. I'm sorry I couldn't spare us from this upcoming moment. She was going to see Cyn. It had been a couple of days, and Grace was getting a touch bolder. Initiating a conversation was something she was capable of now.

She arrived in the creative lounge and saw Cyn, Sami, and a number of inconsequentials hard at work. Grace had to crack a smile. Sitting on top of Cyn's monitor was an orange stuffed octopus. Almost identical to Octavia, aside from the color.

Octavia would never be caught dead in orange. Cyn noticed Grace and lit up.

"Hey! You're back." The digital designer greeted Grace as she approached the computer. "Sami, Grace is back!"

Sami, who was rightfully confused why he would care about a colleague coming to work, gave a half-hearted wave. "Yay, the company can move forward now," he said sarcastically. Cyn wrinkled her nose at him.

"Hey! Not exactly back. Going home in a minute. Just had to pick up my car and prove to the boss that I'm not dead," Grace replied. "Currently."

"Oh." Cyn sounded a touch disappointed. "I suppose your rebelling spirit lives on, then."

"I just have some things I gotta focus on right now." Grace grabbed orange-tavia off Cyn's monitor. "This is cute, though."

"Yeah, I honestly loved yours, and I found this in the store the other day. And check it out." Cyn extended a hand, and Grace handed her the plush. She promptly flipped it inside out. It was now yellow and frowning. Yellow-tavia doesn't have the same ring to it.

"That's adorable!" Grace loved it. "I wonder if mine does that..." She cringed for a second, thinking about how mad Octavia would get if she ever tried such a thing.

"Yeah, it's my little moody octopus."

"My octopus, by the way," Sami interjected, not taking his eyes off his computer screen. Grace and Cyn looked over.

"I literally bought this yesterday, Sami," Cyn protested.

"Not yours." Sami looked up and pointed at Grace.

"You swiped my plushy gift."

"You said you didn't care about it. We talked about this." Cyn shot Sami a look.

"I'd just like Grace here to know that she's a petty thief. She can keep it." He shrugged. "I just want some guilt, that's all."

"Ah, I'm so sorry, Sami! I kind of needed to take her. I wasn't trying to steal. I promise!" Grace got flustered. Even though Sami was obviously pulling her leg, she couldn't help but feel bad. Cyn glared at Sami, who was enjoying the floundering a little too much. He got the message.

"It's fine, it's fine. You're not a thief," he retracted. Grace allowed herself to breathe, but only slightly.

"I can get you a new one," the composer offered. Sami considered, but he could feel the leer of his coworker. He decided he better not accept.

"No, it's alright. He seems much happier with you, anyway."

"She," Grace corrected.

"If you say so." Sami put his head back into his work.

"I'm taking really good care of her! If that helps?" Wow, she genuinely can't let it go.

"It does... a little." Sami nodded.

"Anyway! Whatcha got going on the rest of the day, then?" Cyn pulled them away from the great octopus caper. "Maybe that boyfriend of yours is coming over? What was his name—Chase?" Now if this wasn't obvious fishing, I don't know what was.

"Chase? Ew, no." A visceral reaction.

"Ew? He seemed like quite the catch. Very pretty. You know, if you like guys."

"Pretty boy, you say?" Sami has entered the chat. "Do tell me more."

"He is very pretty." Grace paused for a second. Could she muster that same bravery she had last night? "But, I don't like guys." There it was. She was out to the room. Cyn couldn't hide a smile. "I'll see you all later." Grace's moment of courage was done, and she urgently needed to leave. Cyn waved goodbye as Grace hightailed it out to the parking lot.

"I knew it," said Sami nonchalantly. He looked at Cyn. "So, are you going to...?" He gestured after Grace. Cyn promptly stood up and followed. "I knew that, too." Sami gave himself kudos. Cyn got to Grace just as she was unlocking her car.

"Grace!" she called out. Grace pivoted with lightning speed.

"Cyn. Hi! Yeah, hi! So you're out here now, huh?" There's the bumbling Grace we know. Cyn closed the gap with a charming nonchalance.

"Hi." She chuckled, stopping two feet away from Grace. The way Grace's heart was beating, however, you'd assume Cyn was straddling her.

"What... What's up?" Grace stammered. Octavia looked up from her purse, waking up from her nap. She quickly caught on to what was happening and rolled back over to sleep.

"I'm glad we started talking more," Cyn said clearly. Confidently. A stark contrast to our composer.

"Yeah, totally." Grace nodded. She couldn't help but wonder if this was really happening. Yes, it really was. Unfortunately.

"I'd like that to continue. If you want, we could get dinner this weekend?" Cyn asked the heart-stopping question. She looked right into Grace's eyes while doing it. Her white teeth beaming through soft lips. Grace's mouth hung open for a second, stunned, before finally snapping back.

"Yes. Yeah. That'd be really cool." Nice job, Grace. I honestly didn't think she'd be able to talk for a few hours. Cyn lit up even more.

"Awesome. I can't wait." Cyn charmingly moved her hair behind her ear. "So."

"So." Grace wasn't being cute. She truly didn't know what to say next.

"I'll text you later, and we can figure out where to go on our date?" Cyn, please go easy on the poor girl. Saying the word "date" like that... You may as well slap her in the heart with an electric eel. All Grace could do was nod. She couldn't stop either.

"Cool. Talk later then." Cyn wiggled her fingers to say

goodbye and headed inside Pets YES. Grace nodded for probably a good minute after she left.

"I think she has departed back into the building, dear Grace," Octavia finally spoke up. Sneaky, little plushy. She wasn't sleeping at all.

"Huh?" Grace came back down to earth. "What just happened?"

"I believe you have a date with the young lady."

"Oh god, what did I do?" Grace panicked.

"I am not sure I understand. I thought you would be elated. Do you not wish to copulate with the maiden?" Grace recoiled from Octavia's words.

"Gross, Tavi. Don't talk about it like I'm some pillaging Viking."

"My apologies, dear Grace. By the way you were sweating, I assumed you were lusting."

"Seriously, Octavia. We need to work on how you say things." Grace shook her head and got into the car.

"I have heard I am quite an eloquent speaker." Octavia took offense.

"Not what I meant," Grace said as she looked at the dashboard clock. Almost two o'clock now. She was supposed to go to her brother's house a little before five. An uneasiness set in. "So, I know I should be training and all that, but there is one more thing it looks like I have to do today."

"Another errand?" Octavia groaned.

"Kind of. I need to see my brother tonight."

"Oh, your kin! I was unaware you had such a connection. You do not mention your family much, dear Grace. I believed you to be a lone adventurer like—"

"Don't say it." Grace cut her off before she inevitably uttered the name of a certain Viking. "And that's because I don't really have a lot of family. My parents died in a car crash when I was off at college, and my brother is kind of all I have left. Him and his wife and kids."

"I see," Octavia responded in a soft tone. "Then, I look forward to meeting him!" Grace nervously laughed. Was she really ready to reveal Octavia and the mark all on the same day? Perhaps. She didn't like to keep secrets from Peter, after all. Not when they were face to face, at least.

"Yeah..." Grace said apprehensively. "We'll see how it goes." Grace started up her car and headed back for the apartment.

The afternoon flew by until it was already time to head to Peter's house. Octavia could tell the composer had gotten withdrawn. Quiet. Usually she was quite invested while watching *Pop Love*, but tonight no cheers could be heard from Grace. They were on the Remix High season, too, so that was really saying something. The upcoming conversation was weighing on her. The two hopped back in the car and drove toward the setting sun, until they eventually found themselves in a pleasant little suburb right outside Peter's door.

"Are you prepared?" Octavia wondered.

Grace exhaled deeply. "Yeah, I think so?" She waffled. Instead of questioning Grace's anxiety, Octavia simply gave a heartfelt and heavy pat on the composer's hand, which was resting on the shifter. It was time. A ring of the doorbell set it all in motion. Grace wore her hair up tonight. Hiding the mark wasn't part of the plan. In fact, she was hoping it could get out of the way almost immediately. Then they could all proceed with a lovely evening. Octavia rested quietly in the purse, waiting for her grand introduction.

"Grace!" A warm voice greeted her as the door opened. Peter stood there smiling. "I'm glad you could come on short notice. I'm sure you had plenty of other party plans you could've taken up." Peter laughed. Once again, his lack of knowledge regarding his sister's social life was astounding.

"It's a weeknight, Peter." Grace chuckled.

"Well, you're young. When I was your age, I never let something as silly as a weeknight stop me." Peter playfully elbowed Grace. "Come on in!" Grace nodded and started to move past her brother, who was holding open the door. It was then that Peter saw it. "Whoa." Peter gently placed a hand on her shoulder, stopping her entrance.

"What?" Grace anxiously asked, knowing exactly what the holdup was.

"Grace." Peter sounded serious now. His face lost all color. "Let's maybe chat outside for a minute first." Grace threw it in reverse and walked back out the door. She let out a heavy sigh. At least she was getting her wish. They would talk about it right away. Grace sat down on the front step. Peter joined. Octavia observed.

"So, you saw it?" Grace asked.

"How long ago?" Peter cut to the chase.

"A couple of weeks." Grace couldn't bring herself to look at her brother, and Peter couldn't bring himself to stop looking at the mark.

"Weeks?"

"Yeah, about."

"Grace." Peter sighed. "How could you not tell me you died two weeks ago?" A pit was forming in his stomach. He had lost his parents only years prior. To think the reaper would come for his sister so soon after. A mixture of emotions battled within his heart.

"I... I almost did. I just didn't know how to. I didn't know what you'd think."

"I think my sister died," Peter blurted out. A slight edge was present in his words. Grace finally shifted her gaze towards him, just as he averted his eyes. Tears welling up.

"But she's back now." Grace's voice wavered. She mustered up a smile that went unnoticed. A moment of aching quiet settled between them. Until eventually, Peter turned to face his resurrected sibling.

"Is she?" he asked meekly. That was a gut punch. Of course she was. She was sitting right there, wasn't she?

"I'm right here," she responded.

"You resurrected." Peter shifted uncomfortably. "You know what that means."

"It means I still get to see you. I'm still here with you."

"It's not that simple." Peter tried to stifle the torrents behind his eyes. He wasn't succeeding. "You know it's not that simple, Grace."

"Why? Because of Veritas?" Grace brought it front and center. Peter was a devout follower of the religion. Let's just say the Church of Veritas doesn't look super kindly on the resurrected. It's taboo. There was a belief that those who resurrect did so by striking a deal with something terrible. Personally, I object to that implication. Peter looked down. "It's me, Peter. Your sister."

"How did you come back? What did you do, Grace?"

"Nothing!" Grace protested. Not entirely true, but Grace didn't really remember her time in the great beyond. Peter continued to look away, trying to harden his heart. He had to, otherwise this would kill him. On the one hand, he was spared the tragedy of losing his sister, but on the other, she was now something he couldn't understand or accept.

"What am I supposed to do, Gracey?" Soft words passed through his lips. "What am I supposed to do now?" The tears broke through. Grace placed a hand on her crying brother's shoulder.

"You invite me in and we eat dinner," she pleaded. "That's what you do now, Peter." Grace dared to let a hopeful look spread across her face. Peter, however, just shook his head.

"You know I can't." He let out a heavy exhale. "Not with Lyla and Cody inside." Peter referenced his children.

"What do you mean?"

"They can't see you like this." Peter tried his best to shake off his feelings. "I don't know how I'd explain it." Aggressively, he wiped his eyes with the palm of his hand. "I'm sorry, Grace," he said with an unfortunate resolve.

"No, Peter. Please."

"I don't know what else to do right now. I have to think about them."

"What about me?" Grace questioned as Peter stood back up. He paused for a moment, staring at the ground.

"I love you, Grace, but this is just too much." He walked to the door. "Maybe someday, okay? Maybe someday we can figure this out." Peter took one last look at his sister, who was now hunched over her legs, tears watering the pavement. He wanted to rip his own heart out for this. Which was actually an action I'd like to see at this moment. He should do it. But, regrettably, all he did was pull the door open and disappear inside to his perfect family. Octavia shifted to look up at the shattered composer, facing her worst-case scenario. She pulled herself up onto the edge of the purse. Grace had her head buried between her knees. Something began to radiate from her. Waves of sadness poured out.

"I am deeply sorry, dear Grace." Octavia tried her hand at comforting. "Your brother seems lost. I know you care for him, so this must incite substantial pain." Octavia patted Grace on the thigh. Tears dropped and dropped and dropped until finally they stopped. The tides began to change.

"No, Octavia," Grace spoke sternly. Coldly. She lifted her head up, her eyes filled with something I haven't had the pleasure of viewing for a while. "Don't you see? I'm the one who is lost." Grace breathed heavily, like a bull before a red cape. Octavia sat in silence. She could feel it, too. Rage. "Because of something I can't even control. Don't you get it? Apparently, I'm the one who's damaged. Lost. Not worthy." Grace hurled the insults inward.

"Dear Grace..." Octavia started. She hadn't seen her companion this angry. Though she hadn't been there when Grace died. This was nearly the same rage that sparked her resurrection in the first place. A low pulse circled the composer. Sub frequencies shook the small stones lining the walkway. "You know that is false," Octavia tried to reassure her.

"It's all bullshit!" Grace cried out. The bass frequency was getting stronger, and the doors and windows began to rattle. Octavia observed the effect. She was confused because the composer had never uttered the summoning words, but there was no mistaking it. This was the Sonata Mor. The shaking continued to escalate until Peter returned, panicked. Grace rose to her feet as the door opened. Her fists clenched.

"Grace! Are you okay? I think this is an earthquake," Peter called out. There was still some care in his heart, I guess. Grace turned her head just enough to see her brother.

"Not an earthquake, Peter." Harsh words vibrated through the air. Peter looked around. Sure enough, the rest of the neighborhood seemed fine. This vibration he was feeling came from Grace. Questions swirled around his head.

"Wait. Don't tell me you're doing this?" Peter asked with a slight tremble. This all but confirmed there was something wrong with his undead sister. "Grace, you really did do something, didn't you? Dammit." Disappointment mixed in with the panic. "Stop this right now, okay? Grace!"

Grace inhaled deeply. There it was. The matador swinging that red cape around. It was all she could see. Her heart pumped wildly. She turned to face her brother head on. The sub bass was now reaching audible levels. A low sustained drone. Her eyes were filled with that sweet, sweet anger. Peter's heart hit the floor as he looked into them. This was not the Grace he knew. No, Peter. This Grace is better.

"Grace. Please," Peter pleaded as he stepped backward into the house. Octavia saw the pain in her protégé's eyes. In her opinion, Grace was very close to making a mistake. This wasn't the first time she had witnessed an intense sibling rift. Perhaps that was the reason Octavia decided to play a role she seldom played—peacekeeper.

"Dear Grace, this is not who you are," Octavia said. Peter heard the voice and looked down at the plush. His stress grew exponentially. "He does not deserve this."

"Of course not. He's perfect. He doesn't deserve a corrupted, disappointing freak of a sister, right?" Grace cried through clenched teeth.

"No, dear Grace," Octavia refuted. "He does not deserve to see your power. He does not deserve to see your calling." Grace's lips trembled as she processed the words. "He does not deserve to hear your sound." All at once, the composer snapped to. Octavia was right. As much as I'd love to see where this was going, Peter, at this moment, was undeserving of such a marvelous display.

Grace took a staggered breath in. She looked at her brother, cowering in the doorway. Her heart started to regulate. The pulses of the bass lowered in frequency and volume until everything calmed, settling in its rightful place. Peter's wife, Gabby, came running to the door.

"Babe, are you okay?" Gabby put her hand on her husband's back. He couldn't speak. She turned to Grace. "What happened?" she interrogated. Grace ignored Gabby. She closed her eyes and exhaled. Then slowly reopened them to lock gazes with her brother one last time. A multitude of phrases ran through her mind. Combinations of words she could use to fully explain how she felt at that moment.

"Get bent, Peter," was what she landed on. An insult she would have yielded when they were kids. It was the only thing she could say to communicate her anger, while ensuring she didn't also lose herself. Octavia gave a sigh of relief as Grace scooped her up and returned to the car. Peter just watched, more confused than he was minutes prior.

"Peter?" Gabby called his attention. He looked at his worried partner as Grace drove away.

"Yeah. Let's just go eat," Peter said softly. Gabby gave him a concerned look. "We'll talk later. Go on. I'll be there in a second." Gabby reluctantly agreed and went back to the table to tend to the rowdy kids who, in their mind, just survived an earthquake. Peter watched Grace's car disappear onto a perpendicular street. Slowly, he stood back on his feet.

"Can't bend steel." He recited the other half of their childhood exchange, one last tear dripping down his chin. With that, he returned to the dinner table and to his life.

SEVEN
NOBODY UNDERSTANDS

Grace stared blankly ahead. Octavia sat quietly in the passenger seat as sad indie jams filled the speakers. The sun was nearly set now, and the street lights slowly started to illuminate. Her hands were restless on the wheel, like an itchy trigger finger. Grace wished on everything that she would run into something—anything. A shroud, a disciple, some weird little shit with powers. She just needed an enemy to fight. Her eyes scaled the city streets for any trace of trouble. Octavia eventually realized they weren't returning to the apartment.

"Are you alright, dear Grace?" she finally asked.

"Not really." Grace was honest.

"I am sorry you are feeling that way."

"It's whatever."

"Are we heading homeward?" Octavia questioned.

"Not yet."

"Can I inquire as to our destination?"

"Wherever there's something I can beat the shit out of." Grace revealed her master plan, and Octavia nodded. To be honest, she wasn't fully against the idea. Was it the healthiest coping mechanism? Not if you ask a therapist, but it's one of Octavia's personal favorites.

"That sounds like a lovely destination, composer," Octavia said, giving her blessing. It was at that moment that Grace found a potential hit. Sitting on the shoulder of a passing pedestrian was a cat that bore an unmistakable resemblance to what Grace understood as the "Silence aesthetic". It was Mata. They were going for a dusk stroll with Nova after a very weird day.

"Can shrouds be cats?" Grace asked.

"A feline shroud?" Octavia replied. "I have never witnessed such a thing."

"Oh, then what the hell is that?" Grace pointed as they passed, slowing just long enough for Octavia to hop on the dash for a quick peek.

"Oh! That is a hush. I can understand mistaking one for a shroud."

"A hush? Is that another Silence thing?" Grace asked, hopeful.

"Not really. They are separate, despite both drawing on the void." Octavia dashed Grace's hope. "However, they are very dangerous. They can be catastrophic to any city they dwell in."

Grace tightened. The energy inside her begging to be released. "So, they *are* bad?"

"That's very black and white, dear Grace. A hush is definitely a shade of gray."

"A bad shade?" Grace was looking for any kind of permission. Nova and Mata had turned down an alley a little while ago. Not wanting to lose them, Grace pulled over.

Octavia realized what was happening. "I never trust a hush," she admitted. "It could be worth acquiring more information. If it is causing mayhem, then it is our duty to apprehend it." Grace rammed the car into park. That was all she needed to hear.

Nova was trying their best to find an isolated place to gather their thoughts. Without a car, they were very limited. An alleyway in the city seemed like an okay choice. It was actually the same alley where they had met their new little friend. Part of them wondered if returning to this area might shed some light on the four-legged companion. This was a "killing two birds with one stone" situation.

"Was there a reason you were out here, buddy?" Nova asked. Mata jumped off their shoulder and onto the dumpster. They tilted their head. Nova couldn't resist the cute look and leaned forward for a nuzzle.

"Dumpster diving now, are we?" A gruff voice echoed from a side connecting alleyway. It belonged to a tall, slender man sporting a blood red mohawk. A black bandana was tightly wrapped around the arm of his tattered gray sweatshirt. Three other guys followed behind, all showcasing the same arm bands. Nova turned to meet the voice, and noticed the team uniform immediately. It was identical to the bandana Nova had worn the night before. They had an uneasy feeling. "Couldn't make you smell any worse, though, could it?" The stranger laughed. Nova took a defensive stance. Mata jumped onto their shoulder.

"Oh, come on, Nova. It's just jokes." Mohawk and the surrounding posse chortled.

Nova loosened slightly at the sound of their name. "You know who I am?"

Mohawk scoffed. "What is that? Some kind of threat, mate?" The stranger puffed out his chest in a comical way. "Do you know who I am, oi?" They mocked Nova. Apparently, they took Nova's innocent question as a display of dominance.

"Ooo, Nova acting tough shit, Clay," one of the toadies jeered.

"Is that right?" the mohawk named Clay asked. "Are you acting tough shit?" He got in close. Mata arched their back and splayed their claws. Of course, Clay couldn't see that.

"I'm asking a question," Nova spoke calmly and didn't budge. Their body was filled with potential energy—a loaded spring. Clay glared into Nova's eyes and leaned in, playing a game of chicken. A few tense moments passed before Clay burst out cackling. The posse behind joined in shortly after.

"Oh, damn, mate. That's what I love about you, you know." Clay threw an arm around Nova. Mata jumped up to avoid the bicep and landed atop Nova's head. Sure, Clay's arm wouldn't have actually made contact if Mata didn't want it to, but spiritual beings don't enjoy sharing space any more than physical ones. Nova looked at this new character with confusion.

"You've got bigger balls than the rest of them, that's for sure." Clay gestured to the others, who were all slightly offended, but kept their mouths shut. "Even without any." Clay tapped Nova roughly on the chest and moved away. "Or do you have balls? I can never remember." A shit-eating grin spread across his face. Nova just stared.

Seeing this wasn't getting the reaction he hoped, Clay switched tactics. "We missed you last night, you know?" He took his place back with the crew. "Ain't that right? Weren't you talking about how much you missed ol' Nova here, Brett?"

"What? No." Brett wasn't following the leader very well. Clay smacked him in the family jewels for failing the question. Poor Brett instantly doubled over.

"Of course you were! We all were, right, Derek?" Clay tossed it to another crony.

"Y-yup. Sure was, Clay! We all missed the shit outta ya, Nova!"

Clay shot a glare at the over-eager responder. "You see, Nova? Every member of the Blindspot. Everyone missed you! And we all wondered where you were." The mohawk moseyed back up to Nova while pulling out a bat, which was hanging off his belt like a sword. "We worried about you all alone in the city. Cold. Scared." Clay swung the blunt object around. "And hoarding your haul from the night." He slammed the bat squarely in front of him on the pavement, like a staff. The sound echoed throughout the alley. About time he said it. Let's just say his mohawk isn't the only thing that takes forever to get to the point.

Nova readied themselves. "Just who are you?" they asked sternly.

"Joke's over, Nova." Clay shut it down. "You know who missed you the most?" A dark look spread over his face. "That little bitch you've been fucking." The line was meant to disarm, and it did. Maybe not entirely for the reason Clay was hoping, however. This was the first time Nova had heard of anyone who might be important to them, and that concept successfully put them on edge.

"And that would be?" Nova tentatively asked. They weren't expecting this crew to play nice, but it was worth a shot. This may be the only lead they'd get. This response caused Clay and crew to burst out in uproarious laughter.

"Oh my, my, my, Nova. I didn't peg you for the type. A real player, are we? Almost makes me respect you a bit." Clay flipped the bat back up. "But I'm afraid games are done, and I need my money. And this time, I'm taking a teeny bit more than I usually do. You know, interest and all that. Let's say, one hundred percent?" Clay pointed the blunt weapon right at Nova. "Give me that, and you can walk away with at least one functioning leg and your head, mate."

Nova cracked their neck. They weren't entirely sure who they used to be, but they could feel one thing—they could fight. "You're really annoying. Anybody ever tell you that?" Nova shot back.

Clay chortled. "Oh, Nova." He shook his head and dropped the bat by his side, before turning away. That was, of course, a fake out. Clay came reeling back in, swinging for the fences. Nova read his movements and leaned just out of reach. The cool metal came within inches of their face. Mata sprang into action.

They leaped off Nova and spun around rapidly in the air, winding up for a violent double tail slap right onto Clay's head.

A pulse of void energy shot that mohawk straight into the pavement. Blood sprayed against the walls. I'm not sure he's getting up from that. Mata landed gracefully beside Nova and did a figure eight between their legs. Nova looked down at the creature, feeling an overwhelming sense of pride and astonishment. The little one can dish it out, after all. Nova raised their head to look at Brett, Derek, and the other one. Each displayed a terrified look that perfectly complemented the wet stain spreading on their pants.

"Anybody want to answer my questions now?" Nova offered the olive branch. Derek and the nameless one charged at Nova, while Brett took off in the other direction. I'm surprised. Despite appearing dull, Brett apparently was the only one wise enough to leave. Nova sighed. "Alright, your choice."

Derek swung a punch at Nova, who sidestepped it and grabbed the passing arm. In one movement, Nova shifted their weight to fling Derek against the wall. The nameless one went low for the tackle. Mata bounced up into his stomach as he passed over, their tough skull splintering the poor guy's ribs. He coughed up blood and instantly collapsed onto the floor.

"Last chance," Nova tried again. However, at that moment, a new noise meandered into the alley. Music. A shrieking violin accompanied by a plucky arpeggio crescendoed toward them as a sound dagger whizzed at Mata. The hush swiftly hopped over the attack, causing the wave to crash into the cement. Nova promptly shifted their attention to the sound's origin.

Grace and Octavia stood in the alleyway entrance. A purple aura swirled around the two as a low synthesizer pulsed. It seems Grace caught the hush's display of skill on a few humans and was a little trigger-happy. Of course, she missed the whole first part of the exchange and didn't realize who Mata was messing with. Nova faced the latest threat, as their partner remained attentive by their feet. Derek and the even more unimportant one took this opportunity to limp away down the adjoined alley.

Grace sought clarification. "Can a hush infect?"

I guess she thinks Nova could be a host, judging by how closely their little friend was sticking to them.

"I have never witnessed such a thing. However, that does not mean it is impossible," Octavia answered.

"Who the hell are you?" Nova called out. Their blood was getting to a boiling point. As soon as Grace brought Mata into this, their entire demeanor changed.

"The composer," Grace responded confidently. Once again, she believed she was talking to the hush through its puppet. "And I'm here to end you and the Silence." Damn. Grace is really leaning into this vengeful hero vibe. I've never seen her this eager to just beat something up.

Nova took this remark fully as the threat it was intended to be. "Is that so?" Nova widened their stance. "I don't give a shit who you are. Nobody messes with Mata."

Grace recoiled, confused. "Mata?" she inquired, but the duo was already charging forward. Quickly, Grace summoned a fresh sound dagger and pitched it at the hush. Mata hopped off a nearby wall to avoid it, and ricocheted toward Grace. Octavia slapped the little monster out of the air with a sound tentacle, shooting the poor thing into the brick. Nova found an opening and swung a low punch at Grace. She sidestepped the swing and lightly touched Nova's side. The pulse of soft viola echoed out of her hand and knocked them into the wall alongside Mata. She was definitely pulling her punches with that counter. Grace believed Nova was a puppet, after all. Nova looked up at the composer and her octopus, the aura stormily circling the two. String instruments worked in tandem with a pounding bass drum. Grace approached them, reaching out to form another sharp wave. Mata jumped in front of Nova and bared its teeth.

"Mata, no!" Nova cried out. Mata's protective stance caused Grace to pause. This was new. In all her time fighting shrouds, she never once saw one step in front of their host. This hesitation gave Mata the opening they needed. The hush vaulted in the air near Grace and expanded their mouth wider than their entire body, before violently inhaling all of Grace's sound waves.

"Composer, distance yourself," Octavia shouted. The composer tried to heed the warning, but she was stuck. The sound rapidly funneling inside the small creature tethered her to the scene. Octavia was able to push off Grace and roll away, reserving just enough sound within her plush body. Mata continued until there was nothing left, and Grace was silenced.

"What just happened?" Grace asked, stunned. That couldn't be it, could it?

"You just lost," declared Nova as they rose. "Normally, I'd want to know who you are. But," Nova paused, clenching their jaw, "I can't forgive you for trying to kill Mata." Grace looked at the determined face staring her down. This person also felt different from any puppet she had met.

"Wait, you're not being controlled." It clicked, but all too late. Nova whipped their fist back for a killer right hook. Just as they were throwing it, however, Octavia released the sound she was safekeeping. An a cappella tentacle flashed out and smashed into Nova, tossing them down the alley.

"Composer, we must retreat," Octavia ordered. Grace shot a concerned look at Nova, who was groaning on the pavement. Mata rushed to their side. This truly wasn't like anything she had seen before. Join the club, Grace. "Now!" Octavia yelled. Grace glanced one last time down the alleyway, before escaping to her car.

Nothing about that exchange felt right to the composer. All she wanted was to unleash her frustrations, but here she was again, feeling angry and unsatisfied. Only this time, guilt found its way into the mix too. Perhaps Nova and Mata were not the ideal target for that blind rage. Unfortunately, I think it's a little too late to go back and smooth things over.

"What was that?" Grace posed the question. The street lights brightened their way home against the freshly darkened sky.

"That was the power of a hush," her sherpa answered. Though, I'm not sure that's what Grace was asking. She fell silent for a moment, contemplating. I'm a little worried she may draw the wrong lesson from this. The rage is good, Grace. Sure, in this case, she may have thrown it in a misguided direction, but best not to abandon such a useful and entertaining emotion.

"I was so eager to just hit something," she admitted.

Octavia sighed. "You have been through many ordeals today, dear Grace. Many more than the average human, I am sure," the kraken observed. "It is not unexpected that you would need to release that tension."

"Sure." Grace acknowledged the words, but the guilt still sat square in her chest. "Why do I feel like such a bully, then?"

"What do you mean?"

"I mean, that was weird, right? The way those two fought together. I didn't feel like a hero swooping in to save the day. I felt like some villain stomping down on a random person and their pet."

"It is true. I have never seen a hush be so protective of anything, let alone a mortal," Octavia agreed. "However, if the hush was protecting them, then make no mistake, dear Grace, there is something dark in that person's heart. They are akin to the void."

Grace kept her eyes ahead as Octavia's words circulated in her mind. The way Nova cared about the creature replayed in her memory. Was that really someone with a dark heart? "Maybe." Grace landed in the middle ground. "If I ever meet them again, I'm going to make it right," she promised.

"What if they truly are your enemy?" Octavia raised the all-important question.

The composer pondered for a moment. "Then I'll make sure to take the time to really know that first." She pulled into a vacant parking spot outside her apartment. With resolve, she turned to Octavia. "Before we fight again, I'll make sure I know who they really are."

EIGHT
NOBODY GETS AWAY

Thick snowflakes sleeted down from the midnight sky onto a not-so-quiet road. Cherry Street was the go-to place for college parties and was the current location of a certain murderous trio. Dios sat in a parked car watching all the underage students haul backpacks of liquor to their next destination. The itch to slaughter them all was strong, but the three were here on a very specific mission. They looked at the license plate bolted to the Tesla in front of them—FCK-BOI. It had taken them almost a week to track the car, even with the help of their puppet police officer. Patience paid off as they finally located the vehicle Jake said he had spotted. It should be evident, however, that this was, in fact, not Chase's car. Apparently, Jake wanted to keep that info close to his chest and thought it would be funny to initiate a wild goose chase. Chase would never have a license plate as tacky as FCK-BOI.

Orv was growing impatient. "What are we waiting for? Let's get to slicing!"

"Down, boy. Best not to make a scene, if we can help it," Ira pushed back.

"I'm so sick of not making a scene. What if I want to make a scene? A big bloody scene?!" Orv protested.

"Then we'd have to kill everyone here and all the witnesses," Dom started. "And all the police that showed up. Then our cover would be completely blown, and we'd have to kill the whole town. Which, while it sounds like fun, is not within the wishes of the Silence. Killing is a hobby, not our goal."

"Agh, this sucks!" Orv threw a tantrum as a young man sporting a styled cut and tackily designed button-up shirt approached the Tesla.

"Wait. That's not a girl?" Dom was confused. He knew the owner of the car's name was Blake, and assumed it belonged to the composer, misled by a unisex name.

"It is possible she has allies, you know." Ira sighed. "Perhaps this dashing young fellow is one of them." They watched as Blake got into the vehicle.

"Perhaps."

"Let's just follow him and see where he goes. Maybe he'll take us to our composer friend. If not, we can always have a little chat." Ira smirked. Dios agreed with themselves and followed the Tesla to a set of extravagant apartments.

"Alright, this will work," Dom said as they surveyed the lot. Not another soul was out and about. They'd have the target all to themselves. Dios pulled into the spot alongside Blake. They decided to go the soft route first. This meant using Ira's body. To give themselves options, they wore the clergy outfit, just in case a friendly neighborhood pastor would be the correct cover. After seeing Blake, it was obvious that Ira was the best choice. Ira briefly admired herself in the holy garb before approaching the boy, who was now out of his car.

"Well, hi there, neighbor," Ira said flirtatiously. Blake immediately leaned back and looked her up and down. I guess the whole "innocent woman of the cloth" motif worked for him.

"Why hello, sister," Blake said with a seductively raised eyebrow, and what he perceived to be charm.

"Oh, please, don't call me sister."

"Oh, my bad. Sorry, miss pastor, ma'm." Blake reeled it back. More awareness than I expected from someone with that license plate. Ira moved in close and touched her hand to his chest.

"Call me mommy," she whispered seductively. Blake shivered and came alive.

"Oh my god, yes. Do you want to come up?" Excitedly, he extended the invite.

"Whoa boy, let's wait one second." Ira slowed it down.

"Right. You call the shots." Blake gave a puppy dog look while slipping comfortably into a submissive role.

"Before we have the best night of your life," Ira leaned in and whispered in his ear, "I need to know something."

"Eight inches," Blake reactively answered. Ira gave an incredulous look. "Okay, six," he corrected. "Four and a half..."

"Right." Ira stopped the countdown. "Not that, sweetie, but good to know." She played with the hair behind his head. "See, I'm actually looking for someone. A girl."

"Awesome." Blake's eyes lit up. "Yeah, I have a few on speed dial who would totally be into this sort of thing." Ira tightly gripped the back of Blake's head.

"Ow, ow, ow! Easy," Blake pleaded. Ira's long nails cut the skin.

"Not the game I'm playing, Blake." This was the problem with Ira's femme fatale routine. It always shifted to fatale early. Turns out she has very low patience. Blake's eyes widened at the sound of his name, and his pulse quickened.

"How did you know my name? What the hell is this?" Blake shifted into full-blown panic. "Help!" he screamed. Quickly, Ira covered his mouth with her free hand and slammed him against the Tesla.

"Now, now, we don't need anyone interrupting our one-on-

one, do we?" Ira licked her lips. Blake tried to squirm, but Dios was too strong. "So, about this girl. She would have a lovely, little mark on her neck. An arrow through a crescent moon. Sound familiar?" Blake stopped struggling. He realized immediately this was a misunderstanding. With misguided hope, he believed this could all be sorted out. Ira gave him a look that communicated exactly what would happen if he attempted to scream again. Slowly, Dios removed their hand.

"The mark of the dead?" Blake asked.

"That's the one." Ira booped his nose. He flinched.

"I've never met anybody like that. You've got the wrong guy," admitted Blake. He was, of course, telling the truth, but Dios wasn't known for giving the benefit of the doubt.

"Blakey boy, I thought we could've done this the fun way." She unbuttoned the top of her shirt and reached inside. Blake couldn't help but be mesmerized. His momentary fantasy reprieve was cut short as Ira pulled out a jagged knife. Blake made a desperate attempt to break free, but Dios pulled him back by his hair and pressed him back against the vehicle. They put the dagger up to his throat. "Now we get to do it the even more fun way."

"I'm serious. I don't know anybody with a mark. Please!" Blake cried.

"Our friend said he saw her get out of your car."

"A lot of girls get in and out of my car!"

"And you never noticed any of them having the mark of the dead?" Ira was incredulous.

"Never! And I spend so much time around their neck. I'm not one of those guys that just rushes in, you know? I swear!" Blake desperately pleaded his case. Ira sighed. This guy didn't seem like the valiant type. Definitely not the kind of person that could keep a secret to protect a friend.

"Did that little shit lie to us?" Ira posed to the others.

"Huh?" The question confused Blake.

"Not you, idiot." Ira shushed him.

"I think we've been tricked!" Orv came out. Blake immediately released his bladder upon hearing the second violent voice come from Ira's body.

"I swear to Silence, I'm going to kill him," Dom added.

"What the fuck is going on?" Poor Blake. None of this fared well for him. Dios looked at him with apathetic eyes. He had outlived his purpose. Ira let out a disappointed sigh, before ramming the blade into Blake's chest. A few pained chokes escaped his mouth as he slid down the white Tesla, giving it a red vertical stripe. Just like that, the FCK-BOI was no more. Ira violently pulled the knife from his heart, before sliding her tongue along the stained steel.

"Delicious." She closed her eyes and savored the taste. "So, do we think little Jake even saw a car, or was the whole thing a desperate grab for attention?" Ira asked.

"I don't know, but I plan to beat the answer out of him," Dom responded.

"At least we got a nice snack out of it," Orv rejoiced. Dios returned to their car and quickly left the misunderstanding behind them. This was a very unfortunate detour for Blake, but Jake's antics bought our composer a bit of time. I think this all demonstrates a valuable lesson, however. You really should be careful about what you put on a personalized license plate.

* * *

Across the city, Nova was again walking the alleyways of downtown. This was becoming a routine for them. Every night this week, they had been sneaking out. Well, they thought they had been sneaking out. That shadow creeping at a distance would suggest otherwise. Very little got past Mira. She hadn't found Nova's side quest to be disadvantageous, however, so she was simply keeping an eye on them.

Just what was Nova looking for? Any kind of answer. Who were they and, perhaps more pressing, who was the woman Clay was referring to the other night? He made it sound like she was important, even if he presented the information in a rather crass way. It was the quest for these answers that led Nova to stroll the alleys with Mata, hoping to be jumped by the infamous gang known as the Blindspot.

It seems they also welcomed another encounter with our Grace. They hadn't forgotten what happened and viewed her as the biggest threat of all. Nova hadn't disclosed their fated meeting with the others. There wasn't much trust built yet. For now, they would keep that info to themselves and wait to cross paths with the sound user again. In the meantime, the Blindspot seemed like an easier target to lure out.

Nova had done some digging on the dangerous crew. They were known as Seerstown's largest street gang. The name seemed synonymous with all criminal activity in the city, with a strong implication of violence. Nova didn't know how they were connected to this group, but it made them queasy just thinking about the possibilities. The first night they woke up, they were donning a black bandana. They couldn't rule out the chance that they were a member. Mata pranced happily along every outing. I don't think the search mattered as much to them. The hush was just happy to join.

"That's right, your phone, too." A gruff voice spoke just around the corner.

"Please, I'm begging you. It has photos, pictures of my family. Take everything else. Please, just let me keep that," a woman pleaded.

"Uh, let me think about it." A loud smack was heard immediately after. Nova hastened their steps to the scene. They saw a member of the Blindspot hovering over a middle-aged woman who had just been punched down to her knees.

"Hey, asshole," Nova called. "Want to try fighting someone

who hits back?" Mata jumped up on Nova's shoulder, getting ready. The Blindspot member turned around to face the would-be vigilante. His eyes grew wide at the sight.

"N-Nova," he stuttered. I guess word had spread that a territory leader's head went splat. No doubt that put a target on Nova's back. In the case of a one-on-one run-in, however, that legacy surely gave them the upper hand. The victim took advantage of the distraction and ran for safety. The gang member heard her leave, but couldn't peel his eyes from the new threat. Frantically, he placed his switchblade out in front of him.

"Good, you seem to know me," Nova said. "I have questions." They glanced down at the knife. "Can we put that away?"

"Fuck that!" came the retort. "I heard what you did to Clay, you traitor." Looks like someone found his bark. The mugger readied the blade and took a step forward.

"I wouldn't," Nova warned. The crook halted. He glanced in the opposite direction, contemplating escape. "I wouldn't do that either." Nova advanced.

"Shit," the thug cried. "What do you want from me?" Anxiously, his knees twitched, making both fight and flight impossible.

"Let's start with a name."

"Are you fucking serious? It's Lenny." Lenny found it within himself to be offended. He had a very high self-image.

"Not your name." Nova shook it off. Lenny's ego dropped another couple of floors. "I want the name of a girl. Someone I would have been seeing, maybe." Lenny started to nervously chuckle.

"You're kidding me, right? Did you hit your head or something?" Lenny continued to hold the knife at the ready as Nova came to a stop. They fell silent for a moment. "Holy shit." Lenny had the revelation. "You fucking did! Didn't you? Oh my god." Lenny started to loosen up.

"The name," Nova insisted.

"Nova, buddy. This all makes so much more sense. We're on the same team! You... you just forgot." Lenny lowered the switchblade. "You're part of the Blindspot!" Nova's heart dropped. They knew this was likely, but hearing it out loud hurt. Why would they have joined such a group? Were they actually a bad person? Perhaps they didn't want these answers, after all.

"Listen, you did kind of a fucked up thing, killing Clay and all. But," the gang member held up a hand, "I think your pal, Lenny, can help explain what happened here. You hit your head or some shit, forgot who you were, and ended up on the wrong side of a reunion. Am I right?" Slowly, but surely, Lenny was feeling more confident.

"Something like that," Nova admitted. This was affecting them more than they thought it would. Mata climbed up on top of their partner's head and looked down at them.

"Fuck. I knew it. I knew you wouldn't forget me. Not me, of all people!" Lenny felt a sense of relief. It bears mentioning that there was nothing special about their relationship, even in the gang. Lenny just assumed everyone loved him. He threw an arm around Nova. "Okay, so you've got memory probs. How about you come back to the boss with me, and we smooth all this over?"

Following Lenny's lead, they started down the alley. If they didn't protest, Nova was marching right into the lion's den. But perhaps this was exactly what they were hoping for? What better way to get answers than by going straight to the lair? Their maybe-lover may be there, as well.

"Can you tell me her name first?" Nova needed some assurance. If they were going to take a risk, they needed to know it could pay off. A confirmation that there was actually someone they should be looking for would be enough.

Lenny got reserved. "Ah, yeah, about that." He looked over, seeing this look of hope on Nova's face, which caused pause. "Sasha..." The crook trailed off for another moment. The gears in his head were turning. "Yeah, Sasha. That's your girl!" His demeanor shifted on a dime to an annoying pep. "She started showing up slightly after you joined. Great gal."

"Sasha," Nova repeated. A tingle ran down their spine. The name meant something.

"I can't say she ever cared too much for the Blindspot, though," Lenny continued.

"Where can I find her?" Nova asked as they continued walking. Perhaps they wouldn't need to go all the way to the belly of the beast for info. Lenny seemed an open book, now that he believed them to be friends.

"Uh," Lenny's tone fell again. "Maybe. You know, maybe that's something we gotta ask the boys that saw her last." Nova keyed in on the language. That didn't sound good. They shot a look at Lenny. "Um, just because she stopped coming around when you didn't come back. Yeah, that's all." The mugger tripped over his words. Nova felt uneasy. Looks like a trip to HQ was unavoidable. They wouldn't be going alone, though. Mata was comfortably perched on their shoulder, and, just a few blocks away, Mira was still roaming the darkness. I, for one, cannot wait to see how this turns out.

The crew continued on to a large, multi-story house in the heart of the downtown residential district. Simply looking at it gave Nova a sick feeling. No concrete memories surfaced, but some emotions definitely did. This place filled them with dread.

"Here we are. The big boss's house." Lenny waved his hand out front, like a realtor introducing a property. "I already messaged them we were coming. Gio promised to give you an audience, at least. That's about the best I could do, though, buddy." Lenny was feeling a little guilty. He knew that the chances of the Blindspot accepting Nova's excuse and welcoming them back were slim. However, he also knew his rating would skyrocket by bringing a gang bounty in. That greed overpowered the guilt.

"After you," Lenny offered. Nova controlled their breathing and surveyed the area. Three guys lined a solemn staircase leading up to the main door. There were five sets of windows on the first floor alone. Multiple escape routes went through their mind, but to speak plainly, Nova wasn't planning on running. Mira watched as they entered.

"This is going to be fun," she uttered to herself. I completely agree. Nova immediately found themselves in a grand ballroom. Marble laminate covered the floor, adorned with a gaudy Persian rug. Two spiral staircases were centered toward the back of the room, splitting in opposite directions. This house gave all the correct drug lord vibes. Between both sets of stairs, there, honest-to-god, was a large leather chair. And sitting in that chair was the gang boss himself, Gio. Cronies were lined up on either side of the room and along the stairs.

"The prodigal whatever returns!" Gio exclaimed. He was slouched against the arm rest. Half-assed, he gestured to the front of the room. Nova apprehensively approached. The faint mumblings of a rap song played through the floorboards upstairs. "Our boy, Lenny, here, tells us you have something to say. Something about a huge misunderstanding?"

Nova stood in silence. The surrounding energy was heavy. Every set of eyes stared at the lost sheep with malicious intent, save for Gio, who actively studied the rings on his fingers. After a few moments of quiet, Gio shifted in the comically overdone throne. "Perhaps you want to start by telling me why you painted the streets with one of my lieutenant's brains?" Nova looked around, ignoring the prompt.

"Where's Sasha?" they asked.

The boss scoffed and finally raised his gaze. "Oh, Nova, Nova, Nova." He tsked. "Do you realize the shit you're in right now?" Gio massaged his forehead with his hand. "I really, *really*, don't want to care about you. You know that? You're a worthless, low-level grunt. I barely knew who you were. But then you went and killed Clay and sent three of our boys back with piss in their pants." Brett and Derek both looked down in embarrassment. "And when you do that..." Gio tilted his body forward in the chair and locked eyes with his prey. "When you do that, you get my attention. And now I have to care about a cockroach."

"Sorry about that," Nova started. "Your lieutenant died quickly, at least. Really didn't put up much of a fight. Kind of depressing." They poked the bear. Apparently, they objected to being spoken to like that. Gio stared daggers at the wisecracker. All the Blindspot collectively clenched blades in their fist, waiting for the word. In this moment of tension, a smirk spread across Gio's face.

"Oh, Nova. You are a gutsy kid, aren't you? Fine. You want to know about Sasha?" Gio spoke giddily. "She was here the other night." Nova leaned in. "Yeah, yeah. She came in looking for your ass, I guess. Sly greeted her, ain't that right, Sly?" Gio threw it to a crony sitting on the stairs.

"Oh, yeah." Sly stood up and walked center. He knew the game. "She kept going on and on about how she was supposed to meet you, how you were in trouble, or something. Too bad you weren't here." A pit formed in the house guest's stomach.

"Don't worry, Nova. We make sure anybody who comes here has..." Gio paused for effect, "a good time." Nova's breathing got heavy. They still didn't remember Sasha. Couldn't picture her face at all, but her name alone brought this intense emotion with it. And to hear them talk about her this way was heart wrenching. "Poor thing couldn't handle herself, however. She just kept wanting more."

"Stop," Nova demanded.

Gio leaned even further forward. This was what he lived for. "Everything we had, she took. The drugs this small girl consumed... Shit," Gio continued. Mata arched their back and splayed their claws. The gang lord dramatically fell backward into his chair, threw his hand to his head, and feigned sadness. "See, at the end of it all, the poor girl... She took too much."

"No." Nova shook.

Gio revealed a massive grin as he pulled away his hand. "She's dead. Overdose. I can't help but wonder what would have happened if you would've been here. Maybe you could've stopped it," he taunted. Guilt suddenly ran through Nova's body. If this was all true and they were supposed to be there that night, maybe it really could've been prevented. Anger broke into sadness. The pain of losing someone they loved but couldn't remember.

"There it is!" Gio exclaimed as he loudly clapped his hands together. "I've been waiting for that sad little look." Nova looked away, tears forming in their eyes. "I swear to fucking god, man. Watching people die on the inside... almost as good as watching them die on the outside. For real." Every member of the Blindspot burst out laughing with their leader. Nova stood there, paralyzed. They didn't even understand why this hurt so much.

"Alright, enough of that." Gio silenced his crew. "Thanks for giving us all one last laugh before you die. Now..." He returned his attention to his extravagant rings. "Kill the shit stain." Gio uttered the order and released the hold on every Blindspot member. They rushed toward the target like rabid dogs, excited for the kill.

Nova was still in their own head, numb to the danger. Mata, on the other hand, was ready. Four gang members arrived together. One pinned Nova's arms behind their back, while the others prepared to play pincushion. Mata spun up into the air and swung their tails down at the three charging in front. Two void bombs imploded on contact, shooting an intense gust that sent them all flying through the stairwell's balusters.

"What the fuck?" Gio's mouth dropped. He looked at his peons, who all halted after the display of power. "What are you morons waiting for? Get the motherfucker!" Gio called out. A second batch of Blindspots got ready. This time, some of them hastily exchanged their knives for guns. Mata wasted no time. They pivoted and bashed their head against the crony restraining Nova. A wave shot out of their skull, causing the thug's head to explode like a watermelon. Those head boops are dangerous! The rush of wind and blood splatter snapped Nova out of their funk. They now noticed the little hush fighting with everything it had, and knew they couldn't let Mata carry this battle alone.

Nova glared at the boss. It was time to take the fight right to Gio. Mata landed in the middle of the floor as their partner charged in the direction of the gang lord. Several Blindspots began shooting at the moving target. Mata whizzed their tails like a fan toward the oncoming firestorm, creating a harsh wind that blew the bullets back into the bodies of several gangsters. Love to see a little bit of assisted friendly fire. This is why shooting guns in a ballroom packed with your own team is rarely a good idea.

Nova descended upon Gio, coming in hot with a right hook. With the snap of a finger, the big bad shot up from his chair and slammed a fist into their stomach. They instantly doubled over onto the floor. That was honestly faster than I thought the big guy could move.

"You want to come for the king?" Gio screamed as he towered over Nova. He pulled out a large combat knife and pointed it down at the exasperated opponent. The hush tamer tried to regain their breath as Gio violently swung the blade down. In one fluid motion, Nova was able to roll away and transition into a smooth leg sweep. The Blindspot leader collapsed onto his back for a brief moment, before rebounding with a flip. Seriously, I did not think this guy would be nearly this agile. Nova took advantage of the exceptionally fleeting respite to get on their feet. Gio laughed.

"Not shit," he admitted. "I don't know who the hell you are, but you're not total shit."

Mata could sense Nova was in trouble, but they had their paws full with the seemingly endless horde of Blindspot members. Confusion spread among the gang as an invisible force continued to push them and their bullets back. Member after member would go flying as they attempted to reach Nova. To them, it was utterly bizarre. Despite this, they kept trying. Their leader gave the order, and if he found out anybody tucked tail and ran, it would not be good.

Lenny didn't seem to care as much about the boss's orders. He was already in deep shit for bringing this bomb of a human being into the base, and he knew it. The slippery coward decided to use the fight as an opportunity to escape. On his way out to safety, however, he was greeted with a shadow. Mira rose up from the dark and, in one swift motion, used her nails to rip out his throat. I guess that was the wrong exit route. It was a nice try, Lenny. With this act, Mira was now officially part of the brawl.

As their new teammate started to decimate the opponents, Mata had more space to move on the offensive. A new set of horns grew from their skull as they picked up the pace. The little creature zipped to the left of a cluster of gangsters, pivoted, and shot a straight line through them. Void energy pulsed as the fresh horns penetrated each body, causing the goons to burst. Mira watched in awe as the companion violently fought for their friend. This was exactly what she was hoping for.

In the meantime, Nova held their own. All attempts at disembowelment had been avoided, and they even managed to land a few good punches. However, it was a little disheartening to see how minimally Gio reacted to each hit. It seemed like Nova was just buying time at this point.

Finally, a lazy slash presented the opening they were waiting for. There was no hesitation. As soon as the knife cleared the gap, Nova firmly planted their foot and swung up. One solid uppercut to the jaw should have brought stars into Gio's vision. Unfortunately, the leader was too limber. He bent backward to avoid the attack, and quickly gripped Nova's vulnerable wrist with his free hand. A twisted smile spread across his face. He knew he had them now. Nova stared into his ruthless eyes as a flash of searing hot pain radiated throughout their body. Gio's blade swiped clean across their abdomen.

The boss released his hold, and Nova stumbled backward onto their knees. They looked down to see a massive gash across their stomach, blood pouring out. Their hand quickly pressed against as much of the wound as it could. To say it was an ineffective stopper would be putting it lightly. Gio sauntered over, savoring the moments before he would finish the job. He raised his knife in the air and prepared to ram it into Nova's skull.

"I take it back," he said. "You are just shit, after all." Right as the cold steel was about to crash down, everything fell silent. And I mean deathly silent. The sounds of bloodshed in the room were gone. The hip-hop music upstairs, which had provided a nice backtrack for the fight, had stopped. Gio couldn't hear the sound of his own breath or even the voice in his head. It was all silence. The hair on the back of his neck lifted as an uneasy feeling washed over him. He looked down at Nova, who was panting inaudibly.

"What the fuck did you do?" Gio asked in a panic. He didn't hear the words escape his own mouth, and thus wondered whether he even posed the question. A low grumble entered his eardrum, drawing his attention. Gio whipped around to see a giant demon cat prowling toward him. Mata had grown! They were roughly the size of a car now. The void surrounding the hush was so intense, it created a strong vibration that mimicked a growl. Giant horns protruded on either side of their head, and their long fangs nearly dragged across the floor. The ooze from their eyes formed a black labyrinth against the white skull, and spikes lined their external spine. Their enormous paws pounded against the floor, each step causing a ripple of energy. Gio's body froze with fear as he dropped his knife.

"No... no way. Did she...?" Gio fell backward and cowered before the massive creature. "Fuck! Did she... Did she really send you?" Mata looked down at Gio, and void energy blew a forceful wind toward the Blindspot's fearful leader. "I'm so sorry. Please, you don't have to do this. I didn't mean for her to die, okay?" Frantically, he tried to apologize.

Mata didn't care. Mira observed with bated breath as the hush opened their mouth wide and spawned a tiny black hole in front of their gaping maw. "No!" Gio finally heard his own scream right before getting sucked into the void. An implosion occurred shortly after that shot the pieces of Gio back out all over the ballroom. His precious chair was now decorated with a lovely red mist. Nova gazed in wonder upon their transformed pet. Their lips curved into a small, grateful smile.

"Thanks, buddy." They looked over at Mira next. "And you. You too." Everything got blurry, and Nova collapsed. Mata swooped in by their side, while shrinking back down to house cat size. Mira joined them at the front.

"That was quite the show," Mira complimented. "A bit too much for poor Nova, it would seem," she hinted. Her eyes watched Mata from behind the veil, waiting in anticipation for what the little monster would do now. The hush moved in and immediately began licking Nova's wounds. This was not what Mira was expecting. She thought perhaps Mata was going to devour Nova. Maybe in the end, a hush was still just a wildcard. Her dark intrigue soon turned to genuine surprise, as she saw the knife wound slowly start to heal.

"Good kitty," Mira praised. She knelt down and lifted Nova's head up onto her lap. Gently, she caressed their hair. "I suppose our little warrior will live to see another day."

"That bitch actually did it." A pathetic voice came from the stairs. Sly was propped up against the cracked railing, his hand covering a rapidly bleeding cut on his neck. He stared at the three, each one fully visible, including Mata. Mira looked up at the wretch. Sly let out a laugh of disbelief. "She said she saw a demon cat." Mira gave Nova's head one last brush, before gently setting it back to rest on the floor. She glided over to the dying Blindspot member.

"Who?" Mira asked. Her interests were slightly peaked.

"Sasha," Sly said, the slightest bit of regret in his voice. "Right before she died, she was talking about a demon cat. Bitch was so fucked up from all the drugs we forced on her, nobody thought anything of it." Mira glanced over at Mata, still at work. "Her last words were some shit about saving Nova." Sly chuckled again at the twist of events. The laugh turned into a painful groan. He looked up at the woman in black. "You don't think she really...?"

Mira softly rested her palm on his cheek as she slowly removed his hand from the gaping wound. Sly let out a pained grunt. A reassuring shush pushed through her lips as the blood gushed forth. For a brief moment, she stared into the dying eyes, before placing her nail within the lesion. The sole survivor released one last wail of pain as she dragged her finger across his throat, finishing the job.

She pulled her hand away and let the lieutenant topple down the remaining stairs. If what he said was even remotely true, there could be ramifications if Nova found out. Mira wanted to control how, or if, they would discover this information. A faint groan came from Nova as Mata continued licking—the miracle of healing occurring on the set of the bloodstained ballroom.

"What an interesting development," Mira mused, taking another look at the duo. "Perhaps it was not destiny that brought you together."

* * *

"Too flowery," Octavia critiqued Grace, who was modeling a modest floral dress.

"Flowers are kind of the point of the dress, Tavi." Grace's lips fell to a frustrated frown. This was the sixth outfit she had tried on for the critical kraken. She let out a heavy sigh and collapsed onto the bed. "It's useless. Nothing is going to be good enough."

"It is true I am renowned for my unwavering taste," Octavia acknowledged. "However, do not retreat just yet, dear Grace. Surely, you have a garment that I will approve of." Grace rolled over onto her stomach and kicked her feet, letting out nervous energy. I don't think Grace was worried that her outfits wouldn't be good enough for Octavia. There was someone else on her mind.

"Why am I taking advice from an early world sea beast, again?" Grace sassed. "I mean, do you and Cyn even have the same style? What if Cyn really likes flowers?"

"I have seen this maiden. Flowers are not to her liking," Octavia rebutted. "My taste is paramount. If Miss Cyn does not approve, then she is not a worthy distraction."

"Can we not say it like that? Makes it sound like I'm using her."

"My apologies. I forget you are a romantic, similar to Matteo. Well, if you are looking for a wife, then it is even more pressing that she be deemed worthy."

"Whoa, whoa, whoa, Tavi. Don't whip the W word out on me." Grace returned to her closet for attempt number seven. She knew she wanted a dress, but the options were dwindling. Cyn had never seen Grace in a dress. The corporate workplace environment never seemed like the right place to break one out. Grace is too shy to admit it, but she believes her legs are her best physical feature. Showing them off is definitely part of the plan.

"Wait, dear Grace. What about that one at the end?" Octavia

rolled over to get a better look at a sparkly red dress tucked away in the corner. It was now within view thanks to half of Grace's closet being reassigned to her bed. Leave it to Octavia to pick the flashiest option. Grace pulled out the glittery spotlight. Octavia's eyes literally turned into hearts. I guess it really is true that sea creatures are drawn to shiny things.

"This?" Grace asked nervously. The dress had never been worn. She had bought it in college while entertaining the idea of attending a school formal. It was a rare instance of optimistic courage that fell completely flat when the time came to actually go to the event. A panic attack struck before she even put it on, and it had been a full-time closet dweller ever since. That same panic was welling up now. "This is a bit much, don't you think?"

"If, by a bit much, you mean it is perfectly suited to display your bodice, then yes."

"It's just so..." Grace looked for the words. "Attention-grabby."

"Do you not want the young lady's attention?"

"No, no, I definitely do. But this will have everyone in the restaurant looking at me! Plus, this is only a Sunday night dinner. Which is not even a big deal. Because Sunday is when old people go out to dinner, right? Old people and friends." Grace was spiraling.

"Composer, just try the garment on," Octavia prodded. Grace took a deep breath. "Have we not been training all week? Have we not developed confidence?" Octavia reassured her. It's true that, for the past few days, Grace and Octavia had been heading to an abandoned mall, two towns over, to train. Sorry to skip the training montage on you; it's just so uninteresting. I will say Grace made some good headway with her powers. The experience was also rather empowering for her. Taking some control back after what happened with her brother had helped, if ever so slightly.

"Confidence to fight monsters, Tavi. Not to..." She looked the dress up and down. "Stand out."

"Try it on," Octavia commanded.

"Fine." Grace groaned and disappeared into the bathroom.

"Monsters take many forms, dear Grace," Octavia called out. "Anxiety, for instance, can be a monster. Having the confidence to face monsters, therefore, directly transfers."

"Not bad, Tavi," Grace responded from behind the door. "Perhaps you should go into counseling." Octavia nodded. She believed she could handle counseling easily. She couldn't. Grace returned from the bathroom and stood front and center. The dress really was captivating. An illustrious glitter sparkle above the waist, while the bottom flared out with a more matte red. Small jewels created a series of patterns in the skirt. The hem ended a couple of inches above the knee, allowing Grace to show a bit of her self-identified best asset.

"That is the one!" Octavia exclaimed. Grace did a twirl in front of the mirror and made some silly model-esque faces. She had to hand it to Octavia, the plushy had taste. Something about seeing herself in such a flashy outfit flooded Grace with swagger.

"You know what? I think you're right," Grace agreed. Tonight was a night she had dreamed about ever since Cyn started working at Pets YES. She had a stare down with her reflection, thoughts running through her head. Was this really happening? What if it all goes terribly? And perhaps, even more terrifying, what if it all goes well? What if they kiss? What if Cyn likes this dress? What if she touches it? What if she takes it off? The brakes on the train shattered as it ran away down the track. Grace's cheeks warmed into a rosy blush.

"Oh no, is the dress too warm?" Octavia commented, noticing the crimson hue. Which only made it worse.

"Nope. It's perfect. I'm never taking it off!" A remark to

protest her wild thoughts. Grace ran back into the bathroom to splash some water on her face and put on makeup.

"Oh, good. Overheating is never good, you know." Octavia looked at herself in the mirror and sighed. I think she's a little jealous that humans get to have all the fun wearing sparkly things. "About tonight," Octavia began, "I believe this is one adventure you should tend to alone."

"Huh?" Grace popped her head back into the room. "What do you mean?"

"You do not need a chaperone clouding the atmosphere of your date. I do not wish to be a hindrance."

"Nonsense!" Grace waved her hand to push the thought away. "We can't break up the girl group for something like this, right?"

"It is fine, dear Grace. I can handle myself. It would be best for you to experience the connection purely. I fear you may worry about my presence otherwise," Octavia explained. Grace paused to think about it. It could get awkward. Grace would definitely be thinking about Octavia's well-being, which could influence how she would act. On Octavia's end, she just didn't want to find herself in the middle of an intimate moment, like she almost was with Trish at the club.

"What about the Silence?" Grace asked. "What am I going to do if there's a shroud or something cooking our food?"

"First, you are more than capable of handling a lowly shroud on your own. Second, I will ensure I am at your beck and call, should things get threatening. I will spend the evening with Chase, and we shall remain nearby." It was obvious Octavia did not clear this plan with her date ahead of time. Surely Chase would never have signed off.

"Are you sure?" Grace scooped up Octavia and held her eye level. "We've been kicking it together nonstop. It feels a little weird leaving you behind."

"You have to write your own song, dear Grace." Octavia gave

a pained smile, like a mother looking at her daughter the day she goes to college. Grace moved her forehead to press against Octavia's plushy figure.

"Too soon to talk like that, Tavi. It's just one date." Grace gave a reassuring look and placed the kraken gently on the bed, before returning to her makeup. "I'll text Chase right now!"

Octavia nodded and let out a quiet sigh. She once again viewed herself in the full-length mirror. There were many things reflected in that mirror. A bed overflowing with failed outfits. A new *Pop Love* poster Octavia had insisted on getting. A stack of half-finished books, filled with bent pages. But mostly Octavia zeroed in on one thing. That among all that clutter and life, she stood alone. And no matter what happened during her time on Earth, she knew it always ended that way.

NINE
NOBODY LOVES YOU

Grace watched the clock on her car dashboard. The bright numbers displayed 6:29. She had agreed to meet Cyn at Portobello, the finest Italian restaurant in Seerstown, at 6:30. Grace had a paralyzing fear of being early and seeming too eager, even if she was both of those things. Thus, her eyes remained glued to the time. If she had chosen to look at her phone clock, instead, she would have seen Cyn texted four minutes ago about already being there and getting a table. Her phone was tightly tucked away in her black clutch, however, behind a series of zippers. The clutch was small, but what it lacked in size it made up for in compartments. As soon as the clock rolled over to the magic numbers, Grace decided she could head in.

It was a little weird for her—being there without Octavia. For a long time, Grace was used to doing everything alone, but now it felt foreign. The quiet was strange. Grace chuckled to herself as the image of Octavia's drop off popped into her head. Chase was not thrilled, as one might expect. Regardless, the thought of the two of them hanging out downtown brought a smile to her face. Maybe they'd have their own 90s movie-inspired shopping spree montage, complete with multiple wardrobe changes.

Grace pulled the door open and spotted Cyn almost immediately. She was sitting at a table, her eyes glancing between her phone and the entrance. As soon as Grace stepped in, she gave a large wave. The hostess noticed this and didn't even bother asking the newcomer how many were in her party. Grace made her way back to the table. Cyn stood up to greet her, revealing her date night outfit. She wore a charcoal slim cut blazer over a v-neck white shirt. The ensemble was completed by a dark pair of jeans, a gold necklace, and several rings. It was stunning. Just formal enough, but keeping Cyn's essence. Seeing her like that, however, nearly caused Grace's brain to short circuit.

"Well, look at you, lady in red!" Cyn welcomed Grace with a hug.

"It's not too much, is it?" Grace nervously asked while taking her seat.

"Not at all. You look gorgeous." A charming, toothy smile spread across Cyn's face. Grace managed not to blow a fuse. That was progress. Don't get me wrong, though. She still had to avert her eyes.

"Thank you." She anxiously played with the hair around her ear. "You too." Grace summoned the courage to look Cyn in the eye as she issued the compliment. Yup, she continued to display those pearly whites. Come on, Grace, you can push past that. Don't melt now.

"Thank you," Cyn said enthusiastically. "So, you've been here before, right?"

"Once, I think?"

"It's easily my favorite spot in town. The marinara here is unbelievable."

"Marinara? I suppose wearing red was a good tactical move, then," Grace quipped.

"To be honest, I thought that was the whole reason you wore it." Cyn laughed. "Besides it being, you know, breathtaking." Cyn wasn't letting up on the compliments. Grace's face matched the shade of the dress as she looked down. "You don't like that, do you?" Cyn picked up on the body language.

"What?"

"Compliments. I can tell it makes you uncomfortable."

"A little." Grace nervously laughed. "So does getting called out."

"Oh my god. I'm so sorry. I didn't mean..." Cyn started to apologize.

"I'm joking, Cyn." Grace winked. It was nice for her to see Cyn flustered for once.

"Right." Cyn was relieved. "I've been told I can be pretty forward. So, hopefully I wasn't actually terrible just now, and you're just lying to make me feel better."

"You definitely are forward," Grace admitted. "But, I like that. I've lived a lot of my life wishing I could say what I really wanted. So, I kind of envy you."

"Eh, sometimes it pays to be a little more reserved. That's what I've always liked about you, actually. You're very intentional."

"Always liked?" Grace asked, stunned.

"For a while, yes." Cyn blushed. "That's why I'm glad we finally had our moment to break the ice."

"Ah, yes. Was that when I was talking to the plushy in the staircase, or when I passed out in your car?" Grace mused.

"Both?" Cyn laughed. Grace played with her hands under the table. This wasn't a catastrophe, yet. Exceedingly plain? Yes. Slightly boring? Sure. But it's not terrible, so that's good for our girl.

It continued like this for a while. They briefly talked about work, before quickly moving onto hobbies. Cyn enjoyed playing video games and was making her own graphic novel. Grace watched TV, sometimes read books, and fought demons of sorts. Grace left out that last part, though. Eventually, Cyn realized that no wait staff had been by. Hell, even the complimentary loaf of bread hadn't been brought over. Cyn had a glass of water from before, but not Grace.

"It's been a bit since we sat down, right?" Cyn asked. Grace hadn't noticed. Talking with Cyn made the time fly by. Sure enough, it had been thirty minutes. A passing waiter briefly glanced over. Cyn waved at him, but he quickly averted his eyes. "What the hell? Did he just snub us?" Grace looked down. Her neck was feeling awfully hot, as she had the realization. She was so concerned about everyone staring at her because of the vibrant red dress, that she forgot how the little black mark under her ear stood out far more.

"I'm sorry." Grace apologized.

"What?" Cyn was confused. She saw Grace instinctively raise a hand to cover the mark. "Oh." It dawned on her. "Oh, hell no." Cyn was furious. She bolted up from her chair and stormed up to the check-in.

"Excuse me. We've been waiting for a while. Could you have someone come by?" Cyn kept a calm facade. She wasn't certain everyone in the place was a bigot. The hostess looked at Cyn and then leaned to see who she was with. She gave a fake smile.

"Yeah, I'll get right on that." The staff member said the words, but did not take action. She returned to look ahead at the front door, awaiting whatever new guests may come through. Cyn watched her for a second, and then glanced at the entrance. It was obvious nobody was coming in.

"And you're going to do that, when?" Cyn poked. The hostess shot her a glare.

"When I get to it. Now please feel free to go back to your table with your little dead girlfriend," she sneered.

Cyn returned the meanest look she could. "Oh, I see. I didn't realize this place was staffed with assholes!" She shouted that last part loud enough to make a scene. The hostess quickly buried herself in the reservation sheet, trying her best to pretend nothing was happening.

"Cyn, it's okay." Grace got up.

"No, it's not." Cyn rejected the premise. "You're all a bunch of miserable, little cowards," Cyn blasted the staff. Grace didn't shrink. The entire restaurant was now staring at them. Judging them. Yet, Grace stood tall. Cyn's bold display was inspiring. There it was, her complete unwillingness to hold back. Now it was Grace's turn.

"You know what? Let's blow this Popsicle stand!" Grace shouted. I suppose on some level, Grace thought that was cool. It wasn't. However, Cyn found it adorable. A surprised smile came across her face.

"Yeah! I hear Portobello has rats, anyway!"

"Big ones," Grace added.

"And they cook them."

"Into the gnocchi soup." Grace locked eyes with the other tables as she performed the rest of the show. The two defiantly grabbed their coats and marched out the door. The patrons and staff watched, stunned, as the girls stormed out. As soon as the doors closed behind them, they both burst out laughing.

"Oh my god, you were amazing!" Cyn exclaimed.

"Me? No. That was all you!" Grace returned the sentiment

"No, no, no. You are a creative genius. I can see why you're in marketing. Big rat gnocchi soup." Cyn kissed the tips of her fingers. "Chefs kiss, madam."

"I was just working with what you started." Grace did a little curtsy bow. Cyn's face glowed.

"Hey, let's go somewhere else," Cyn suggested.

"Yes, please. I am literally starving," Grace admitted.

"Perfect. Some place fancy, or fast, then?"

"Fast, please."

"You got it. Let's take my car." Cyn extended her hand out.

The composer looked down at the offer, and her heart started to race. Was she really getting this worked up over something so grade school? Finally, she reached forward and interlocked her fingers with Cyn's. The two girls reciprocated rosy smiles as they made their way to their second attempt at dinner.

* * *

Meanwhile, Chase clutched a gun and tried his best to keep a steady hand. He let out a slow and controlled exhale, before releasing a hail of bullets upon attacking alien invaders. The game was called Area 51 Outbreak, and it was one of the oldest in the entire arcade. Octavia watched as Chase missed more than half of his shots, resulting in a particularly mad looking alien closing the gap and lasering his head off. His character's head, of course. Like I said, this was an old game. Nowhere near the level of sophistication needed to laser Chase's actual head off.

"Somehow, that was even worse than your last attempt," Octavia critiqued.

"I know," Chase groaned. "This isn't really my thing."

"I should hope not," Octavia concurred. Chase glared at her. "You are the one who decided to come to this bombardment of color and sound. Do not get upset at me over your decision," Octavia reminded him.

"Two minutes away," Chased grumbled. "You insisted we find a place two minutes away from Portobellos."

"Should trouble strike, we must be close."

"Sure. It just kind of limited where we could go." Chase swiped his arcade card to boot up another life.

"There were several clothing peddlers and that building with the captivating aroma."

"Yeah, I'm not going clothes shopping or to a cafe with a stuffed animal. Sorry."

"How dare you!" Octavia took offense. "You know I am not a stuffed animal. I am…"

"Octavia, master of water and sound. Right? We all know." Chase waved her away with his plastic blue gun.

"Ruler of sea and melody, you imbecile." Octavia huffed. She watched Chase take on the early-level aliens, his health dwindling rapidly, as a majority of his shots failed to find their mark. "Your aim truly is dreadful."

"It's the damn controller sensor. I swear it's off by inches, at least," Chase replied, defending himself. He was also right. As mentioned, this machine was ancient. Nostalgia was the only thing tethering Chase to it.

"Sounds like an excuse. It is alright to have awful hand-eye coordination."

"Okay, that's enough." Chase slid the gun into its plastic holster as a spiky invader punched him to death. He snatched up Octavia and brought her over to the actual oldest game in the arcade: Clown Revenge. Three rows of clown pins stood at attention. Paying your credits would give you nine wooden balls. See where this is going? Chase swiped his card, and the projectiles slid down the ramp.

"What are we doing now?" Octavia sighed.

"Just watch." Chase scooped up each wooden ball and, one by one, knocked down each terrifying clown. Octavia couldn't help but be impressed.

"Chase, this is much better. You should only do this one," Octavia praised.

"See, my hand-eye is great." Chase felt validated. A little childish to prove your point this way, but whatever works. "I was the ace pitcher for Seerstown High. Still hold the record for fastball." He mimed a pitch.

"I do not know what any of that means, but good for you." Octavia lightly clapped her plushy appendages together.

Chase's face dropped. "Of course you don't." He took Octavia and sat at a table. A quick check on his phone revealed that only twenty minutes had passed. He groaned.

"Is that Grace?" Octavia inquired.

"No, just checking the time." Chase let out a sigh. He did not have enough credits on his card to last all night. Not with how quickly he kept dying.

"Oh." Octavia sounded disappointed. Chase picked up on her tone.

"You miss her, huh?" he teased. Octavia scrunched her face and looked away. "It's okay if you miss her. You two have spent, like, every waking moment together for the last however many days, right?"

Slowly, the kraken turned back. "It feels strange, I admit. However, it is not as if I do not know how to be alone."

"Really?" Chase was a little surprised. He wasn't completely aware of Octavia's backstory and assumed she spawned into existence the second Grace got her powers. Which was partially true.

"Oh, yes. Matteo was quite fond of his alone time, actually. Or his time with his maidens. I frequently had to entertain myself." Octavia nodded in remembrance.

"Right. Matteo. And that is..."

"A previous composer," Octavia responded.

"There were others?"

"A few before Grace. I have been alongside them all. Aside from the very first, that is." This line caused Chase to sit back in his chair, finally realizing the scope of Octavia's existence.

"Wild. So you were a part of a lot of people's lives, then. That's pretty cool."

"True. I have been a part of *their* lives," Octavia moped.

"Is that not cool?" Chase asked the clarifying question. He could tell something was bothering her.

"Being alongside them has always been wonderful." Octavia gave a pained smile.

Chase paused for a moment. He thought carefully. "Are you worried you're only a part of Grace's life?" he finally asked. Octavia looked up in shock. She did not expect Chase to be so astute. I suppose this is him showing that bartender intuition.

"Perhaps," she acknowledged.

Chase nodded his head. "You know, one date doesn't mean she doesn't need you."

"I know. However, while she lives her life, what am I? As they all start to live their lives, what am I? If I am not there to guide them, or protect them..." She trailed off as she looked down at her plushy body. I never knew Octavia felt this way. Sure, she willingly entered into this deal, but that doesn't mean it didn't cause her pain. Chase fell quiet for a moment. If he had a dish towel, I half suspect he would sling it over his shoulder right about now.

"You know, I was dating this guy once," Chase began. "We were together for years, actually. Pretty much the entire time I was in high school. Right up to senior year." Octavia raised her eyes to look at Chase. "He was a big deal when I met him. Rookie of the Year on the baseball team, and I was just a nobody. But, for some reason, he noticed me and we started dating."

"Thank you for sharing." Octavia said what she believed she was supposed to. She wasn't entirely sure why Chase launched into his dating history.

Chase chuckled. "Yeah, sure. But the point I was going to make was that he was this powerful presence, and I was just this random kid who had nothing to offer. So, he became my identity. I was Scott's boyfriend. And that's all I was." Octavia withdrew again. She was starting to understand. "In fact, it got so bad that all of his things became my things. He's the reason I started to play baseball."

"I still do not know of this baseball," Octavia interjected.

"Ironically, that's what ended up driving him away." Chase ignored her. "Turns out he didn't want to date himself. That's actually exactly what he told me when we broke up." He sighed in remembrance. "And that's when I realized I had to figure out who I was, you know? Away from him."

Octavia nodded. "I see."

"Grace is great. She's full of surprises. Annoyingly cheery and somehow insanely dependable."

"That she is," Octavia proudly agreed.

"But she's not you. You're your own... person?" Chase stumbled. "Octopus?"

"Kraken."

"Right, kraken. You're your own kraken, with or without Grace. Maybe it's time you find out what you like to do on your own?" Chase leaned in close and gave a sly smirk. "I mean, you're the goddess of the ocean and music." He spoke confidently and incorrectly. Octavia burst out laughing.

"That was the worst attempt yet, dear Chase."

Chase tilted his head in confusion. "What do you mean?"

"Sea and melody," Octavia reminded. "Seriously, it is exceedingly simple, and it even rhymes. I am not sure how you forget it so easily."

Chase rolled his eyes. "Oh, come on, you know what I meant. I'm trying to be inspiring here. Can you give me a break?" He brushed the laugh away. Octavia wiped a joyful tear from her eye.

"I know. It was quite a poignant tale until the end," Octavia offered in consolation.

"My point is that you're pretty cool all on your own," he summarized as he reached for his phone.

"Thank you," Octavia said. She resigned herself to a satisfied smile as she looked up at him. Composers were interesting companions, to be sure, but perhaps there were other friendships she could form this time around.

"Ah, shit," Chase cursed.

"What is it?"

"They're on the move. We gotta go." Chase picked up Octavia and grabbed his jacket, which was still hanging off the Area 51 Outbreak machine.

"Where are they off to now?" Octavia asked. Chase let out a snicker.

"Lucky Strike."

* * *

Cyn and Grace arrived at their backup plan. The only establishment they could think of in town to get the fastest food possible—Lucky Strike. Yes, it was a bowling alley. However, did you guess? It was quite the look—both girls all dressed up in the rundown lanes. If Grace's dress was an attention grabber in Portobellos, it definitely caught some eyes here, especially paired with the bowling shoes. She didn't care anymore, though. All anxiety was ironed out during the previous restaurant debacle. This place seemed more accepting and brought the burgers and fries out within minutes.

"Now, this is what I'm talking about." Cyn gawked over the greasy burger. Grace took a bite and melted into her scoop chair.

"Yes! Nothing beats a divey burger."

"Not even rat gnocchi?"

"Not even rat gnocchi." Grace giggled.

"You're okay with this, right?" Cyn asked nervously. "Like you're not going to go home and journal all about how you just had the worst first date of your life?"

"No," Grace quickly responded. "I don't journal. I may make a video blog about it, though," she teased.

Cyn playfully elbowed Grace. "Oh, god, please don't tell me you're a vlogger."

"Not a chance. I can barely talk in front of people. You think I'd make a video for thousands?"

"Thank god." Cyn laughed. "I'm sorry. I just can't keep up with that lifestyle. You'd leave me in the dust."

"Nah, I'd feature you in one video, and all my gracelits would fall in love with you. You'd start a channel and overtake me in a month."

"Gracelits?" Cyn gave an amused look.

"Yeah, that's probably what my fans would call themselves, right?"

"It's not bad, but..." Cyn turned her whole body to face Grace. "You don't think they'd call themselves Grace riders?"

Grace thought for a moment. "Oh my god, you're right! How did I not think of that?"

"I don't know. And you're the marketing girl," Cyn razzed. "Perhaps I'll tell Tania and I can just take your job, too."

"I think you've earned it fair and square." Grace played into it.

"Nah." Cyn paused for a moment. "If I did that, then I wouldn't get to work with you. That would kind of suck."

"Yeah, I guess it would," Grace agreed. While she hadn't been loving her job lately, she had to admit that Cyn working there was a big draw.

"Speaking of. Think you'll come back anytime soon?"

"Yeah, I do," said Grace. "Until I find something I really love, at least."

"Yeah? Any idea what that would be? What you could fall for?" Cyn asked, slightly flirtatiously. Grace was mesmerized by the beautiful girl eating a French fry in the most enticing way she'd ever seen. To say Grace wanted to be that piece of crunchy potato was an understatement.

"I'm not really sure. I've never really thought about passions," Grace responded, avoiding the obvious double meaning of the question.

"Finding a calling is tough," Cyn empathized. Grace pondered for a second. Technically, she has a calling. She may have fallen into it, but Grace is a composer. I still don't know if she is thrilled about that or not. The problem is that composers typically don't get the chance to chase outside interests. Grace doesn't fully know the history there, but I think deep down she can sense that to be true.

"What about you?" Grace shifted it back on her date. "Is the graphic novel your dream?"

"Yup!" Cyn beamed. "I like that I get to do graphic design in the meantime, but I love creating unique, meaningful things, you know? The art of telling a story can be so impactful. Not that making a graphic of a house cat in the jungle for a new cat toy isn't impactful." Cyn laughed.

"That's amazing. The novel," Grace specified. "Well, all the work you do, really. I really hope I can read the novel someday, though."

"Do you get into that kind of thing?" Cyn asked.

"Sometimes." Grace poked her fingers together. "I have to be honest, though. I rarely finish things I start. Books, TV shows, you name it. I get roughly halfway if I'm lucky."

"Ah, problem with the follow through?"

"I just really like the beginning of things, you know? They're the most fun part."

"I get that."

"I think if I could finish anything, though, it'd be something you made." Grace blushed at her own cheesiness.

"I'm honored." Cyn gave that signature smile while their eyes locked. The tension was thick. Both felt the magnetic pull of the other, but neither wanted a first kiss to be between the bites of a cheap burger. I firmly believe that's the only thing stopping them.

"I'll be right back." Cyn excused herself to go to the bathroom, only taking her gaze off Grace when she absolutely had to. She felt an intense need to floss and brush her teeth with a single-use toothbrush. The idea of kissing Grace with anything in her mouth was a horrifying image for her.

Grace waited patiently in the bowling booth, butterflies circling her stomach. She knocked down seven pins while taking her turn in their game, which they had briefly paused to eat. That was due to Cyn's insistence that she couldn't bowl and touch food at the same time. Grace popped a mint into her mouth. In case another moment was to arise, she needed to be ready. This was going better than she ever thought. Her first date with a girl. It was electric. Cyn swooped back into the seat next to Grace.

"Okay, so I just saw the most eclectic group of people on my way back." She was giddy.

"What do you mean?"

"It's gotta be the strangest bowling team I've ever seen." Cyn nodded her head in a direction. Grace followed the line to a crew a few lanes over. It truly was an unusual grouping. A police officer, still wearing his uniform, a nun of the Church of Veritas, a large imposing pro-wrestler, a teenage boy sporting a letter jacket, and what appeared to be a Girl Scout of some sort.

"Wow, they must be in an interesting league, huh?" Grace joked. However, the smile quickly left her face. See, attached to every member of that lane was a trace. What's even worse was that they were all now staring at her. A lump formed in her throat. "I think we should go," Grace warned.

"Nah, I think they're harmless. Just your average breakfast club!" Cyn thought they were still playing around.

"No, seriously, Cyn." Grace stood up. The league of extraordinary infected rose simultaneously and began to walk toward the girls. Cyn noticed this and stopped laughing.

"Uh, are they coming over here? Do you think they heard us?" she whispered, embarrassed they might have been caught gossiping.

"We have to go." Grace whipped out her phone and shot a

text to Chase. It read "aaa." This was a code they had developed. It just needed to be any letter or number repeating three times. This was largely because of Grace's insistence that they consider a scenario where one was blindfolded or restrained and couldn't see the screen. In theory, it was a pretty practical code. I'm not convinced it would work nearly as well if one was, in fact, blindfolded and tied up, however. Grace grabbed Cyn's hand and began to book it out of the bowling alley.

"What are you doing? Do you owe them all money or something? We have to return the shoes!" Cyn was a whirlwind.

"No time. Explain later." Grace kept going to the door, but the puppets cut them off, making a line in front of the only exit.

"Grace, why do all these people look like they want to hurt you?" Cyn gasped. "Is this a mark thing?"

"Kind of." Grace stepped in between Cyn and the group.

"Grace, what are you doing?" Cyn called out in concern. "Let's just get management over here to tell these jokers to leave."

"Yeah, I don't think that's going to work." Grace got ready to call forth the sound. However, she was so busy looking at the four directly ahead of her that she didn't see the pro-wrestler charging in from the rear. Cyn did spot the imposing man making his move. Quickly, she pivoted a foot out front and whipped her elbow around to come crashing into the throat of the wrestler. He fell backward onto his back, gripping his neck. Grace whipped around just in time to see the aftermath.

"What just happened?"

"Big guy tried to attack us!" Cyn shouted.

"And you knocked him down?"

"Yeah." Cyn glanced over at Grace's stunned, albeit impressed, face. "So, I may have forgotten to mention I know Krav Maga." She took a defensive stance. Grace felt fiercely attracted to her at that moment. Stay focused, Grace. There's a pre-teen running at you.

Grace caught on and spun around the Girl Scout going in for the tackle. This led the scout right to Cyn, who quickly placed her palm against the tiny attacker's face and turned her away. The poorly balanced puppet crashed into a table.

Grace looked around for any trace of the shrouds. Of course, none of them were there. Which made sense. See, if you read between the lines—and read the scared look on everyone's infected faces—it seemed news of the new composer had spread. A girl with the mark of the dead, of which there were very few in Seerstown. Some lesser shrouds of the city decided that a herd mentality was best going forward, thus the unusual gathering of puppets. The actual foes were likely staying out of sight.

"Is there a problem here?" Lucky Strike's manager came over, hands in her pockets, annoyed to be pulled away from her TV in the back. The police puppet drew his firearm and aimed it at the manager, who immediately threw up her hands. After the intruder got the message, he turned the gun on Grace.

"Oh, hell no!" Cyn cried out as she ran and looped her arm around the officer's elbow. She pulled up with her other hand to loosen his grip. The pistol fell to the floor. Letterman and Cyn both looked at the gun and then at each other. Boy wonder made a play for it, diving forward. Cyn extended her leg just far enough to reach it and sweep it away. The firearm flew off a small flight of stairs onto a lane, causing it to discharge onto a lone pin. The words "Spare" flashed across the screen as the tenants of that lane looked up in horror. They all scampered away. The manager also took the opportunity to flee the scene.

"You're really good at this." Grace was enthralled. So enthralled that the Sonata hadn't even been activated yet. I wonder if she's worried about using it on humans? She has gotten a little stronger. I don't think Grace could emotionally handle any collateral damage. Pity. Instead, she opted for her mild physical prowess. With Cyn at her back, she felt confident she could at least take on the nun and Girl Scout.

"Thanks," Cyn replied, returning to the stance. "I got you," she said as she rammed her knee into muscle man's chest cavity. Just when he had finally regained the ability to breathe, too. He folded over and fell into another table, which splintered into several wooden pieces. The holy woman swiftly grabbed a sharp piece of the wreckage and began thrusting it toward Grace. Nimbly, the composer danced around it. Growing up Veritian, Grace found it hard to fight back against this particular infected. Cyn, on the other hand, was able to push past it. She spun in and clamped the stake-bearing arm tightly in her armpit, before head-butting sister silence right in the habit. Hitting a nun still felt off, but to be fair, that nun was trying to skewer her date.

With Grace having some space, she now had a moment to follow the traces. They all led to the bathroom. Wait. Really? That's not very far. I guess these are weaker shrouds, after all.

"Got ya." Grace pumped her fist. "It's my turn, Cyn." She smirked.

"Let's see what you got, girl," Cyn encouraged as she high-kicked the star athlete right in the chin. I don't think she's really ready for this.

"Sonata Mor." Grace spoke the magic words, and the chorus erupted immediately. A low staccato saw bass mixed with a kick drum set the foundation for violas and violins to play a triumphant harmony. The coup de grâce, however, was the light piano melody sprinkled throughout. Cyn's jaw dropped as she looked upon the composer. The sound waves radiated off of her. Grace giggled. She couldn't deny it was fun revealing the power. In what was a truly confusing move for Cyn, however, Grace gave a cheesy wave before taking off toward the bathroom.

"I'll be right back!" Grace shouted.

"Ok," a stunned Cyn replied. She snapped out of her stupor just in time to sidestep a punch from the policeman. This was followed up with several quick punches to his face and neck. He fell to the ground with the others. All the puppets groaned as they pulled themselves back up. Cyn nervously readied herself for the next round.

Grace burst through the bathroom door, quickly surveying the room. Each trace led to its own stall. It was nice they were giving each other space. She walked up to the first stall and peeked through the little slit between the door and wall. Not usually an action I'd condone, but in this case I'll let it slide.

Sure enough, there was a shroud shaking inside. Grace formed a sound dagger. The music changed to be more legato, something soothing and connected. In a swift motion, Grace hurled the sound into the door. The waves collided with the stainless steel, spread around the stall, and reformed on the other side, where it continued its trajectory and sliced through the shroud. That was a neat new trick. The Girl Scout was now free. The other shrouds must not have cared for Grace's new move, however, as they all decided to pop out in unison.

"Whoa, hi." Grace stepped back. "Sorry about your friend." All the infectors rushed forward, ramming into her. Grace flew out the double-sided bathroom door and slid by Cyn's feet.

"Whoa, you okay?" Cyn asked as she tripped the attacking nun and pushed her to the ground.

"Oh, totally." Grace groaned as she stood. The four remaining shrouds poured out of the bathroom and surrounded them.

"What the actual..." Cyn's jaw hit the floor. This had been a very revealing couple of minutes for her.

"I'll explain later. Now duck," Grace called out. Cyn listened and dropped down as Grace shot a wave of sound toward a shroud just behind her. A sustained violin screeched as the frequency cut the puppeteer in two. Cyn's expression was quite the sight. Awe, terror, disgust, pride. A lot of things to say with one face.

"That was…" she started but was interrupted as the wrestler grabbed her. Cyn tried to use her training to break the grip, but before she knew it, he was lifting her into the air, getting ready to slam her down. Grace panicked. How could she take out the puppet without harming the man or Cyn? She didn't know how to manipulate the sound delicately enough to do that.

"Grace!" A voice screamed out from the entrance. It was Chase. She looked toward him as he pitched Octavia with his signature fastball. The plush soared through the hall until she was caught securely in Grace's right hand. The composer twisted around as a sprouting sound tentacle shot out and swept the wrestler off his feet. He flew up in the air and released his grip on Cyn. Octavia launched a second tentacle that caught Cyn and lowered her down safely.

Cyn took a moment to regain her balance. "Thanks," she managed to get out.

"You are welcome," Octavia responded. At this point, it didn't even surprise Cyn that the plush octopus could talk. Because of course it could. She partly wondered if the one she had on her work desk had the same potential. Cyn watched as her date and a plushy brutally bludgeoned each of the remaining shrouds with a rapid barrage from three—that's right *three*—tentacles. Operatic singing now accompanied and followed the driving piano melody. This song was powerful and energetic. The crash of a cymbal rang out as the last shroud was demolished.

A light metallic shimmer filled the atmosphere as the melody beautifully resolved. After a beat of silence, a heartfelt piano solo began to emanate from the composer. A modest postlude to the number. I suspect the reason for the sound change was that Grace had returned her gaze to Cyn. Grace wore a cheesy smile that made Cyn almost forget that this girl just killed a bunch of monsters. The song gradually faded, and the aura retracted until it disappeared.

"Whoa," was all Cyn could say. Slowly and confidently, she

glided up to Grace, stopping directly in front of her. Adrenaline still pumped through her veins. She brushed Grace's bangs away and behind her ear. Her hand stopped and ever so softly rested against Grace's cheek. "That was amazing."

"That's what I was going to say." Grace nervously giggled. Her heart was pounding. Cyn was only inches away from her at this point, and Grace was enthralled by her green eyes. Her lips parted ever so slightly.

Cyn looked down at their pink hue. "I'd very much like to kiss you now," she said, flashing that flirty smile.

"Yeah, that'd be..." Grace started as Cyn leaned in, closing her eyes. "Cool," she whispered. Grace wrapped her arm around Cyn's waist as their lips came together in a spectacular show of sparks. A ballad radiated off Grace, her heartbeat present in the melody. Cyn glided her fingers through Grace's hair as their tongues danced and explored. Poor Octavia was still in Grace's grip. This was exactly the moment she was trying to avoid. The plushy wiggled to send the message to Grace, who promptly let her go. Seems like Grace had better use for that hand anyway, as it lifted to the small of Cyn's back.

"Way to go, Grace," Chase said, cheering on his friend.

The two suddenly realized just how public the affection was, and delicately pulled away from each other.

"Wow." Grace reached a hand to her lip, trying to memorize the feel and taste. She had never experienced a kiss like that before.

"Yeah, wow," Cyn agreed. Grace turned to face Chase, who was uncomfortably close wearing a dumb smirk.

"What is wrong with you?" Grace hit him in the chest. She was a little upset they got brought back down to earth so quickly.

"Ow! I think you mean to say—hey thanks, Chase! I would've been in big trouble without you, Chase." He took offense. Fully unaware that his moment-killing streak remained strong.

"Yeah, yeah," Grace begrudgingly acknowledged. "I will admit that was pretty stellar timing, and quite the throw."

"Chase was the ax pitcher for the baseball," Octavia incoherently bragged on his behalf.

"What?" Grace couldn't even begin to understand that sentence.

Chase gave the octopus a friendly wink. "Still got it, I guess," he gloated.

"Oh, you're the guy who was waiting outside Grace's apartment." Cyn entered the exchange when it clicked.

"You're Grace's driver from that one time!" Chase also pieced it together. "Damn, Grace, you move quick." Grace gave Chase a look. Maybe he wasn't fully putting it together.

"You can call me Cyn." It hurt Grace just a little that a nickname privilege she waited a year for was being handed out so readily.

"Chase." He waved two fingers to say hi.

"Oh, I know your name." Cyn chuckled. "I was convinced you were her boyfriend for a while."

"Me and Grace?" Chase guffawed.

"You'd be so lucky," Grace teased. Octavia jumped onto Grace's shoulder and audibly cleared her throat. "Oh, right. And this is Tavi." Grace gestured up to her.

"Dear Grace, please. I am Octavia..."

"Queen of sea and melody!" Chase triumphantly added. Octavia snickered. He was getting close. Queen was acceptable. The kraken turned back to Cyn and puffed herself up as big as she could. Which was, of course, still very, very small.

"Nice to meet you. That is quite the title," Cyn spoke cutely, as one would to an adorable little puppy.

Octavia did not care for that. "It is a title I earned through much bloodshed," she asserted.

"Aw, I'm sure it was!" Cyn scrunched her nose. The stuffing nearly burst out of the kraken.

"Ha ha, what Cyn is trying to say is that she is impressed by your totally real history of being a badass." Grace nervously tried to patch it up. "Right, Cyn?" she coached. "She's killed, like, so many monsters."

"Oh. Yes. Absolutely. I am humbled." Cyn understood and immediately shifted her tone, and even threw in a slight bow. Octavia appreciated the alternative approach. She was a sucker for any show of reverence.

"Please rise, Miss Cyn. No need for such displays. You are dear Grace's maiden, after all." Octavia accepted her.

"I'm what now?" Cyn asked with a smirk.

"So anyway," Grace abruptly interrupted. "I suppose this kind of puts a weird spin on the rest of the night, huh?" They looked around at the completely cleared out bowling alley, save for the five puppets who were waking up.

Cyn tensed up and prepared to fight. "Here we go again."

"Wait, wait, wait!" Grace frantically waved her arms to halt her. "They're harmless now. Probably. I guess I don't really know what kind of people they are without the Silence."

"The Silence?" Cyn wasn't ready to relieve her stance just yet.

"It is true, Miss Cyn. The shrouds controlled them," Octavia added.

"The creatures we were fighting. They infect people and control them," Grace elaborated.

"Oh." Cyn slowly put her arms down. With everything she just witnessed, why wouldn't she believe that possession was also on the table? "That sounds intense." She kept a watchful eye on the five, just in case. Grace knew Cyn needed the full story to relax. *I'm assuming she'll also want to clear things up for the newly severed, as well.*

"Alright." Grace cleared her throat. "Everyone gather round, I guess. It's story time."

* * *

"Jake, you little shit!" Dios kicked the flimsy front door off of the Evans' household. That entrance really can't catch a break. The three were there looking for an explanation regarding their recent wild goose chase.

"Melting your facade so soon, Dom?" Ira mocked. Dios was using Dom's body in casual pastoral dress. If the neighbors just saw the local priest kick down a door, it may hurt the cover. Dom couldn't care less at that moment.

"I know you're in here, fucker. I can sense you." Dom was rabid. Dios grabbed a nearby vase and chucked it against the back wall. "Come out."

Jake appeared at the top of the stairs. His smugness fully recovered. "Is that Dom acting like a wild animal?" he poked. "That's usually Orv's role, isn't it?"

"Start talking," Dom demanded. There was no time for games.

"About what? The weather? It's a bit sunny. I think we may get that early spring we're all hoping for." Dios punched the baluster, taking a significant chunk away. "Can you chill, please? I still have to live here, you walking pile of waste." Jake got a little tweaked.

"Bold move, by the way." Ira came in with her usual calm and control. "Hiding out where you killed daddy dearest."

"I already took care of any potential problems." Jake brushed it off. "I should be fine here until my new silence develops."

"You didn't." Dom came back breathing flames. "Don't tell me you used Isaac to clean up your mess." Isaac was the name of one of their police puppets. Typically, he helped with the ever-important job of getting rid of crime scenes before anyone got involved.

"He's the Silence's lapdog, not yours Dom. I'll use him whenever I need."

"We can't just call on him for risky bullshit. What do you think is going to happen when your precious dead father doesn't come to his court hearing? If we lose such a valuable puppet because you have no impulse control..."

"Impulse control? Don't make me laugh. You three are the worst of the lot when it comes to control. If there're any eyes on Isaac, it's because he's been covering for a serial killer for years. Please. If he gets burnt, we'll just make a new toy." Jake glared from above. His spatial position added to his confidence. Dios growled at the boy.

"I'm going to slaughter you," Orv spat.

"Now, now, everyone," Ira interjected. "As much as I like to watch you two argue with a literal child, we're not here about Isaac."

"Right. You fucked us!" Dom screamed. Jake grinned.

"So you simpletons really went after that license plate, I take it?" He burst out laughing. "The one that literally said 'fuck boy?'. Wow, you really are idiots."

Dios picked up a large splinter of the busted stairway. In one motion, they snapped their wrist, and the splintered wood extended all the way up to Jake. It collided with the void shield and snapped.

"Did I strike a nerve?" Jake was enjoying this. Dios retracted the makeshift weapon and tossed it to the ground.

"Why are you such a piece of garbage?" Dom grumbled. "Did you even see a car?"

"Perhaps. I'd love to tell you, but I have other plans." He looked down at his nails in disinterest.

"Care to share with the class?" Ira prodded.

"I'm going to kill her myself. I do come from a legacy of successful composer killers. She's mine."

"Your great grandma got lucky with a cheap shot on her own brother a hundred years ago," Dom chortled.

"Not to mention dear old mom is in town, too. I believe that gives her the same credentials as you," Ira noted. The mention of his mother caused Jake's face to drop.

"Don't talk about that bitch," he snarled.

"Your mommy issues are that intense, huh?" Ira twisted the knife.

"She's precisely why I will never tell you anything. As long as that whore is around, I'm working solo."

"All you have is a sad little shield," Dom mentioned.

"Which the composer already broke once," Ira added. Jake bit his lip in frustration.

"I'm going to awaken soon," he claimed. The three burst out into laughter.

"Let's not rush puberty, Jakey," Ira said. "It could be a long while before you've got the juice needed. Meanwhile, she gets stronger every day." Dios began advancing up the stairs. "I get that you want to be the big man. I really do. But, if your mother is correct." Jake spat at the mention. Dios was all the way on the second floor now. "If Mira is correct." Dios placed their hand on the boy's shoulder. "If this composer could be the maestro, then we can't waste time on silly little pissing contests." Jake scowled at Dios, who knelt down to his level.

"She's mine to kill," he insisted.

"Sure, sure. Tell you what. How about you agree to play nice, and we let you have the killing blow?" Ira offered. Jake looked away and pondered the deal. It would be a surefire way to ensure his legacy. He carefully weighed his options.

"Deal." The word fell out of Jake's mouth as he extended a hand. As Dios went to shake it, he withdrew. "But the slut stays out of it," Jake stipulated.

"Sure," Ira lied. Jake gave a scrutinizing look, before finally shaking on it.

"That's our big boy," Ira praised. "Now, about that car."

* * *

While Dios was away, Mira enjoyed their bed in a way they never did. She lay there completely naked, save for her signature black veil and the spiral mark at the center of her chest. A handsome young man nestled beside her. Both breathed heavily after an activity I didn't feel comfortable intruding upon.

"That was amazing." The stud was seeing stars. A dumb, satiated smile sat comfortably on his face. Let's call him Jeff. His real name isn't important. Jeff turned to adore his afternoon delight. Mira, however, simply zoned out, staring at the ceiling. Her breathing returned to normal, while her ecstasy dissolved into a blank numbness. Only moments ago, this woman expanded Jeff's horizons to heights he never dreamed possible. A pleasure so delectable, it seemed forbidden. Now she was motionless and dull.

"Are you okay?" he asked, concerned. "What happened?" No response. "What's going on, baby?" Gently, he reached over and placed a comforting hand on her.

Mira reacted like a mousetrap. Her eyes shot toward him with piercing disdain. "You disgusting worm. Do not touch me."

"Whoa, whoa! Not into that sort of thing," Jeff said quickly. Mira pushed him off and sat upright. He moved to the corner of the bed and pulled a sheet over his lower body. "What the fuck got into you?"

"A defiler got into me." Mira stood. "A disgusting man."

"Alright, you know what? This just got too weird for me. That's the last time I go home with some random, slutty nun," he said with conviction, though I doubt he will ever encounter this scenario again. One, because it was incredibly contrived, and two, because Mira had a habit of doing this, and it seldom ended well. As he started to get up, she gripped his throat and forced him back down. The man tried to pull away to no success.

"Are you ready to pay the price for your lust?" she asked, while staring into his soul. He looked back, terrified. "The lust you forced upon me, dragging me down into your filth." Mira's claws dug into his neck. He choked and thrashed to no avail until finally, he went limp. She released her grip and allowed the body to collapse onto the bed. "Disgusting." Mira looked down on her victim, before slowly making her way to the mirror. She stared at her exposed figure and wept.

"Foul. Unworthy." She hurled the insults at her reflection, while violent arms wrapped around her body. Nails tore fresh wounds alongside layers of deep scars as she dragged them across her back. Mira winced through the pain. "Pitiful and low." More degradation as red rivers flowed along her skin. She continued to lock eyes with her likeness in the mirror, until finally her nails retracted from her flesh. Her hands slowly dropped to her sides. The penance had been served. Slowly, she put the signature black dress back on over the dripping wounds.

"I vow to never again fall to the temptation of the flesh." Mira spoke the oath she'd recited so many times before, while looking down upon the unfortunate lover. Poor Jeff. Eventually, she would need to deal with his body, but the thought of touching it made her ill. Later, perhaps.

Instead, she went to the rectory kitchen. The activity had left her famished. Sex and murder builds quite an appetite, I'm sure. To her surprise, she saw Nova sitting at the table eating a bowl of cereal alongside Mata.

"Look who's up," she said with a fresh attitude. "I thought you were still recovering in bed?" Mira spoke nervously as her activities got a little loud despite her best efforts. "Have you been up long?" she probed.

"Don't worry, I didn't hear anything," Nova coyly responded.

Mira accepted the olive branch of ignorance. "Oh, wonderful." She grabbed a cutting board and ingredients for a stir fry. "Cereal as your first meal after waking?"

"I've never been one for cooking."

"That's why you have me, dear," Mira said sweetly.

"I can fend for myself. Besides, you were..." Nova paused.

"Busy." Mira dropped the knife at the implication. "Are you okay?" Nova spun around to check on her.

"Yes, yes. Of course." Mira pasted on a smile. She recovered the cutting utensil and wiped it off before slicing the veggies. "You'll need your strength back quickly. Mata did a wonderful job healing you, but you should eat something better than cereal to fully recover."

"Thanks." Nova was grateful. Not just for the meal, but for everything Mira had done. They don't know how someone with her demeanor managed to hold her own in a gang fight, but Nova knew she did it for them. Nova glanced at Mata, who was laying loaf style on the table. They moved their bowl over to the hush. It was mostly milk now.

"Hush's care not for milk," Mira mentioned, seeing the offering from the corner of her eye.

"I've been wondering what Mata eats. I haven't seen them eat anything yet." Nova sighed. This wasn't actually true. Mata enjoyed a big helping of Grace's sound just the other day. However, Nova still assumed the ethereal kitty would need physical sustenance, so they had been periodically offering random scraps to no success.

"A hush feasts upon sound," Mira whimsically informed them.

"On sound?"

"Correct."

"How?" Nova was intrigued.

"Some believe they pull it into their body from the vibrations in the air. When it feasts, I wouldn't be surprised if things got just a little quieter around them," Mira said playfully. Nova looked at the cat-like creature.

"Sound, huh?" They drifted away in their thoughts and fell quiet.

Mira noticed. "Something on your mind?" she asked.

Nova thought carefully about this next sentence. They

mulled over whether they could trust Mira. If this was Dios, the answer was much more cut and dry, but Mira helped save them. She appeared to actually care. "Do you know anybody who can use sound?" Nova finally asked. Mira perked up. "As a weapon?" Nova looked over at the excited woman in black.

Of course, Mira did not display this full excitement. Instead, she played it carefully. "Have you met such a woman?"

"How did you know it was a woman?" Nova asked. Just as they suspected, the strange sound wielder was part of this weird, new universe they found themselves in.

Mira scooped a helping of stir fry onto two plates and placed them on the table before seating herself. "She's called a composer."

"A composer..." Nova looked down. "Is she dangerous?"

Mira leaned in close. "Incredibly," she whispered. Mata got up and shook their body into a stretch.

"She tried to kill Mata."

The cat was out of the bag. This was the best sentence Mira could have heard. Gently, she cupped Nova's hand within her own. "You poor thing. To think you'd have a run-in with such a villain. You and Mata are okay, that is all that matters." Manipulative words flowed into Nova's ears, and I'm afraid they were more inclined than ever to believe them. Mira leaned back. "How did you manage that, by the way?" she pried. "Getting away from her, that is."

"I don't really know. Mata must've eaten the sound, I guess? The music stopped after Mata inhaled it all. Then she... the composer, just looked at me." Nova remembered the look. It was one of worry. "And then she ran."

"Is that so?" A twisted smile spread across Mira's face as she glanced at her adorable secret weapon. "Sounds like you were lucky, then."

"We were defenseless. Why didn't she kill us?" Nova wrestled with their memory.

Mira stood up and walked behind them. Firmly, she placed her hands on their shoulders. "It seems our brave little warrior over there drained the composer of all her sound. Without that, dear, she is powerless." She leaned in to whisper, "Rest assured, if she had even an ounce of strength left, she would have finished the job with no mercy." Nova shuddered at the thought. "You've got quite the partner there." Mira grabbed the remainder of her plate and put it on the counter.

"You barely ate?" Nova pointed out.

"Oh, I am alright. Besides, I just remembered something important I should tend to." Mira floated out the door with a renewed burst of energy. She stopped at the entrance to look back. "You, on the other hand, need to eat every last bite. I'll check on you later." She wiggled her fingers to say bye and was gone.

Nova was a little thrown off by the sudden exit, but their rumbling stomach motivated them to stay and finish the warm meal. While they ate, their mind drifted back to the night prior, and to one thing in particular: Sasha. It was the name that had been bouncing around in their brain ever since it was uttered. Nova kept trying to conjure up an image, a memory, or anything. Unfortunately, they had no luck. Mata decided the table life wasn't for them anymore, and they jumped down to rest on Nova's lap, nestling in comfortably. Nova, of course, began petting them.

"I wonder what kind of person she was?" The rhetorical question was directed at the content creature, who was utterly unburdened by such troubles. Nova was envious. Their brain would not free them of these thoughts. Should they try to track down Sasha's family? Get answers? The only thread they had to their past was now part of a major crime scene. There were no survivors last night. I mean, surely not every member of the Blindspot was in attendance. However, I can't imagine too many low-level crooks would be willing to continue carrying the gang's flag now. Cutting off the snake's head tends to lead to the body's death. This left Nova with the increasingly unsettling thought that they may just have to let it all go. What was the point, anyway? Sasha had died. Was chasing after some dead girl really that important? Their heart would not allow them to say no.

After Nova polished off their plate, they went for a stroll down to the worship space. Mata pranced behind. The two grabbed a seat in the front pew. Veritas stared down from the giant colorful mural. Nova looked up into the eyes that always appeared to be looking right back at you. This was becoming somewhat of a regular occurrence for them. Something about the space seemed calm and safe—as long as its pastor was absent, of course. It did make a certain amount of sense. The church was specifically designed to harbor these feelings. It really was a gorgeous little place. No wonder someone like Brody wanted to keep it sparkling. The primary purpose of the building was still the worship of Veritas, which ultimately made it a massive waste of beauty.

Nova always felt a myriad of emotions sitting in that pew looking up at the big guy himself. A delicate balance of peace and judgment. Despite this, it remained the calmest place, and thus an ideal location to soul search.

The staring contest with Veritas ended, and Nova allowed their eyes to wander. Mata naturally was curled up on Nova's thighs. *I swear all hushes do is sleep and destroy.* There was enough of the latter perpetrated the night prior, so it was time to catch up on the sleep portion. Nova surveyed the oak pews, the marble altar, the gold candelabras, and finally the community billboard. The billboard was a pleasant reminder that there were actually people living normal lives somewhere in this city.

Today, however, there was something a little extra in store for Nova. Dead center on the board was a missing persons poster. The name "Sasha Conrad" filled the bottom of the page, centered under a picture of a pretty young woman. Blonde curls framed her delicate pink face. Nova stood up immediately, causing the poor hush to roll onto the floor. Mata landed on their feet and shook themselves off.

"Sorry, bud," Nova said while gravitating toward the picture. They grabbed it off the board for a closer look. The paper was slightly beat up, and the back was littered with grime. Surely this hadn't been sitting in the church long enough for that? Nova came here every day. They would have seen it. Regardless, the lowly state of the poster did not matter. What drew Nova's attention was the image. There goes their heart again. An aching pain pulsing throughout their body. If hearing the name had an effect, that sensation was only amplified by seeing her face. Without a doubt, Nova knew this woman. Perhaps even loved her. That assurance was all they had, however. No memories surfaced, just those annoying feelings.

Peeking out from behind one of the stone pillars was Mira. She watched as Nova found the present she left for them. A smile spread across her face that almost seemed genuine, if not lacking tact. Then, in an instant, she vanished. Off to clean up the rest of her mess. She reappeared in the hallway to Dios's room, plastic lining, garbage bags, and saw in hand. Just as she was ready to get to work, the door swung open, giving way to a very annoyed looking Dom.

"What the actual fuck?" Dom swore.

Mira frowned. She did not enjoy her dirty laundry being so public.

"For real, girlie. It's not even my birthday." Ira laughed. She enjoyed seeing this side of Mira. Something that only increased the discomfort of the lady in black. "For the record, though, I prefer my playthings to be alive first."

"I'm going to take care of it now." Mira dismissed them.

"That's not the point," Dom yelled. "I'm all for fun and games, Mira."

"Pfft, you're the least fun of the three of us," Ira corrected.

"But," Dom reinserted himself, "do it in your own room, bitch."

"We want to kill next time!" Orv spoke, missing the entire issue.

Mira turned her nose up at Dios and pushed them away. "As if I would do something so degrading in my own quarters," she replied.

"Oh, so you just turn tricks in our bed?" Dom persisted. "I guess you really are just a slut."

Mira spun on a dime and glided toward Dios, gripping their neck. She rammed them against the opposing wall. "Silence your vile tongue, snake," she scolded.

Dios chuckled. They always loved getting Mira worked up. Seeing cracks in her holier-than-thou persona was what they lived for these days. They did not wish to fight, however, so they simply put their hands up. "Yes, mistress," Ira teased. "Can we at least have some fun before you finish the job? I see your new toy is already broken. Maybe we can be of service?" She winked seductively as the body switched to Ira's. "Look, you can even choose your flavor."

Mira released her grip in disgust. "Just leave me be. Your room shall be ready again soon." She shooed them away.

Dios wasn't about to let the fun end that easily. "If we leave now, you won't get to hear about our day," Ira continued. "With your son."

Mira's fists tightened. "Are you incapable of even the slightest amount of tact?" Mira scowled.

Dios cackled. "Oh, your relationship never gets old. I could watch the abuse and neglect for hours on end," Dom mused. The glare Mira was giving told them to move on, which Dios obliged. "The composer's car. We've got it." A satisfied smirk spread across Dios' face as they knew they hooked her in.

"Very well." Mira swallowed her pride. "I'm listening."

TEN
NOBODY IS WAITING

Grace laid in bed, curled up in a comfy ball. A pillow was squeezed tightly in her arms as she stared giddily at her phone. Illuminated on the screen was a single text.

"Good morning!" A smiley face emoji punctuated the sentence. The good smiley face, too. There is a difference, I guess. The message was from Cyn, and Grace had been staring at it for at least a half hour. And that's after she spent the previous thirty minutes coming up with a delicately crafted response. She settled on "Mornin!" with the same rosy-cheeked emoji. A true work of art.

"Still daydreaming?" Octavia observed as she crawled into the room. After her earlier attempts at crafting a response were denied, Octavia huffed off to the couch to watch a rerun of her favorite idol anime. To be fair, Octavia's tone was a little old-fashioned for modern dating.

"I just can't believe it." Grace obsessed over the text. "Like, did last night even happen?"

"I assure you it did. And what a battle it was!" Octavia hopped on the bed, ready to relive the glory. Grace rolled over onto her back, nearly crushing the poor stuffy, the pillow still fully gripped within her arms.

"The date, Tavi. Did I really go on a date with the girl of my dreams?" Grace's eyes sparkled.

"Oh." Octavia was disappointed. "Yes, I can confirm that also occurred. Is she really the maiden of your dreams?" Grace responded to Octavia's question by squealing into her pillow like a schoolgirl. Her phone vibrated, and she nearly jumped through the roof. "Oh my god, it's her!" Cyn's name flashed across the notification screen.

"Sublime." Octavia groaned and slid off the bed. "I shall see you in another hour." She wiggled her way back to the TV.

"So, last night really happened, right?" Cyn's message said.

"See! She can't believe it either." Grace shouted to the octopus now in the next room. Octavia was already booting up *Pop Love* and chose to ignore the composer. Grace gave a little shrug. "Wait, she can't believe it either?" The sentiment seemed unbelievable. Was it really possible Cyn was just as excited about the date as she was? If that is true, I really, truly am glad we are only witnessing one side of this display. Watching Grace be lovestruck is about all I can handle at this time. Just like that, Grace was back in generator mode, coming up with the perfect response. This could take a minute. Eventually, she responded with the masterful: "I think so." She ended with the thinking emoji. There was a brief pause before a wave of courage flooded her. Back to the keys. "I had a really amazing time." A red heart capped the sentence. Bold, Grace. Before she could talk herself out of it, she struck the send button. She exhaled. They kissed last night. It was time to stop playing things timidly. The blissful staring at her messages came to a halt as three knocks hit her front door. She gave her phone one more excited glance, before swinging her feet over the side of the bed and getting up. Quickly, she threw on a pair of yoga pants and tied her hair up.

"You have yet another visitor," Octavia said as Grace walked past. Her eyes stayed locked on the TV screen. Grace opened the entrance to a completely put together Trish. The instinct to slam the door shut was intense, but she managed to override it.

"Hey!" Grace said, trying not to think about what she herself looked like. Trish was wearing an adorable oversized purple sweater that hung over a pair of black leggings. Her hair was up in a claw clip. I think Grace was hoping Trish would look a little less cute after her date with Cyn. Her attractiveness, however, had not diminished.

"Hi," Trish responded with a shy smile. "Sorry to intrude, but I have something I really need to talk to you about." She fidgeted with her fingers. Uh-oh. Grace still hadn't had the almost-kiss chat with her. She wasn't exactly avoiding it, but her nerves definitely kept her from making it a priority.

"Yeah, that's probably a good idea." Grace knew she couldn't run anymore. She stepped aside and waved her hand to welcome Trish in. The two made their way to the living room couch.

"Oh, hi Tavi!" Trish cheerily greeted the Octopus like a guest on her kids' show.

"Greetings, Miss Trish," Octavia returned the greeting. Her eyes did not leave the screen. She also did not intend to invoke the name of Trish's children's show, either. That was just a happenstance of Octavia's formality.

"This show looks cute," Trish said, trying to connect with the kraken.

"This show is immaculate. Humanities perfected art," Octavia responded. Once again, her focus did not waver.

Trish nodded. "Sure, sure. I can definitely tell." She couldn't tell. And for good reason. *Pop Love* was a good show, sure, but it had never graced a single top ten list. "So, anyway." Trish turned her attention to Grace. "I have to tell you something I think you should know."

"I went on a date yesterday," Grace blurted out. She wasn't

able to hold it in. Hearing Trish admit her feelings would only make it harder to say later. Trish was taken aback and didn't seem to know how to respond. Grace took this as an invitation to word vomit. "Sorry. I know we had our almost-moment. We never talked about it, I know. I really should have said something sooner. I really like this other girl. Her name is Cyn, but you don't really need to know that, I guess?" The wheels were off the car. Trish just watched the display. "It wasn't like I didn't *want* to kiss you. Of course I wanted to. I mean, look at you! You're gorgeous. Everybody wants to kiss you. It's just, I really really like this girl. Cyn. Once again, I guess you don't really need to know her name, but..."

"Grace." Trish put us all out of our misery. "It's okay."

"It is?"

"Yeah. I mean, sure, I have been kind of wondering if there was anything happening between us since that moment, but that's not exactly what I came to talk about today." Grace's lips puckered in embarrassment. This is why listening is important.

"Oh." Grace melted into the couch, trying to disappear.

"I mean, don't get me wrong, I love to hear that you wanted to kiss me." Trish giggled. "I'd be lying if I said I wasn't hoping for one that night."

"Sure, sure." Grace nodded numbly. Octavia subtly turned the volume up. Trish realized Grace was adrift and offered a life jacket.

"We can still be great friends. Besides, it's not like anything actually happened." This snapped Grace out of it. Trish was smiling warmly. On the inside, it seems this news may have impacted her more than she's letting on, however. This was a girl who has had a lot of practice taking high roads.

Grace returned the smile. "Yeah, I'd like that." The two sat for a moment while Glitter performed their newest hit at the school festival in the background. "So, what *did* you want to talk about, then?"

"Something less fun." Trish shifted uncomfortably. "I saw a shroud." She spoke the words that caused Octavia to pause her show and tune into the conversation.

"Wait, what?" Grace was confused. "Like a new one? Not the one I killed?"

"Yeah, at yoga this morning." Grace twitched. Of course Trish did yoga.

"But you haven't been severed. So, how is that possible?"

"One does not have to be severed to see the unseen, dear Grace." Octavia decided to contribute her expertise. "One only needs to be exposed to the truth, which Miss Trish, here, was."

Grace nodded, digesting the info. Then it clicked. "Wait. That means..." The color drained from her face. "The whole club...?"

"Yes. Anyone who has had the pleasure of hearing your sound will have the veil ripped away!" Octavia said with pride.

"Oh no, no, no." Grace got up and started pacing. "That's so many people who have to be flipping out now."

"Not this again." The kraken sighed. "Dear Grace, knowing the truth is not a punishment. You have liberated these minds."

"Not like this. They're all going to piss themselves when they see another one out in the wild."

Trish stood up and placed both hands on Grace's shoulders to stop her. "I didn't piss myself when I saw it."

"But that's because I had a chance to explain it to you!"

"No. It's because I got to see you kick the shit out of one of them," Trish affirmed. "Everyone in that club witnessed what you did. If they see another out and about, they'll know it can be defeated."

"It is true, dear Grace. You were inspirational," Octavia added. Grace was taking everything in. She still didn't love that she couldn't do an introductory seminar for every soul with newly opened eyes, but the words were comforting. "It is the age of a composer. The truth of the Silence will be exposed. It must be."

"What if people aren't ready?" Grace asked.

"It does not matter, dear Grace." Octavia hopped along Trish's arm to place a plushy, tiny tentacle on Grace's shoulder. "It only matters if you are ready."

"And after what I saw, I definitely think you're ready." Trish winked.

"Thanks," Grace timidly responded. Once again, she's really not used to this level of affirmation. I do fear that it may be making her a little weak. She cannot afford to be weak right now. Not with the events that will unfold after she receives this text.

A vibration rattled her phone on the end table. Grace darted to the device. "Hold that thought." She held up a finger to pause the conversation.

Octavia groaned. "Make yourself comfortable. This will take a while," the octopus advised the visitor.

"It's Chase," Grace spoke softly.

"Oh, if that is the case, then Grace shall be done momentarily. She hardly ever puts effort into communication with Chase," Octavia corrected.

Grace gravely presented the phone to her mentor. The message simply read "999".

"The warning signal?" Octavia gasped.

"I think so," Grace confirmed.

"Is everything okay?" Trish asked nervously.

"We must make haste," Octavia urged.

Grace threw her coat on. "I'm sorry, Trish. I promise we will figure out how to take out your yoga shroud later."

"It's okay. I totally understand. Please, just make sure he's okay. And..." Trish paused for a moment, worry present in her eyes. "You stay safe, too. Okay?"

A brave smile spread across Grace's face as she gave an assuring nod. "I'll be back soon." She put it out into the universe. I really hope she's right.

* * *

Two floors, white siding, red shutters, and an above ground pool. These were just a few features that made up Sasha's house. Nova checked the address on the missing poster and compared it with numbers on the mailbox. It was a match. This was it.

They stared down the long walkway leading to the stained wooden door. What waited behind remained to be seen. Perhaps all they'd find was a set of worried parents. At best, maybe answers. Mata gave Nova a reassuring nudge against their calf.

"Here goes nothing," Nova said to the hush. "Thanks for coming with me." They smiled briefly at their companion. With the missing poster firmly in hand, Nova traversed the sidewalk. A ring of the doorbell queued a rapid heartbeat. Mata took their usual spot in Nova's hood to provide the most efficient emotional support. After what seemed like an eternity, the door opened. A middle-aged man in modest square spectacles came into view.

"Stephanie?" His mouth hung open.

"Um, no. Sorry," Nova said, confused. "I'm actually here about this." They presented the poster. The man didn't bother looking at the picture of his daughter.

"You miserable little shit." His lip quivered, and the words alone made Nova take a step back. "The nerve of you coming here. After everything you've done. And you dare to show up with my Sasha's missing poster?" Tears filled in his eyes. Nova tried to speak, but their mind went blank. "Get out of here and go back to whatever backstreets you're sleeping in." He spat on the floor and began to head inside.

"Wait! Mr. Conrad," Nova called out, afraid to lose their chance.

The pained father stopped in his tracks. "Just go, Stephanie."

"My name's Nova."

This caused the man to scoff. "Whatever you say." He started to shut the door.

"I know what happened to Sasha," Nova revealed.

Mr. Conrad paused again. This time he turned around to face them, tears streamed silently down his cheeks. "What did you and your miserable friends do to my little girl?"

"I didn't... It wasn't me. I... I was looking for her," Nova stumbled.

"Looking for her?" This seemed to surprise Mr. Conrad. "She left late that night. The last time I saw my daughter, I knew she was going to see you. It was always to see you." Outrage coated his words. "I told her you were a lost cause, that the girl she knew wasn't there anymore."

"I don't..." Nova blurted, before reeling it back in for a softer tone. "I don't remember any of that." Now Nova's eyes got a little watery. They didn't exactly understand why. Mr. Conrad looked at them, trying to figure out what game they were playing.

"What do you mean?"

"I can't remember." Their voice shook. "I know I knew Sasha, but I can't... I can't remember."

Mr. Conrad shut the door behind him as he took a stance firmly on the stoop. "It's been a while since I saw you like this." He analyzed the vulnerable human being in front of him. "You usually come around here acting like some big shot, pissing the ever-loving hell out of me. Despite all that, Sasha still believed she could 'save' you." Mr. Conrad sneered. He walked past Nova and sat on the cold stone step and buried his head in his hands. "I just want to know where my daughter is."

Nova took a seat beside him and exhaled. "She did come looking for me," they revealed. "But I wasn't there to meet her. I don't know why. I just remember waking up on the pavement that night. I can't remember anything else." Mr. Conrad looked over at Nova, trying to determine if this was all just some story. "I... I tracked down the gang I guess I used to run with." The explanation painfully poured from their mouth. "And," Nova did not want to speak these next words, "I found out... I found out that Sasha...That night, Sasha..."

Before Nova could even say it, Mr. Conrad knew. He closed his eyes as drops of sorrow fell. "No, no, no," he repeated. "Please, no."

"I'm so sorry." Nova gently placed a hand on the father's back as he leaned forward and bawled into his arms, trying to stifle the sound. "I'm so sorry I wasn't there." A teardrop slid its way off Nova's chin. The two sat there on the unusually warm winter's day as the news settled in.

Eventually, Mr. Conrad pulled his glasses off and wiped his eyes. "Her body?" is all he said.

Nova couldn't look at him. "I don't know," they responded. Mr. Conrad took a deep breath and shook his head. "I only know the last place she was."

"Okay." Mr. Conrad accepted the compromise. He stood up. "You tell me that, and maybe you can start to make amends for everything you have done to this family." Nova rose to meet his eyes. Mr. Conrad pulled a pen out of his breast pocket and handed it to Nova. They took it and wrote the address of the drug lord's house on the back of the missing poster, using the archway as a backing.

The face of Mr. Conrad's daughter greeted him as Nova returned the poster. Gently, he placed his hand against the paper as droplets wet the page. "You really don't remember?" he asked solemnly.

"No memories, but," Nova started, "I remember how she made me feel." They looked down at the picture of the girl, then up at her father. "I think I loved her."

This caused Mr. Conrad to close his eyes again, trying to hold back the endless waterfall. Finally, he opened them and stared directly into Nova's. "This girl. The one you grew up with. The one who stood up for you in school. The girl who helped you with your homework. The girl who gave you everything, despite getting nothing in return." His voice broke. "What you did to this girl..." Mr. Conrad shook as he pointed at the picture. "That was *not* love." The words flew out like knives into Nova. With one final look of disdain, Mr. Conrad disappeared back into his lonely house. The door slowly came to latch.

Nova couldn't move. The interaction sunk deep into their skin and tightened their muscles. Mata got up on their shoulder and tried to nuzzle their face to little effect. Nova took a deep breath. "I guess I was a real piece of shit," they said. Mata turned their head inquisitively, before brushing along Nova's neck. Nova reached behind and scratched Mata's back. "I guess we better go."

The return from the house felt like a walk on the clouds. Nova's body was so numb they couldn't even feel their feet touch the ground. As they began their trek down the street, however, they noticed the weight of fresh eyes staring at them. They turned to see Jake Evans standing in the broken down entryway of the house next door. Unlike the Conrad estate, their neighbor's yard was in complete disarray. Nova did not recognize the boy, but Jake seemed awfully interested in them. This drew Nova in.

"Can I help you?" Nova asked as they advanced toward the Evans's household.

"Funny. You're the one coming up to my house. Shouldn't I be asking you, Nova?" Jake dropped the name. Nova and Mata both perked.

"You know me?"

"Oh, come on. It hasn't been that long." Jake eyed up the duo. He seemed slightly confused. "Though there seem to be some significant changes in your company."

Now it was Nova's turn to be confused. "What do you mean?"

"Well, you have a hush on your shoulder, for one. And... no strings attached," Jake observed.

"You can see Mata?" Nova completely glossed over the remark about the strings.

"You named it?" Jake laughed. "What a concept. A hush with a name." That's what I thought at first, too. "Well, in that case, yes, I can see Mata." Jake turned and walked back inside. He waved a hand, welcoming his visitors in. Nova and Mata hesitantly followed the strange boy. The interior of the house matched the exterior—a complete mess.

"You live here?" Nova inquired as they tapped the obliterated stair rail.

"For now." Jake ushered them into the massive living room. "Can I interest you in something to drink?"

"No, I'm okay."

"Fair enough." Jake took a seat in a chair. Nova followed suit and sat on an opposing loveseat.

"So, are you going to tell me who you are?" Nova dove in.

"Really? You don't remember?" Jake seemed a little hurt. "I'm Jake. I've been neighbors with your little girlfriend for years."

"You knew Sasha?" Nova dialed in.

"Of course. Like I said, we are neighbors," Jake confirmed. Nova flinched at the use of present tense. "You seem like a lost little puppy. Do you remember anything?" Jake asked with genuine curiosity.

Nova looked away, getting frustrated by how many times they've had to deal with this. "I remember my name and other small things, but everything else is gone."

"Fascinating." Jake was enthralled.

"So, you knew me?"

"Sometimes we'd talk while you were waiting for Sasha." Jake sounded almost nostalgic.

"Were me and Sasha... Were we good together?" Nova needed to know.

"Hell if I know." Jake shrugged. "She seemed happy. You seemed happy. Well, until..."

"I joined the Blindspot," Nova said finishing the sentence. I'm not convinced that's where Jake was heading with that.

"Right." Jake took the suggestion. "You joined the Blindspot and things changed. You started coming around a lot less frequently."

"What the hell was I thinking?" Nova shook their head. "Why would I get tangled up with a group like that?"

"For starters, you were kicked out of your home," Jake answered. The directness surprised Nova, sure, but it was the contents of the words that really hit. There were many times Nova wondered about their family. Deep down, they always knew it probably wasn't a happy story.

"One night I saw you in the rain waiting outside her house. You had just been given the boot," Jake continued. "You were pitiful. Weak. And so angry. I..." Jake trailed off for a moment. "I knew you couldn't make it on your own." Nova hung on every word. They looked at Jake with a face that urged him to continue. Jake sighed. "And you must've known that, too. So, you joined the Blindspot." He quickly pivoted away from his original thought. That last sentence sounded much less sincere than the lead up.

Nova sat with the info for a bit. Mata chilled on their shoulder, trying to provide a consistent presence. "Surely, Sasha would've helped if I had just asked, right? Offered me a place to land on my feet?" Nova tried to piece it together.

"Not with that dickbag as her father." Jake sneered. "You needed something else. Someone else to help you." He looked at Nova, deep in thought. I can almost sense a new emotion radiating off Jake. Guilt, maybe? A buzz in Jake's pocket took his attention away. He checked his phone, and a much more familiar look returned to his face—a large smug grin. "I'm sorry, Nova. Something has come up." Jake shot up and moved past his visitors, who were still digesting the info.

"Can you tell me more sometime?" Nova quickly asked.

Jake stopped in the doorway. "I don't think I'd be able to tell you much more," he said somberly. "But it really was nice to see you again." Jake turned his head to give a smile. Not even a creepy one, either. This was a smile far more fitting of a boy his age.

"Nice to meet you," Nova responded in kind, the only truthful way they could. Jake exited, and the two now sat alone amidst the wrecked Evans' house with a lot of new things to think about. Perhaps they'd take the long way back tonight.

* * *

BANG BANG BANG! Grace banged on the entrance of Chase and Tommy's apartment. "Chase, are you in there?" she shouted, ready to break the door down if there was no answer.

Luckily for the landlord, Tommy answered the call. "Grace? What the hell, sis?" He sounded annoyed. Grace moved past Tommy and immediately began to look around. "Sure, waltz on in."

"Is Chase here?" she asked while frantically searching.

"What? No. He bounced a bit earlier, for groceries or something." Tommy halted Grace by putting both hands on her shoulder. "You're acting mad strange. What's going on?"

"I think Chase may be in trouble."

"Chase? He was here literally minutes ago. Chill." Tommy disregarded the concern.

"I got an alarming text from him," Grace continued.

"What'd it say?" Grace showed him the message. "Well, that's just a series of numbers, isn't it? Getting a little hysterical over three nines, yeah?"

"It's code. You wouldn't get it. He's not answering his phone. Can you just tell me exactly where he was going?"

"Gracey girl, you need to chill your tits. Chase is a big boy. He's fine. Now, I'm kinda in the middle of something." Tommy gestured toward a paused video game. His achievements scrolled across the idle screen.

Grace almost blew a fuse. "Classic, Tommy. Not your problem, so it's not a problem." Grace pushed Tommy's other arm off her.

Tommy chuckled. "Damn, bro. The claws? What got up your tree?"

"You. You don't take anything seriously."

"Whoa, full on assault here. I'm just trying to enjoy my day off. You're the one who came storming in spilling nonsense." Tommy shook it off. "Twisted way to treat your kidney twin."

Grace let out a sharp exhale. "Oh, screw you, Tommy."

Tommy got in her face. "Grace, I'm about to toss you out."

"At least you'd finally be direct."

"Alright, I'll bite, what's this really about?"

"You, Tommy. You don't give a shit about anything. You're a bad friend." Tommy turned away and paced in the kitchen. Grace was finally letting it out. Everything she'd been feeling regarding this particular friendship.

"I'm a bad friend? Real rich, Gracey. I've been there for you your whole damn life. I'm the first person you told about being a lesbian. Do you remember that shit?" Tommy tapped the counter aggressively.

Grace took a deep breath and slowed down. "You've had your moments," she admitted. "But lately, you've been a ghost. I hardly see you anymore. And I died, Tommy. I literally died, and I haven't heard from you in weeks. *That's* a twisted way to treat your kidney twin."

Tommy stopped tapping. She had a point. "What do you want from me, Grace?" He sounded exhausted. "I don't know anything about that. I don't handle death well. You know this."

"Then maybe learn. Or at least try. Dammit, Tommy, you've done nothing! All the while, Chase has stepped up beside me where you should've been." Grace moved in.

"Yeah..." Tommy got withdrawn. His eyes fell to the floor. "Yeah, that's a little off the rails." The nervous tapping started again. "So, Chase. He's really been showing for you?"

"Yes! He's part of the girl group. And I need to know where he went."

"Okay." Tommy let out a heavy sigh. "I really don't know, Grace. Like I said, I think maybe groceries? But I wasn't really listening." He sounded slightly ashamed this time.

Grace shook her head. "Shit." She looked down in her purse at Octavia, who had been a silent observer. "What do we do now?"

"I am sorry, dear Grace. I am not sure." Octavia was stumped. "If only he still had a trace."

Grace collapsed into a kitchen chair and entered her brainstorm. She massaged her temples with her hands, while tilting her head backward. "If only," Grace agreed. Tommy just stood there awkwardly. Sure, it was a little weird his uninvited guest was making herself at home right after that fight, but he felt like he owed her this much. "Are traces only used for shrouds?" Grace asked.

"I am not aware of any other kind. A trace is the spiritual link betwixt two beings. There is nothing else that bonds to a host in such a way," Octavia answered.

A spiritual link. That phrase replayed in Grace's head. Her generator mode was in full force. "Lots of things are linked," she stated. Keep going Grace. This is a good line of thinking. "Maybe not in the same way, but we're all kind of linked, right?" Grace shifted upright and looked around. To be honest, she wasn't fully sure what she was looking for. Grasping at straws would be the most appropriate term here.

"Yeah, that's true..." Tommy responded, befuddled. Poor guy thinks Grace is still talking to him.

"Technically, that is sound reasoning," Octavia, the real collaborator, said.

"So, maybe I am looking for a trace, just a different kind."

"I suppose that is possible," Octavia agreed.

"So, what if I did that thing again?" Grace posited.

"What thing?" Octavia and Tommy asked in unison.

"That thing we did in the club, when I discovered my instrument."

"Alright, sis. You've officially lost me." Tommy couldn't keep up.

"That could work," Octavia encouraged. "There is no music this time, however. You will have to focus on the organic timbre of the room."

"Alright, I think I can do that." Grace gave a hearty exhale, before allowing her eyelids to calmly collapse and her body to become still. Her focus shifted to the noise of the room. The heater hummed softly. Tommy's fingers impatiently tapped the counter. A couple of birds chirped outside. Each sound appeared separately at first, but soon they began to meld together, forming lines of melody and harmony in asynchronous beauty.

Grace became lost in the frequencies. They enveloped her, and she could once again feel the individual waves of sound waxing and waning against her skin. Slowly, but surely, Chase's voice started to whisper in her head. A low hum added to the natural symphony. She could sense it—a new sound wave. It felt strong. Linear. She opened her eyes to see a purple wave extending from her heart. It bounced around in a path before her.

"Holy shit. It worked." Grace was in disbelief. "Tavi, it actually worked!"

"Who?" Tommy butted in. Grace ignored him.

"You found a trace?!" Octavia exclaimed.

Grace moved her head up and down in excitement. "Yes! And I'm like 99% sure it goes to Chase."

Tommy stopped trying to understand at this point. "You know where he is then, yeah?" he said.

"Yup," Grace responded. "Alright, Tavi, there's no time to waste."

"Full speed ahead, dear Grace." Octavia hopped out of the purse, causing Tommy to jump. She held out a tentacle in front of her. "Onward!" She charged. Grace pumped her fist, and the two took off in pursuit. The door slammed behind them, and Tommy was left dumbfounded.

"Who the fuck is Tavi?" He shook his head and went back to his video game.

ELEVEN

NOBODY LIVES

All the lights were dimmed in the Church of Veritas. Candles burned brightly in their stead. There was a hallow emptiness as the pews remained barren. A lone spotlight shone upon Chase, bound to a chair at the foot of the altar. Who says Dios doesn't have a flair for the dramatic? The captive groggily opened his eyes to see Dios sitting opposite him, scrolling through a phone.

He recognized the figure as his vision sharpened. "Father Dom?" The trio wore Dom's face and a long, black, pastoral robe.

"Welcome, my son." Dom played the part, raising his hand in blessing. As Chase came to, he began to take in more of the scene. All at once, he became astutely aware of the rope binding him to the wooden chair and a pounding sore spot on the side of his head. His heart raced.

Dios delighted in the shift in expression. "Someone spicy looking for you at the bar," Dom read a text message, revealing the phone to be Chase's. "You really think I'm spicy?" Dios shifted into Ira's skin as she spoke. She held a hand up to her chin. Chase's panic ramped up after the little show. "Thank you! You're not so bad yourself."

"Help!" he cried out.

Ira joined in and screamed at the top of her lungs. Their sounds echoed off each other in the rafters. She let out a giggle. "It's useless, boy. Let's just say that we are in the presence of some significant soundproofing, compliments of the Silence." Dios moved in closer while continuing to examine the phone.

"So her name is Grace, huh?" Ira inquired, looking for a read on the hostage's face.

Try as he might, Chase was unable to hide the visceral reaction. "What? No," he sputtered out, but his actions gave a different answer.

"Thought so." Ira laughed. "You know, we were half expecting a long, drawn out interrogation." Dios unsheathed a crooked blade as they walked behind the prisoner. They leaned over and lightly traced the dagger over his exposed clavicle. His breathing hastened as he felt the cold steel.

"All that work to knock you out and bring you somewhere secluded, and it turns out all we had to do was look at three missed calls and the tippy top text on your phone." Dios moved their other arm around to show Chase the screen. They placed Ira's face against his.

"What... what do you want?" Chase tried to regain composure.

"Oh, sweetie. We already have what we want. But if you wanted to be an extra good boy, you could go ahead and tell us what 999 means." She referenced the message. "Code?" Chase fell silent. "Obviously it's code. I've gotta say, I'm impressed you managed to get a text out. Someone's got a keen intuition. Not the first time a girl's stalked you, huh?" Ira made a pouty duck face briefly, before letting out another giddy laugh. "She's going to try to find you now, right?"

Dios slithered around to look at Chase, a horrific grin spread across their expression. The captive tried to avert his gaze.

"That's it, isn't it? Perfect." They pulled away, allowing Chase a brief reprieve from the sharp feel of the blade.

"That saves us a lot of time." Dom took control. The body shifted back to his. "Sadly for you, that means there's really only one role left for you to play." Dios turned and licked their lips. "Demoralization." They held their dagger up to the spotlight, admiring the bright gleam coming off it. Frantically, Chase tried to squirm out of the restraints.

"This may sting a little bit," Orv mocked, as they lowered the blade to meet Chase's neck.

"No, no, no," is all he could say on repeat as he hyperventilated. Dios laughed in unison, savoring the moment. A moment that would be cut short.

"You greedy assholes." A shout burst out as the church doors swung open. Jake paced through the pews all the way up to the altar. "I knew I couldn't trust you."

Dios groaned. "You have got to be shitting me," Dom grumbled as he lowered the knife. "I locked that fucking door, didn't I?"

"Like a locked door is a problem for me." Jake brushed it off. "Isaac told me you inquired about that license plate. You know, the one we were going to track down together?"

"That goddamn puppet," Dom cussed.

"Listen, little buddy," Ira spoke. "You know we're a solo act." Jake raised an eyebrow. "As solo as we can be," she clarified. "But I promise we planned to tag you in on the fun part."

"Bullshit. I've learned better than to trust you dipshits." The boy sneered. "Why do you think I asked our infected friend to let me know if you made a move?" At this point, the little psychopath noticed Chase wriggling in the chair. "That's not the composer, morons."

"Well, no shit." Dom shook his head.

"Your tip led us to this dream boat." Ira winked at the hostage. The gesture was not returned.

"So, naturally, we're going to torture him until we get info on the girl, right?" Jake assumed.

Dios let out a frustrated exhale ,and Dom grew impatient. "See, this is why we do things on our own. I don't have time to catch you up. We've already done that." They were on the cusp of a much anticipated kill. Every moment they don't murder our friend over there, their itch intensifies.

"What about me?" Mira's voice floated into the conversation. She emerged from a darkened corner, frustration emanating from every pore of her body. "Do you have time to catch me up on your impatient and petulant actions? I mean honestly, bringing the boy here?"

"Ugh," Dom groaned as Mira marched right up to the altar. Without skipping a beat, she wound up an open palm and smacked it across the trio's collective face. "What the fuck, Mira?!"

"You dare jeopardize us with a kidnapping? After all the groundwork we've laid?" Her shadow rose high above her, looming over the object of her frustration.

"Groundwork? You mean that fucking moron and their dumb little cat?" Dom shot back. The words sprung an internal reaction in Jake. "Newsflash, Mira. They're both useless."

"A moron and their cat?" Jake prodded.

"Hush that devilish tongue, boy," Mira scolded. "You do not belong here."

"That's not your call, mother harlot," Jake growled. "You're the one who is not wanted. Can't you see?"

"Oh god, both of you! Shut the fuck up," Dom screeched.

"Neither of you are wanted," Ira clarified. Claws were out, as the three bodies formed a standoff, contempt bouncing between the lot.

"Dios, take care of this mess right now." Mira tried to regain control. "We have not earned enough goodwill from Nova for them to overlook innocent blood." Jake glanced at the mention of the name.

"You are not the Silence, Mira. Stop acting like you have any authority here," Dom rebelled. "I don't care what anybody thinks. Especially not that little shit." Dios gripped their blade and pivoted toward Chase. "We will kill because we want to, and I'm so tired of talking."

Chase shifted. All that time bought by the bickering, and sadly, he wasn't able to make even a dent in the restraints. Don't worry, though, this isn't over for him just yet.

A long, drawn out bass note filled the room as a haunting vocal melody danced in the acoustics. Right before their very eyes, a sound tentacle shot past the three bodies and wrapped around Chase—chair and all. It whipped him across the church, sliding the seat alongside a back pew. Grace stood at the entrance, Octavia resting in her palm. Two tentacles protruded from the plushy.

"Let's cut to the chase," Grace quipped the truly awful play on words. Octavia quickly used the second tentacle to untie their friend.

"Marvelous," Ira shouted while Dios clapped their hands. "Our girl knows how to make an entrance." Grace gripped Octavia and got ready.

"Oh my god, thank you, thank you, thank you!" Chase showered her with gratitude. "I thought that was the end."

"I'm sorry it took me so long, Chase." Grace gave him a quick smile, keeping Dios in her field of view.

"You ended up being a better lure than we hoped, boy." Ira laughed. "We didn't even need to do anything else. Did she put a tracker on you? Jealous much?"

"Grace, we have to get out of here. You're the one they want," Chase warned.

"These must be the disciples I've heard so much about." The

composer controlled her nerves. They really stepped into a beehive here.

"Be on guard, dear Grace. They are on an entirely new level," Octavia advised. To be honest, I think she can tell they are in over their heads. Grace surveyed those standing before her. Mira and Jake reluctantly lined up beside Dios to face their enemy. This just became an all-hands-on-deck situation. Or so it would seem.

With Grace in clear view, Dios finally had the chance to really get a good look at her. Her face tickled their memories until it all clicked. Their jaw dropped as they made the realization. They were the ones who created the composer. Well, at least the ones who showed her the door.

"I've been waiting for this reunion." Jake stepped forward. "You won't escape again." I'm pretty sure he has that backward, but alright. Grace recognized the boy immediately and could feel Octavia tense up. The kraken was once again confronted with her own personal vendetta. Things were different this time, however. Octavia knew she couldn't be rash.

"I'm afraid the concert must come to an end now, composer," Mira joined in. The makings of a grand battle royal were underway. That is until Dios came to a resolution.

"Sorry, crew," Ira called to her comrades. "Turns out this is personal." They reached their hands inside their robe. In an instant, syringe needles extended out of both sides of the cloth and pierced Jake and Mira in their necks. Each instinctively put a hand up to their throats as the needle retracted back into the garb.

"What the fuck?" the boy swore. Mira began to tremble. She looked at Dios, fearful and angry. Dios pulled their hands out of their robe, revealing two red-stained syringes.

"You didn't." Mira stumbled backward into a pew as Jake fell forward, both still conscious, but just barely.

"Blood of the devout," Dios spoke in unison, each too excited to deliver the news. In this case, Dios meant the blood of a devout Veritian. Truly blessed blood is hard to come by, but when it exists, it can be a powerful, albeit non-lethal, poison for those connected to the Silence.

"All thanks to Jakey-poo over here." Ira rubbed it in as Dios squatted down by the boy. He would be shaking right now if he could move.

"Remember dear Brody? That pathetic moron you killed literally on the altar?" Dom laughed. "I wasn't going to let the blood of such a devout sacrifice go to waste. After all..." Dios moved to Mira now. "You never know when you'll have to put a colleague in their place." Dom gave a smug look as Mira's eyelids got too heavy and closed. Grace watched the mutiny unfold and realized this was their chance.

"You need to go," she urged Chase.

"What? No, I can't leave you with them," he resisted.

"Yes, you can. You've had my back a lot, and I am so grateful, but I can't have you in this fight. This one is too much."

"It is true. Now is your opportunity to escape," Octavia agreed.

"But..."

"No buts! Get out of here." Grace gave him a reassuring look. "I'll find you when I'm done."

Chase took a deep breath. He'd seen that face before. Confident Grace was here, and that was someone he could trust. "Give them hell, Grace." Chase returned a purposeful nod before escaping through the large doors. Grace returned her attention to the bickering ahead.

"You lied to me!" Jake screamed at Dios as he clung to consciousness.

"Get over it, shitstain," Dom jovially shot back. "This is unfinished business for us." Those were the last words Jake heard before passing out. Dios moved to the front of the altar and faced their target.

"Sorry, it turns out we don't play well with others." Ira giggled. "Let's finish this, yeah? Just us girls." She challenged Grace. "And the two other men inside me," Ira added.

"Huh?" Grace was confused, but had little time to contemplate the double entendre. Dios pointed their knife out in front of them, before extending the blade rapidly toward the composer. Octavia quickly reacted, batting the attack away before it made contact. The elongated steel ricocheted into a pew, where it lodged into the solid oak. Dios adjusted their grip and slashed back across the entire church, effortlessly slicing through the seating. Elegantly, Grace limboed under the dagger as it passed overhead.

"Extra long knife. Got it." She identified Dios's power. Well, part of it, anyway.

"Not bad," Dom commended. "Though if you died right away, it wouldn't be fun now, would it?" Dios retracted the blade and charged at Grace. The composer formed sound knives and threw them at the advancing threat one by one. A plucky synthesizer played over a harmony of strings. The bass came in pulsing waves every time a dagger went flying. Dios dodged left, right, and left again, before swiping a lit candle off a pew. Swiftly, they elongated the wax toward Grace.

Octavia took the bait and knocked the decoy away, but Dios had already dispatched a secondary hidden assault with the knife. Grace was just able to deflect it with her sound at the last second, but it caught the edge of her palm, drawing blood. The string instruments briefly fell out of tune.

"Shit." Grace clenched her hand, but had little time to recover before Dios was upon her. They shortened the blade, before slashing diagonally in a violent motion. Grace dodged backward and fired a sharp wave. Without missing a step, Dios caught the noise on the tip of their dagger and snapped their weapon behind them, flinging the sound away. It crashed into the marble altar, causing a sizable crack.

"Oh, my parishioners are not going to be thrilled about that." Dom tsk-tsked as they twisted the knife back around. It shot out toward Grace once again. However, this time their veiled movements made the trajectory unpredictable. She couldn't avoid this one. The blade pierced her shoulder and pinned her against the wall. She dropped Octavia and let out a scream. Dios extended the candle again and promptly swept the plush all the way across the church like they were playing golf. They knew separating them was important. In a desperate attempt, Octavia released the remaining sound reserved in her body, shooting a pointed tentacle at the foe. Dios gripped the incoming sound.

"So this is the great Octavia?" Ira mused. "I'm not impressed." Dios clasped their hand and dispersed the frequency.

"No!" Grace screamed in pain, unable to run to her companion. Octavia winced. This was not good. She needed to close the gap before it was too late. Grace's aura wasn't extending far enough to meet the kraken, so the tiny plush had to crawl her way back.

Dios stepped forward, retracting the blade as they moved, keeping it firmly within Grace's shoulder. In a desperate play, Grace tried to toss a sound dagger. A premature cymbal crashed as Dios nonchalantly batted it away.

"It's good to see you again, you know." Ira smirked as the body changed to reflect her image. It got the reaction she wanted. "Your tip about that DJ. Spot on. He was something else."

"The woman at the bar?" Grace's face dropped.

"That's me." Ira lifted her free hand to her chin in an adorned fashion. "I knew you'd remember this beautiful face." Dios was a foot away now. "But let's see if you remember this one..." An evil grin spread as Dios changed again. This time, they displayed a scarred and mutilated mug. Heavy eyebrows and no hair accented a broken nose and loose teeth. Orv was finally out in plain view. This was the moment they were truly waiting for. As Grace looked at him, she remembered. How could she not? This was the face of her killer. Her eyes grew wide, and her body began to shake.

"Do you recognize us?" Orv's words danced out in his deranged voice. "We're the ones who gutted you!" Sharp, cracked, and crooked teeth made up Dios' twisted smile. They savored the reveal. Octavia was almost there, but she was running out of time. She had to make it. Another composer would not die on her watch. This one had to be different. Dios noticed the composer shaking and let out the signature unison cackle.

"Yes, show me your fear," Orv licked his lips. "I want to taste it." Only Dios made a grave judgment error. They thought they had won and could now enjoy the fruits of victory. However, Grace wasn't shaking because of fear. Oh no. This was not a tremble. This was an earthquake, and I have been waiting so long to witness it again. This was Grace's pure, unfiltered rage, and it had finally found a worthy target.

A dark swelling of staccato trumpets came into forte. The music became strong and purposeful. That was not at all what Dios was expecting. The brass emitted a loud punch as Dios felt something pierce their skin. They looked down to see Grace gripping a spear of sound, half of which had gone through their abdomen. Black blood dripped onto the floor.

"You undead little bitch!" Orv screamed. Grace screamed as she ripped the spear out through their side. Dios howled in pain. A beat dropped as Grace's waves danced across the air and connected with Octavia. The purple aura enveloped the plush wholly and expanded to create the visage of a sound kraken right there in the church. Not exactly full-size Octavia, but close. She also now had four tentacles instead of three, which all came crashing down to the ground, crushing rows of pews. Levitating at the center of the waves was Octavia's little stuffed body. A beautiful operatic voice rang out in an almost heavenly overtone as a massive tentacle sideswiped Dios, sending them flying. The mighty swipe also pulled the blade from Grace's shoulder, freeing the composer.

"This is more like it!" Octavia exclaimed. It had been a long time since she'd been able to go into kraken mode. She looked down at the composer with pride. Of course Grace could handle it. Why was she worried? Dios frantically rose to their feet and backed up to create more distance.

"You think that's impressive?" Dom heckled. "You got in a cheap shot."

"All that changes now is that we finally have a real fight." Ira livened up. "This is the thrill of the kill we've been waiting for!" Dios's eyes were lit. They discarded their robe, revealing two more jagged daggers looped into the side of the traditional pastoral collared shirt and slacks. Dios unsheathed each blade and readied them. Grace looked upon her killer with revenge pumping through her heart.

"Few have the pleasure of reuniting with the perpetrator of their demise." Octavia stoked the fire. "Let us revel in the vengeance fate has afforded us."

Grace spun her new weapon in the air like a baton, before gripping it like a javelin. "I couldn't agree more," she said as she catapulted the sharpened noise toward the wounded Dios. They just barely dodged the spear, but ended up in the path of another sweeping appendage. One voice split into a chorus as the sound collided with the trio and smashed them against the bulletin board. Grace charged forward, seizing her chance. As the composer closed the gap, a driving bass drum accented her steps. She formed another spear and held it at her side. This resembled more of a jousting type attack. That was a versatile instrument she had.

Dios seemed eager to show off their own new trick, however. They regained their balance and proceeded to split their two knives into three separate blades each, all of which extended out on different trajectories. Two shot out down the middle, while the others hinged at a forty-five-degree angle, creating a web of steel. Grace pivoted off her foot to sidestep the center daggers. A sound wave blasted beneath her, giving extra air to a backflip, allowing her to leap over the adjacent slashes and land firmly on her feet. Now that was a perfect ten.

"Nice try," Grace mocked as she sped ahead to take advantage of what she perceived to be an opening. Dios, however, manipulated an extended blade to twist back around toward the composer. It collided with the sound spear at the exact moment Grace thrusted forward. A saw synth screeched as Dios' knife snapped, knocking Grace slightly off her mark. The spear pierced Dios in the shoulder. Not exactly where she was aiming, but she'd take it. It was a very eye-for-an-eye moment. Not the ultimate one, of course.

Octavia followed up by hurling down a tentacle. It tore through the brick wall behind Dios as it crashed upon them. A loud thud accented the beat, and debris littered the air. Grace, in sync with Octavia, jumped away just before it slammed down.

"You are quite the warrior, dear Grace," Octavia praised. "Seeing you now, I cannot help but be reminded of..."

"Don't you dare say, Ragnar," Grace cheekily warned.

"Your potential," Octavia finished. "Your strength stands alone, composer." Grace smiled at Octavia, a sense of pride welling up. The moment was short-lived, however, as a barrage of blades blasted out from behind the settling dust. Grace reacted quickly, forming another sound spear. Trumpets and violins played a heroic duet as she spun the instrument around like a fan, knocking each blade away.

"You miserable little slut!" Dom screamed as Dios stepped into view. "Who do you think you are? We already killed you once. We will kill you again." Venom dripped from their mouth. Grace and Octavia looked at each other as a spark connected between their minds. It was time to end it. It was time for *the move*. This was something they had been working on in training. Albeit to limited success. Regardless, they both still believed now was the right time to break it out. Grace gripped her spear tightly. It would be different with this weapon, but she felt ready. She was still seeing red. A loud, explosive sound wave propelled the composer forward at full speed.

"You think you can just keep coming at us?" Ira jeered. The daggers each spread into ten blades, all shooting off in various trajectories. "Not this time."

"Get minced, bitch," Orv added. In this moment, confronted by so many opportunities to be sliced and diced, Grace closed her eyes. Which, admittedly, probably seems unwise. However, at that same time, Octavia let out a bellowing aria that filled the room. Grace felt the sound as it bounced off every surface. It was as if she was submerged in water, and every ripple danced against her skin. Each blade was a void in the noise—their path predicted by the displacement of sound. It was almost like she could see the future.

Effortlessly, she dodged left, up, and down until she finally vaulted off a pew where Octavia gripped her tight. The ruler of sea and melody lifted the composer over the remaining blades and into the heights of the steeple. The lone spotlight outlined her silhouette as Dios looked to the skies. Grace opened her eyes to admire the view from the vault of the church, before turning the spearhead downward.

"This time, you're the ones who die," Grace promised. A powerful voice sang beautifully alongside a harmony of brass and synth as Octavia swung down her tentacle with Grace in tow. The composer took aim, and in a tonal crash, the spear struck Dios right through their heart and smashed them into the floor.

Grace glared down into Orv's eyes. The eyes that struck fear in her only weeks ago. Her teeth clenched as she twisted the sound wave and let her rage pulse out into the noise. The vibrations spread throughout Dios, creating a shock effect. They let out a collective yell as they gripped the instrument and tried to dispel the frequencies. Grace's sound held strong. The trio gave a collective grunt, before gradually loosening their hold and going limp. The music slowly resolved, and the aura around Grace and Octavia diminished.

Slowly, Grace's breathing and heartbeat regulated. She raised her head and surveyed the wrecked church. I don't think they'll be able to have service here next weekend. She spotted Mira and Jake and realized they still needed to be dealt with. Grace had never seen the woman before, but she was well aware that Jake was bad news. If this was the company the woman in black kept, it was highly likely she'd be a problem for Grace someday. Still, she didn't feel right doing anything while they were incapacitated.

"You truly are remarkable, dear Grace." Octavia took her place on Grace's shoulder as she drifted down from the sky.

"You too, Tavi. That form was so badass!" Grace booped her companion's head. "And hey, that move worked out almost exactly as we practiced."

"That was nothing like what we rehearsed," Octavia disagreed.

"Sure it was. You grabbed me and smashed me down. I mean, sure, you were able to get me much, *much* higher because you went all super-sized, but still."

"The original maneuver was designed to be much more elegant."

"Tavi, you literally swing me like a hammer. It's not elegant."

"There is elegance in power." Octavia stuck to her guns. Grace giggled. The two turned around to determine how to handle the others. Unfortunately, this was a mistake. Behind them, an enormous shadow emerged from Dios's flesh. A massive snake-like figure coiled around and split into three cobra heads, spikes lining the body in a spiral pattern.

"How dare you turn your back on us," Dios spoke as one, each voice adding to the uneasy timbre. Grace spun around just as a spike extended out of the figure. Thinking quickly, she sidestepped the upcoming attack. Unfortunately, this put Octavia right in the kill zone, and the prong skewered her. Grace watched in horror as Octavia was raised up in the air and a purple liquid leaked from her body.

"Tavi!" she screamed. Her sound immediately erupted, and the aura returned. Another thorn shot out, but Grace bashed it away with a fresh spear. The fire was back as she glared at Dios and saw them for what they really were. While Dios can take the shape of Dom, Ira, or Orv, this was their true form. The one gifted to them by the Silence. The three-headed serpent. Each snake head held a different consciousness.

"Oops," Ira hissed. "Did we just impale your bestie?" Grace let out a yell and began launching javelins in an unbound fury. One after another, her sound took on a stabbing staccato pulse. Kick and snare banged out together on the beat. This music was loud and abrasive. Dios slithered around the assault. They moved effortlessly up on the walls and ceiling, going in a giant arch over Grace and ending up behind her.

"Did you really think you had won?" Dom mocked. "You only defeated a flesh suit, peasant."

"Now we will tear you limb from limb with our teeth," Orv spat. Grace stared down at Octavia's motionless form. Tears formed in her eyes. Desperately, she tried to transfer her aura to the plush, but the kraken's body wouldn't accept it.

"Come on, Tavi. You can't do this. I need you," she cried. Dios lowered their heads and slid rapidly across the floor in Grace's direction. Quickly, she summoned her instrument. Dios staked a spike into the ground and used their momentum to pivot their tail around at Grace, who managed to vault it like a rope. Once again, that seemed to be thanks to the new technique of using sound as a booster.

While she was jumping over, however, a thorn extended upward toward her. She swiped the spear at her feet to knock it away. This caused her to lose her balance and fumble the landing. Frenzied strings played over a double time kit as she tried to recover. Stay focused Grace. Rage is good. Blind rage is not.

Dios slithered up the wall and flung down at the staggered composer. Orv's mouth was wide open, with his fangs stretched downward. Grace regained her footing just in time to launch a sound wave right into his jaw. It punctured through Orv's lip and out the back of his head, disorienting the rest of Dios, who came crashing down. They missed.

"Fuck! That hurt!" Orv cried out.

"You'll pay for that," Dios spoke in unison as they stood tall on their tail. The spikes on their belly spun around like a drill, before elongating outward. Grace was suddenly in a blender as the lengthy blades fanned the room. The composer fell flat to avoid the rotating death parade. Kind of an easy way to negate that tactic, if I'm being honest. However, it left Grace in an incredibly vulnerable position.

This is what the snake was hoping for. Dios retracted the spikes and charged full speed ahead at their unguarded target, their fangs at the ready. Sinking their teeth into the composer would be the most satisfying victory for them. Grace tried to form a spear, but only a knife took shape in the sound. She had used too much, and without Octavia, her ability to be amplified was severely hindered. While on her back, she readied the dagger. This had to be enough. There was no time to move. Dios was almost upon her. Do-or-die time. Suddenly, a medium-sized stone smashed into Dom's snake head and ricocheted onto the other two. It threw off the snake's aim, and they clumsily collided into the wall. Grace looked toward the stone's origin point. Chase stood there panting. His legs were shaking.

"Get away from Grace, you slippery little freak!" Brave words rang out from a cracked voice.

"Chase…" Grace was touched and horrified that Chase came back.

"You're not fighting this alone." He nodded his head assuredly as Grace got back on her feet. "Though, I thought you were fighting a pastor. Not a giant snake monster."

Grace almost dared to smile as she thanked him, but before she could say anything, a spike ejected from the recovered snake and shot clean through Chase's heart.

"No!" she screamed out. The brave young man staggered backward, looking down at his chest. Blood cascaded out.

"I'm sorry, Grace." His voice quivered as he looked to his friend. "I just couldn't run this time." He dropped to his knees and collapsed. Grace wailed. Dios did not stand on ceremony. Three spikes extended toward her. With ferocity, she wildly swung her knife, which successfully knocked one blade fully away. The other two, however, rebounded into her flesh. One pierced through her right leg and the other through her stomach. The blades retracted, and Grace toppled to the floor.

Her song was now only carried by a solitary violin. It played a sad melody. Soft. Slow. This can't be it. Grace looked at Octavia and Chase, who were both laid out in front of her. These were her partners. These were the friends who died for her. Her eyes slowly shut, and they disappeared. She felt it again. Anger and rage. The immense frustration of being helpless. Despite that, the violins stopped playing, and the aura vanished.

Is this really the end? I can't believe it. You've been entertaining, sure, but if you die now, Grace, that's it. That's all there is to it. I can't bring you back again. There are rules. So, hold on to something. Find anything you can fight for, because this can't be your finale. You've been courageous. You've been strong. You've been surprising. But, most of all, you've been annoyingly kind. Virtuous, even. That's not normally something I care for, nor was it something I expected when I met that girl so full of fury. However, watching your brand of virtue, I have to admit I kind of enjoyed it. So, please Grace. Don't let some snake of the Silence take you out. Can you find it? The will to keep playing your song?

Grace's eyes shot open. They landed on the three-headed serpent, who was cackling and reveling in their kill. A low vibration began to emanate from her body, followed by a light piano melody. Grace moved her arms to her side and pushed up with all her strength, letting out a pained groan. Dios stopped laughing and watched what they deemed a pathetic last attempt.

"I've got it," Grace responded. "The will to fight. To play on. I've got it." Dios heard the proclamation and burst out in their inharmonious guffaw.

"Wow. Cool. We don't care." Ira rolled her eyes. "Who do you think you're talking to, anyway?" Ira questioned. "All your friends are dead, girlie." Grace stood on her feet. Her song was growing stronger. A cello bowed a legato harmony. The aura flickered around her.

"Nobody," she answered confidently. As my name left her mouth, the music erupted. A symphony of strings, brass, and synth played a triumphant melody. A timpani exploded the beat as the waves amplified across her entire body. Her hair turned that marvelous shade of purple. The mark of the dead extended throughout her skin, connecting in a crescent moon shape beneath both ears. Arrows dipped down through the crescents like a pair of painted earrings. The serpent's eyes grew wide as they witnessed the transformation.

Grace could feel that this sound was different. It coursed through her veins and plugged firmly into her heartbeat. Never had she felt more in tune with the music. A new frequency danced before her eyes, enticing her to take hold of it. She accepted its invitation and gripped the density of noise. A crescent moon bow spread out in either direction, so that she grasped it in the middle. It was beautiful. The bow of Aelia. Now that's something I haven't seen in ages. I knew you were special, Grace. Now take the vengeance you deserve.

The sound wave spiraled off Grace and engulfed Octavia's lifeless body. It circled her. Sparks flashed around the plush, levitating it until it erupted into a shower of sound. Octavia fell from the spectacular display and bounced off the floor. Groggily, she got up and shook herself out.

"Did you just drop me, composer?" Octavia smirked.

Grace's heart leapt. "I promise it's the last time." She beamed. "Now, Tavi. Take a minute to recover." Grace turned her eyes to her enemy. "I've got this." Octavia looked upon her mentee in awe. It was truly a magnificent sight. The kraken had never witnessed this before.

"You think a little bow is going to scare us?" Orv hissed. Dom's head glared at the composer. Ira seemed to be the only one who fully understood.

"She's the goddamn maestro!" Ira broke the united front. Grace reached out her right hand and pulled back an arrow of sound. She placed it neatly on the shelf of the bow. Dios rapidly slithered toward the maestro in a mad panic, while spikes extended out before them.

Grace took a deep breath and felt the sound. A powerful gnawing synth added to the melody as she drew the bow back. When Dios was mere feet away, she released the arrow. It immediately split into three. As each soared through the air, sound waves pulsed off them, disintegrating the advancing blades until they found their mark in the scaly flesh. One for each neck. They pierced the snake with a powerful momentum that carried the slithery body all the way away and up. Dios collided against the mural of Veritas. The arrows acted as nails, hoisting them up against it.

"Fuck," Dom yelled. "What is this shit?"

"Not death! Not death!" Orv pleaded. Ira fell silent. For the first time, she had nothing to say. Grace took a powerful stance and looked upon the thrashing pinned snake.

"Why aren't you dead?" she asked. It was a good question. Normally, that arrow is a kill shot. However, killing a disciple of the Silence isn't so simple, Grace. You must pierce them with immense sound, right where the void is connected. In this case, just above their collective lungs. Best not to leave this to chance, however. Use everything you've got.

Grace nodded. She retracted the bow and looked over at Octavia, extending a hand. "What do you say? Ready for our ultimate performance?" Octavia's eyes lit up.

"Absolutely, dear Grace. This is what I live for." Octavia hopped into Grace's palm. The kraken could feel it immediately. Music and power unlike anything she had ever experienced with a composer. Sound waves levitated Grace high above the ground as she held her companion out in front. Eight massive tentacles emerged from the tiny stuffed body with barely enough room in the cathedral to accommodate them. They intertwined and curved in a bow-like shape. The operatic voice joined the chorus. Grace reached forward and summoned an immense sound arrow through Octavia's form. She took aim at the serpent. Dios wriggled desperately, a green aura suddenly visible around them. It swirled their body, culminating in a dense mass right above the lungs. The kill zone.

"This is not how we end. You're just some worthless piece of shit, nobody," Dios protested. "We will not be forsaken! "

"You know, for a disciple of the Silence," Grace said, drawing back the bow, "you sure don't know how to shut the fuck up." She let loose the arrow. It soared through the air with a melodic explosion of strings, percussion, brass, synth, and voice, before finding its mark right above Dios's lungs. Each head looked down in horror. A sound wave pulsed outward from the bolt, disintegrating their entire body in an instant. Black goo remnants stained the colorful Veritas mural.

It was finally done. Revenge was exacted, and a major player in the Silence's army was eliminated. Vandalization of a Veritas worship space was just the cherry on the sundae.

The aura and hum circling Grace and Octavia faded as they softly returned to the ground. Grace's hair transitioned to its usual chestnut color, and the mark retracted to its original size. There was no time for celebration, however, as the sound of the massive church doors latching shut rang out in the vast, leveled space. Grace whipped around to see Nova standing in their view. Mata jumped off their shoulder and arched their back.

"You're the one I ran into in the alleyway. With the hush." Grace was tense. She used everything on that last attack. Luckily, Nova didn't know that.

"And you're the composer." Nova controlled their breathing. This was the great enemy they'd been warned about, and after witnessing Dios's final moments, they weren't itching for a fight, either. They noticed Mira and Jake passed out in the front of the church. Jake's presence came as a surprise. There would be questions later. But first, there was only one question that mattered to Nova. "Are they alive?" they asked tentatively. Grace looked toward the idle threats.

"I think so. The snake pastor dosed them with something." Grace treaded carefully. Her mind was on one thing right now— Chase. Perhaps there was a way to save him, but time was not on her side. Nova nodded their head. It didn't surprise them at all that Dios would pull a stunt like that. The unholy trinity always gave them a sick feeling.

"I just want to take my friends out of here." Nova proposed the compromise. Was that a deal Grace could afford? Killing Dios was a major win. Perhaps it was time to call it and focus on recovery.

"Composer, think this through," Octavia cautioned. "We may

not get this chance again." She looked with contempt upon the passed out boy. The last thing the kraken wanted was to let him escape, but she could feel it. Their sound was all dried up.

Grace paused for a moment and then stepped aside, giving Nova a direct path to the altar through the debris.

Nova eyed her up and down. "How do I know you won't shoot me in the back?"

"Do I seem like the type?"

"I don't really know you, but you just killed a person of the cloth." Nova was partially joking. Dios' death didn't actually phase them. In actuality, they quite liked that Grace took care of them.

Grace gave an inquisitive look. "Did that look like a person to you?"

"Nope," Nova concurred. "Never did." With that, Nova and Mata began their guarded trek to the front of the church. They locked eyes with Grace as they passed, but both parties put faith in the ceasefire. Nova picked up Mira and threw her over their shoulder. Mata wriggled under Jake and then expanded their body so that he was resting comfortably on their large back, nestled between a set of bony spikes. Nova gave Grace one last look before heading to safety through the side corridor. Grace's bluff worked, and they were in the clear. She turned her attention now toward Chase. Quickly, she sprinted over and knelt beside him. Two fingers to his neck revealed there was no pulse.

"Alright, Chase. Time to wake up," she pleaded while rolling him over onto her lap. His shirt was drenched in blood. "You can't die on me." Grace's voice shook. "I'm so not okay with that." She closed her eyes and tried to tap into the noise of the room. There was nothing left in the tank. She couldn't get a read on anything anymore. "Chase. Come on, man." Grace turned her plea to the sky. "Please, help him." I know what you're asking for, Grace. It doesn't work that way. "Please!" she screamed.

"Dear Grace..." Octavia placed a consoling tentacle on Grace's leg as she looked upon Chase. A deep ache formed in her own heart. "He was brave."

"Don't talk like that."

"He saved your life."

"Stop."

"He has given you an enormous gift."

"He's not dead! He can't be." Tears began to drop onto Chase's forehead. "I told you to run." Grace's voice quivered. "Why didn't you just run?" She and Octavia mourned. Heads down, crying for their friend. This was the first person who really accepted Grace after she resurrected. I suppose his loss truly is unfortunate. All remained quiet as a warm gold light flickered across the lifeless corpse. What's this now?

"Composer." Octavia rapidly tapped Grace to get her attention. Grace lifted her head in time to catch the glow. It radiated for a moment before painting the air directly above Chase. An ancient symbol floated above his body, before shattering into a million colorful particles that showered Chase. As they descended on his flesh, a mark of that same symbol formed on his neck, directly under his chin: a sword piercing through the sun, two rays branching out into a pair of angelic wings. It extended down into his clavicle. Now that's not very discreet.

Octavia hopped on Grace's shoulder to observe the scene. Her eyes widened when she saw the branding. I can imagine she has mixed feelings about what this means. Sure, Chase will return to life in a few moments. A second chance has been gifted to him. It's the gift giver that concerns Octavia and me. A golden blade. For the first time in millennia, Veritas has chosen a champion.

Chase's eyelids fluttered, and he sucked in a violent inhalation of breath. He shot up, nearly head butting poor Grace. She didn't even let the guy finish coughing the blood out, before tightly wrapping her arms around him in a bear hug.

"You're back!" Grace squealed.

"Back?" Chase sounded groggy. He took a moment to familiarize his surroundings. The decimated church slowly brought the memories back. "Last thing I remember was opening the doors to this church... And then this giant snake. You were fighting a giant three-headed snake?" The tale sounded outlandish to him. Surely this wasn't actually the last thing he remembered.

"Yes!" Grace gave a radiant smile. "Then you threw this rock at it like a badass."

"Oh, nice." Chase nodded before shooting a horrified look at Grace. "Wait. I did what?"

"You fought like a true warrior," Octavia praised.

"Weren't you dead when that part happened, Tavi?" Grace mentioned.

"Tavi died?" Chase was trying to catch up.

"I do not die, dear Grace. I was severely wounded and out of commission, but as long as your sound exists, so do I remember?" Grace did not remember.

"Wow." Chase let everything sink in. "So you're telling me I basically fought a hydra and lived?"

"Well..." Grace cringed. "You, um, kind of died, I think." This statement was greeted with a bewildered look. "But only for a little bit!" Grace hastily added.

"I died?" After looking down at his bloodstained shirt, he determined the intel must be accurate. "Wait, does that mean..." His hand went up to the side of his neck.

"Not exactly." Grace wasn't sure how to explain this.

"I'm not a resurrected?"

"Well, you have a mark, but it's not the same as mine. It's kind of right here..." Grace moved her hand up and down her throat.

"It's on my throat?"

"Like, the whole thing." Grace handed him her phone. He flipped the front-facing camera on and examined his new beauty feature.

"I can't have a giant ass mark on my throat. This is totally not my image," he vented. "This makes it look like I'm in the Blindspot or something!"

"I think it's kind of cool," Grace consoled him. "Plus, you're not dead. So, that's a plus?" She shrugged.

Chase exhaled, before letting out a laugh of disbelief. "Yeah, I guess that's true." He looked at Grace warmly. "I'm glad you're alive, too. And you." He nodded at Octavia, who returned the gesture in kind.

"Aww." Grace lit up. "Girl group hug!" She pulled Chase and Octavia in for a big squeeze.

"Yeah, yeah, yeah." Chase wiggled out of the overly-lovey moment. I get it, Chase. "Can we get out of this creepy church now?"

"Yes, please," Grace placed Octavia gently on her shoulder and stood up. Chase saw the blood on Grace's own shirt.

"Um, are *you* okay?"

"I should probably go to a hospital," Grace said matter-of-factly.

"Why didn't you start with that?" Chase berated her. "Let's go! Can you walk?"

"Easy peasy. It's really not as bad as it looks." Grace was telling the truth. Her form change actually did a decent job of regenerating some of the tissue already. Though, it was by no means a full heal.

The three made their way to the doors. As Chase pulled them open, he turned back for one last look at the stained Veritas mural. He locked eyes with the portrait.

"Come on, before anybody sees us leaving this mess!" Grace rushed Chase along.

He snapped his attention back. "Right. Sorry," he apologized as they exited the church. The doors closed on the battlefield, and the three began to reminisce and laugh, filled with the adrenaline of a hard won fight. As they made their way to the hospital down the street, the conversation quickly shifted to Cyn. Of course, Grace would start talking about her so soon after nearly dying again. Her phone revealed seven unread messages. Which meant she had a lot of responses to brainstorm. Still, it was nice to see her have something to go back to, I guess. Something to look forward to. She's definitely earned it.

Grace reached a new level today. Which, I honestly didn't see coming. A delightful surprise, to be sure, as there's never any telling what may follow a resurrection. Most of the time, it's entirely dull, unfortunately. But this instance... This was worth it. The first maestro in ages—the second one ever—now walks the earth. The next series of events are sure to entertain, and I, for one, cannot wait to watch them unfold.

The Silence must know about her awakening now, however. Killing such a strong disciple will surely create waves. No doubt that slimeball will throw everything it has at her, but let's see how she handles that. I have to say, though, for the first time in a long while, I feel good about our chances. Grace will keep growing, and when all is said and done, I promise you the Silence will be destroyed. And it will be destroyed by Nobody.

ACKNOWLEDGMENTS

The experience of writing this novel has been life changing. Not only have I, personally, been able to complete something I have always dreamed of doing, but I also had the privilege of discovering immense support from those in my life. I want to express gratitude to all those who have been there for me, and I would like to take a moment to call out a few amazing people!

First and foremost, I want to extend a massive thank you to Eliza. When I first asked them to read my book, we had just started to become friends. I was initially only looking for assorted feedback on how my very first novel read, and I knew Eliza had a propensity to tell it like it is and not hold anything back—a trait I would come to feel very conflicted about later on in this process. Little did I know that our friendship would blossom and I would end up finding my biggest supporter. I bothered Eliza *a lot*. And not only about the book. They provided feedback, brainstormed, developed amazing assets for the cover, and provided consistent motivation and encouragement. I still remember when they took the time to send pictures of what each character looked like in their mind. It was so surreal. Someone was genuinely choosing to talk about my book in a fun, hypothetical way. I'll never forget that feeling. Some pictures completely missed the mark, however—Seth Green as Chase... not a chance, Eliza. Regardless, your support means the world to me and this book crossed the finish line thanks to you!

I am extremely grateful to my sister, Melanie. She also allowed me to bug her incessantly—mostly regarding the cover design. Thank you for not only being a support with this novel but also being one of my largest familial supports period. You were the first person in my family I came out to for a reason, and I will always treasure our bond. I'd also like to take a moment to thank my father, Gary, who read this entire book despite being a Catholic, right-of-center, heterosexual man—not my largest demographic. I know you and mom don't always understand me, but you take the time to support me, regardless. That means something and it matters.

My dear friend Amber also read this book and provided valuable feedback. When she told me she enjoyed it, I knew I had something that wasn't complete garbage. She has read many literary works—let's be honest, a good majority have been fan fiction—and has tremendous taste. I am honored that you took the time to read my story so thoroughly. Perhaps, if I am fortunate enough to inspire fan fiction, you can find the best ones and share them with me.

Lastly, I want to thank my ex-wife and my daughter. I saved this part for last, because I knew there would be tears and I did not wish to write too much with watery eyes. To Karen... Our marriage may not have survived until the completion of this book, but I will never forget everything you have done for me. You have had to put up with far too many big dreams of mine over the years and have seen my ambition wane almost every time. Nonetheless, you have always supported me. Thank you for that and for being an amazing mother to our daughter. I will always treasure our memories and our friendship.

To my daughter... This whole thing happened because of you. Before you came along, I lacked any semblance of a drive to make my dreams a reality. I had resigned myself to obscurity. You changed all of that. You deserve *everything* and that includes a mom who will work hard and show you that following your heart is important. Even if this book burns up in irrelevance and completely fails, I hope you always remember how important it is to chase what you love. You are only two years old, and I can already tell that you have a unique and beautiful fire for life. My greatest wish for you is that the wonder in your heart continues on forever and ever, and that you find something that truly inspires you. Drain the marrow out of life and remember, you can do difficult things.

A final shout out (I promise this is really the last one) to the person reading this. You are a lovely human being and that color you're wearing really works on you.

Thank you all. I love you!

ABOUT THE AUTHOR

Natalie West is wonderful, but pretty uncomfortable writing about herself. So, it's a good thing this is a completely objective third person take on her life and is not, in any way, written by her. No, not at all.

Anyway, she was born in Wisconsin, but spent many years in the Arizona desert finding herself. Eventually, she returned to her cold homeland with a beautiful, smart, and creative daughter. That little girl is her world and a big reason this book was written in the first place. Writing has always been a passion for Natalie, with her first novel "releasing" in the 8th grade. It was about as good as you'd expect. Nobody read it and that's a very good thing. Many attempts to write another novel have followed, but all floundered until she wrote the very book resting in your hands.

In addition to writing, she has always been drawn to the art of creating music. If you read this book, that connection is probably not surprising. The marriage of these two passions has long been a dream of hers. Natalie is exceptionally queer and strives to provide her personal perspective through the characters she writes. In fact, some characters in this story are probably a little too similar to her... No, there will be no mention of names. This is Miss West's first published novel, with hopes for many more to follow!